Cat & Cat

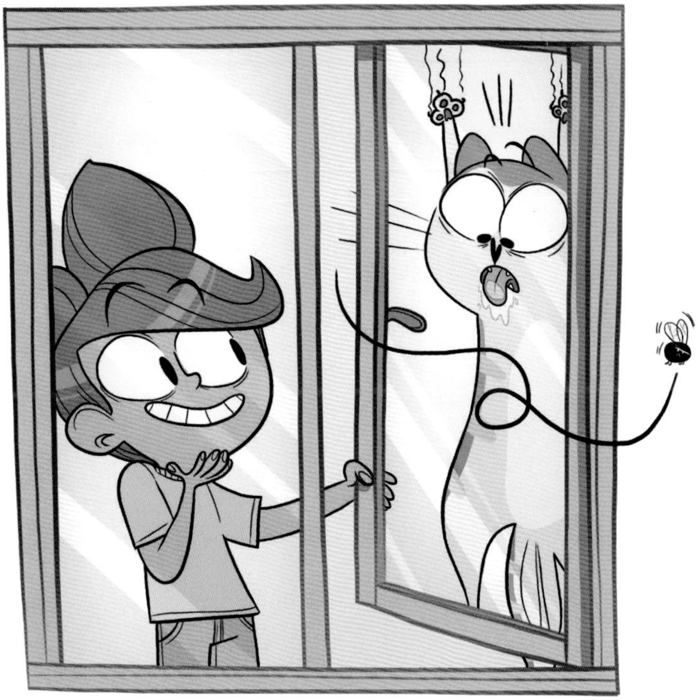

PAPERCUTZ™

MORE GREAT GRAPHIC NOVEL SERIES AVAILABLE FROM

PAPERCUTZ™

THE SMURFS #21

CAT & CAT #1

BARBIE #1

THE SISTERS #1

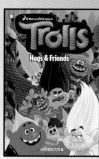

TROLLS #1

GERONIMO STILTON #17

THEA STILTON #6

THE ONLY LIVING GIRL #1

DINOSAUR EXPLORERS #1

SCARLETT

ANNE OF GREEN BAGELS #1

DRACULA MARRIES FRANKENSTEIN!

THE RED SHOES

THE LITTLE MERMAID

FUZZY BASEBALL #1

HOTEL TRANSYLVANIA #1

THE LOUD HOUSE #1

MANOSAURS #1

THE ONLY LIVING BOY #5

GUMBY #1

WWW.PAPERCUTZ.COM
ALSO AVAILABLE WHERE EBOOKS ARE SOLD.

Cat & Cat

1. GIRL MEETS CAT

CHRISTOPHE CAZENOVE
HERVÉ RICHEZ
SCRIPT

YRGANE RAMON
ART

PAPERCUTZ
New York

To my parents,

To Kali, Patate & Pitou, Toudougras

To Kalysia, Homer, Clovis, Flûte, Hermès…and all the Ronrons!
To Qwertt, Minimia, Chablis, June & Guiness.
To Ricqles, who took good care of Taz, Mitsy, Gimli, and K2000.
To Olivier, Kiwi's official veterinarian in real life, and Sushi's in the comicbook.
To Kiwi, my valiant, affectionate bunny, who waited patiently for me to finish this comicbook
to get out of his cage again.
To Nuggets, Moumoute, Batman, Tweedledee & Tweedledoo, Watson, Chaussette & Mascarpone,
Pompidou, Adolfina, and all the cats abandoned in streets and elsewhere.
To my friends and all those who enjoyed this book.
To my cat. Thanks.
Thanks to SaruJin and Guillaume T. for their help prepping for setting the color when finishing the book.
http://www.yrgane.com
– Yrgane

For Céline, who loved doing the butterfly and who'll love not doing it anymore…
– Hervé

Cat & Cat

#1 "Girl Meets Cat"
Christophe Cazenove &
Hervé Richez – Writers
Yrgane Ramon – Artist
Joe Johnson – Translator
Wilson Ramos Jr. – Letterer

Special thanks to Catherine Loiselet

Production – Mark McNabb
Managing Editor – Jeff Whitman
Editorial Intern – Izzy Boyce-Blanchard
Jim Salicrup
Editor-in-Chief

Papercutz books may be purchased for business or promotional use. For information on bulk purchases
please contact Macmillan Corporate and Premium Sales Department at (800) 221-795 x5442.

Hardcover ISBN: 978-1-5458-0427-8
Paperback ISBN: 978-1-5458-0428-5

Printed in China
February 2020

Distributed by Macmillan
First Papercutz Printing

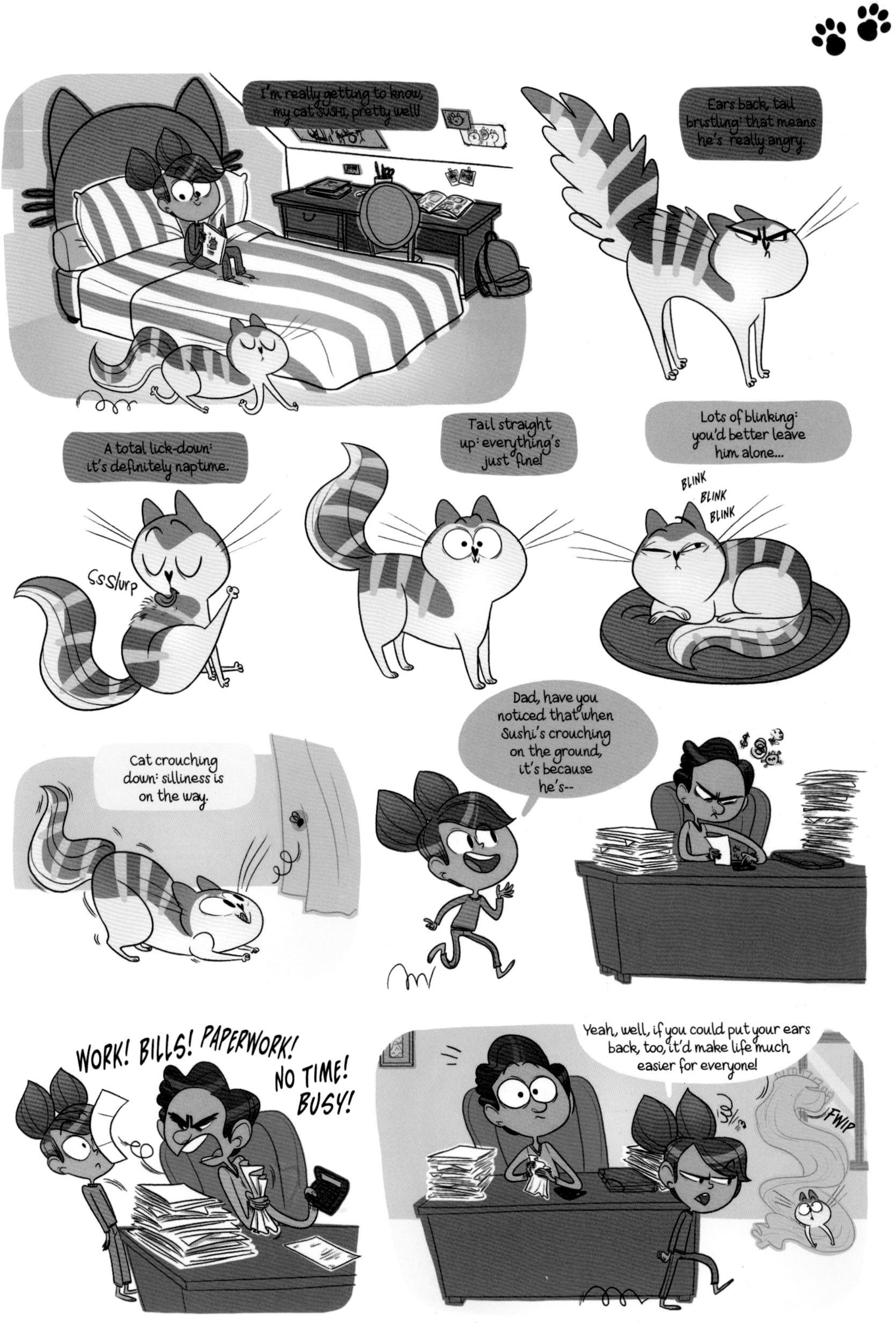
I'm really getting to know my cat SUSHI, pretty well!
Ears back, tail bristling: that means he's really angry.
A total lick-down: it's definitely naptime.
SSSlurp
Tail straight up: everything's just fine!
Lots of blinking: you'd better leave him alone...
BLINK
BLINK
BLINK
Cat crouching down: silliness is on the way.
Dad, have you noticed that when Sushi's crouching on the ground, it's because he's--
WORK! BILLS! PAPERWORK!
NO TIME!
BUSY!
Yeah, well, if you could put your ears back, too, it'd make life much easier for everyone!
FWIP

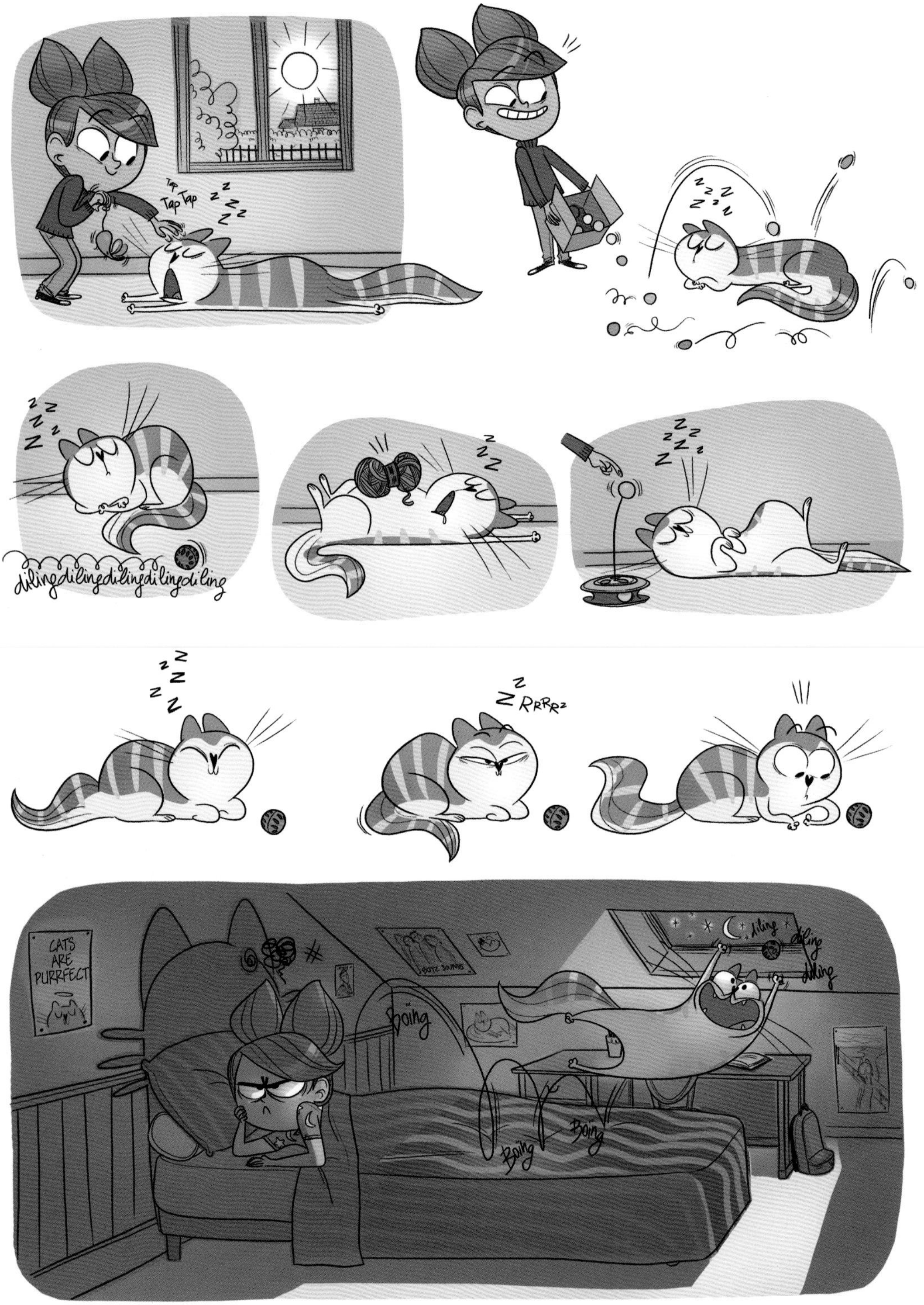
Tap Tap Tap
dilingdilingdilingdilingdiling
CATS ARE PURRFECT
BOYZ SOUNDS
diling
diling
diling
Boing
Boing
Boing

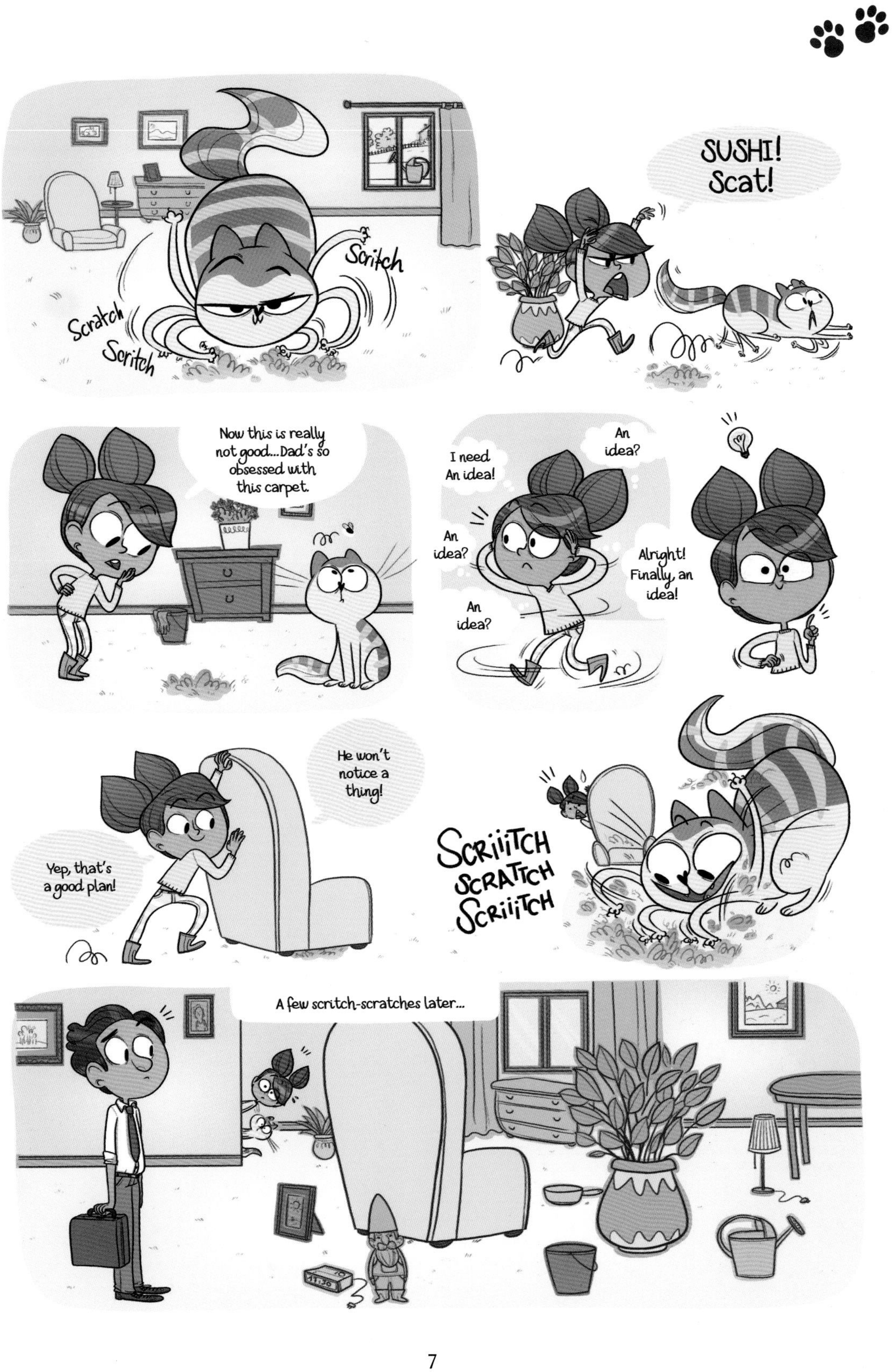
Scratch
Scritch
Scritch
SUSHI! Scat!
Now this is really not good...Dad's so obsessed with this carpet.
I need An idea!
An idea?
An idea?
An idea?
Alright! Finally, an idea!
He won't notice a thing!
Yep, that's a good plan!
SCRIIITCH
SCRATTCH
SCRIIITCH
A few scritch-scratches later...

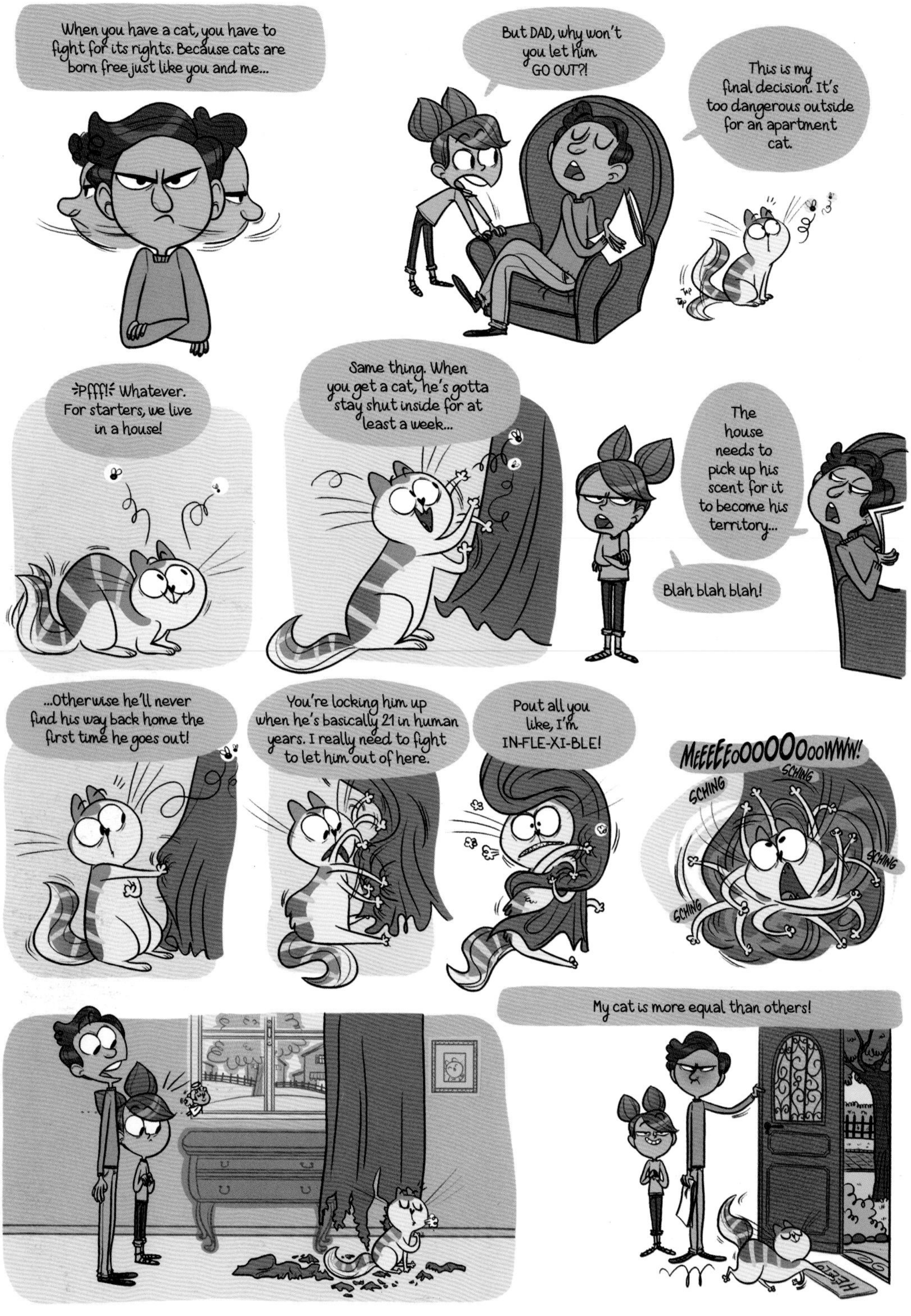

When you have a cat, you have to fight for its rights. Because cats are born free just like you and me...
But DAD, why won't you let him GO OUT?!
This is my final decision. It's too dangerous outside for an apartment cat.
TAP TAP
Pfff! Whatever. For starters, we live in a house!
Same thing. When you get a cat, he's gotta stay shut inside for at least a week...
The house needs to pick up his scent for it to become his territory...
Blah blah blah!
...Otherwise he'll never find his way back home the first time he goes out!
You're locking him up when he's basically 21 in human years. I really need to fight to let him out of here.
Pout all you like, I'm IN-FLE-XI-BLE!
MEEEEEoOOOOOooWWW!
SCHING
SCHING
SCHING
SCHING
My cat is more equal than others!

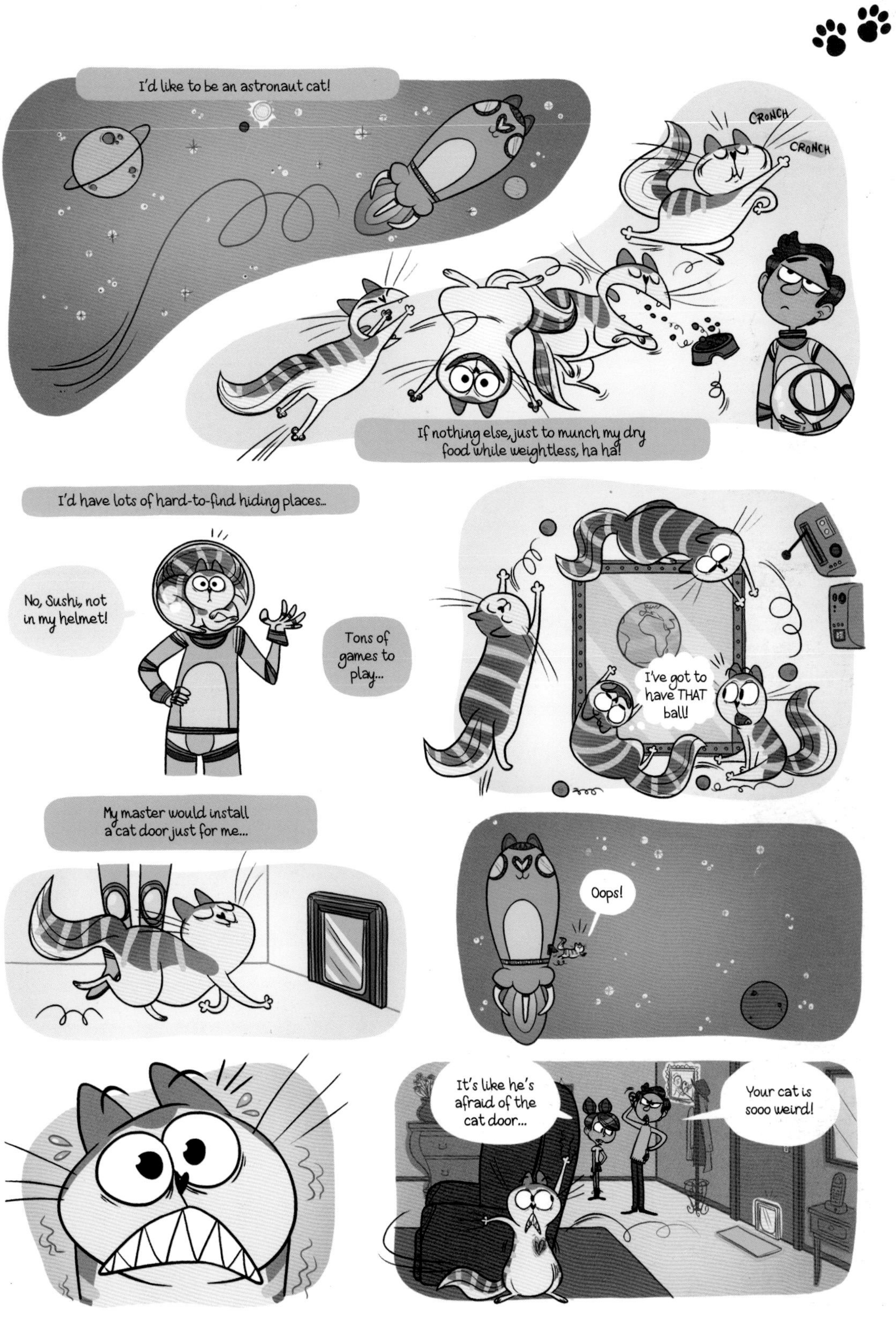
I'd like to be an astronaut cat!
CRONCH
CRONCH
If nothing else, just to munch my dry food while weightless, ha ha!
I'd have lots of hard-to-find hiding places...
No, Sushi, not in my helmet!
Tons of games to play...
I've got to have THAT ball!
My master would install a cat door just for me...
Oops!
It's like he's afraid of the cat door...
Your cat is sooo weird!

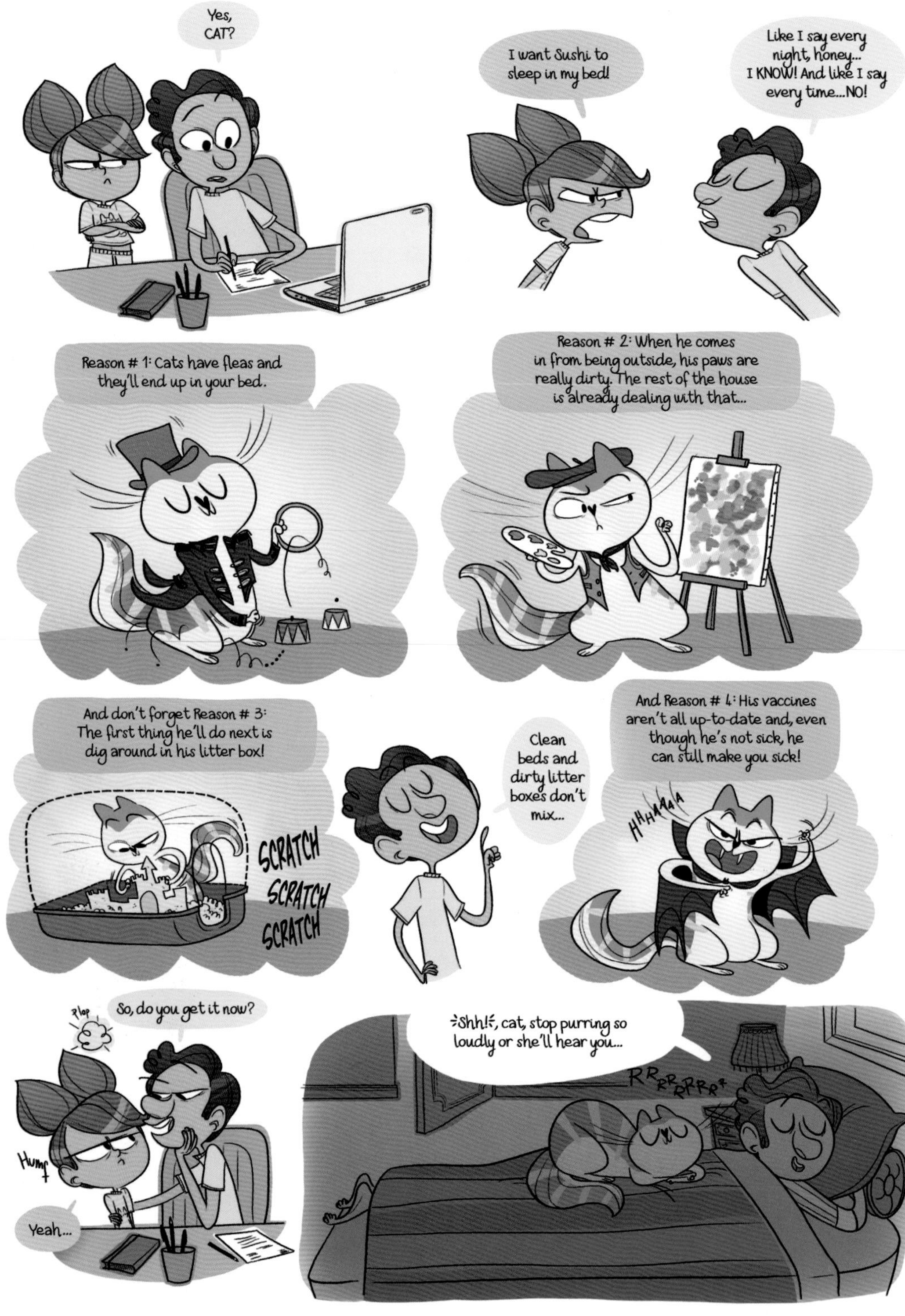
Yes, CAT?
I want Sushi to sleep in my bed!
Like I say every night, honey... I KNOW! And like I say every time...NO!
Reason # 1: Cats have fleas and they'll end up in your bed.
Reason # 2: When he comes in from being outside, his paws are really dirty. The rest of the house is already dealing with that...
And don't forget Reason # 3: The first thing he'll do next is dig around in his litter box!
SCRATCH
SCRATCH
SCRATCH
Clean beds and dirty litter boxes don't mix...
And Reason # 4: His vaccines aren't all up-to-date and, even though he's not sick, he can still make you sick!
HHHAAAA
So, do you get it now?
Hump
Yeah...
Shh!, cat, stop purring so loudly or she'll hear you...
RRRRRRRR

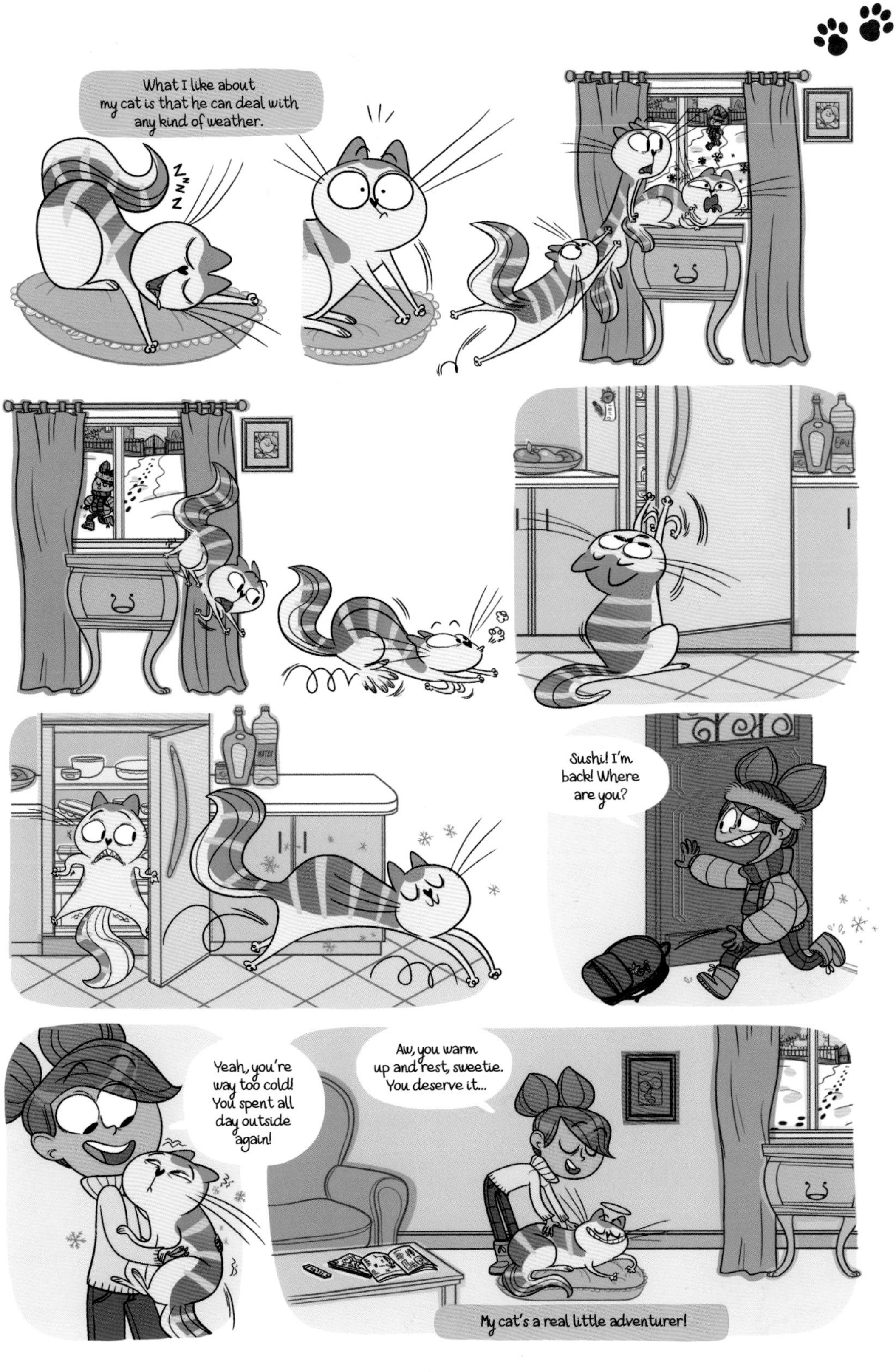
What I like about my cat is that he can deal with any kind of weather.
ZZZ
Sushi! I'm back! Where are you?
Yeah, you're way too cold! You spent all day outside again!
Aw, you warm up and rest, sweetie. You deserve it...
My cat's a real little adventurer!

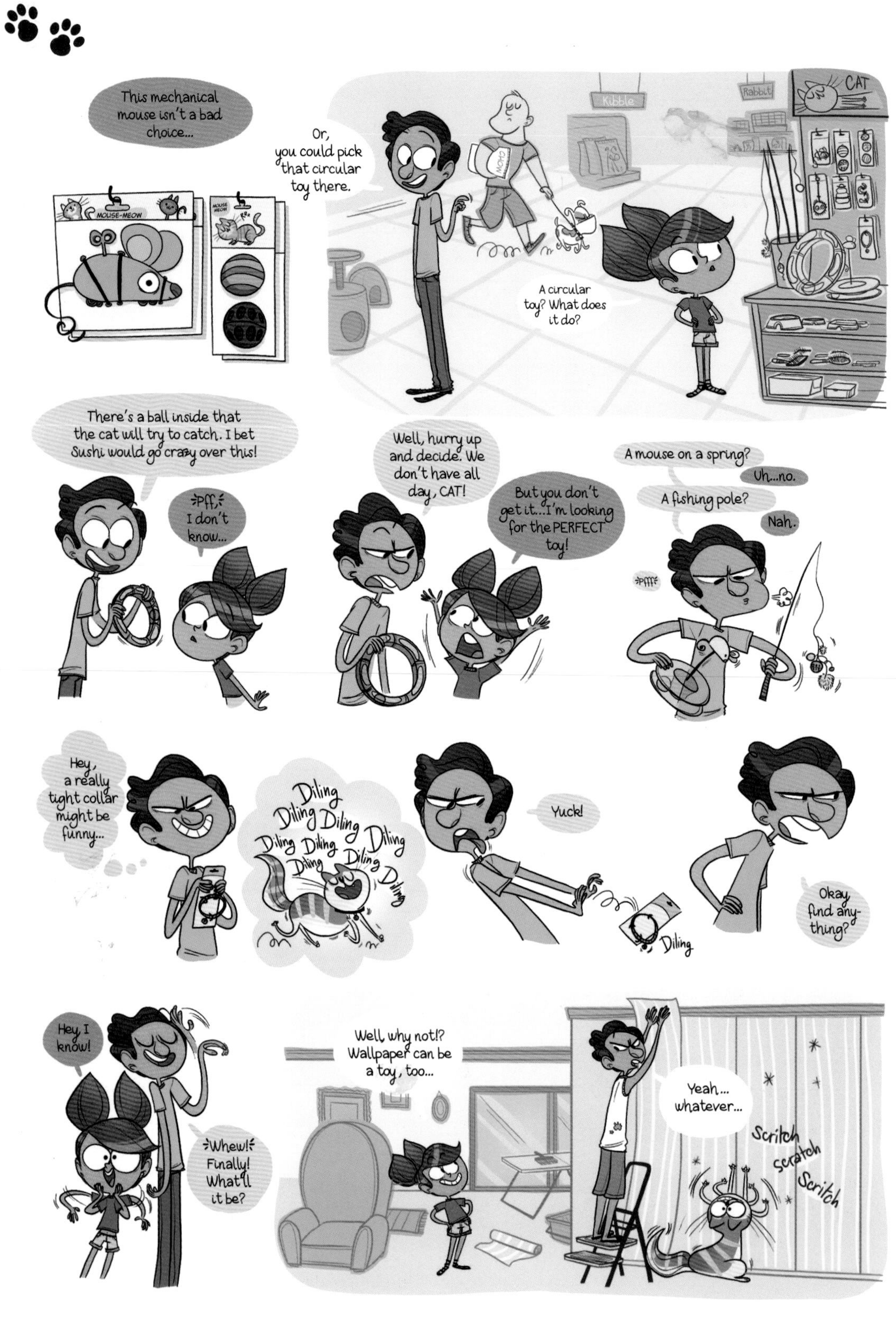
This mechanical mouse isn't a bad choice...
MOUSE-MEOW
Or, you could pick that circular toy there.
Kibble
Rabbit
CAT
CHOW
A circular toy? What does it do?
There's a ball inside that the cat will try to catch. I bet Sushi would go crazy over this!
Pff, I don't know...
Well, hurry up and decide. We don't have all day, CAT!
But you don't get it...I'm looking for the PERFECT toy!
A mouse on a spring?
Uh...no.
A fishing pole?
Nah.
Pfff
Hey, a really tight collar might be funny...
Diling Diling Diling Diling Diling Diling Diling Diling Diling
Yuck!
Diling
Okay, find anything?
Hey, I know!
Whew! Finally! What'll it be?
Well, why not!? Wallpaper can be a toy, too...
Yeah... whatever...
Scritch scratch Scritch

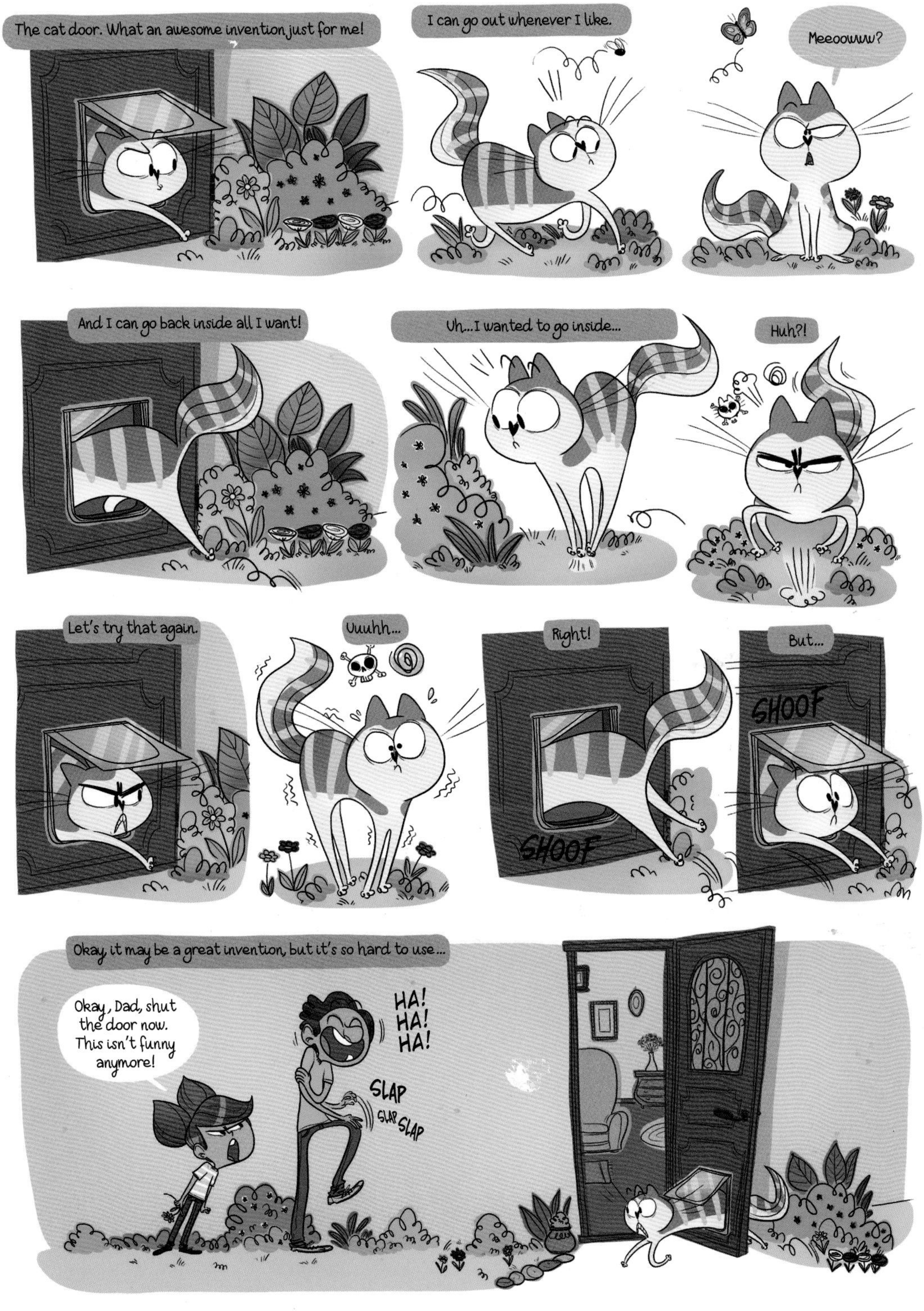

The cat door. What an awesome invention just for me!
I can go out whenever I like.
Meeoouuu?
And I can go back inside all I want!
Uh...I wanted to go inside...
Huh?!
Let's try that again.
Uuuhh...
Right!
SHOOF
But...
SHOOF
Okay, it may be a great invention, but it's so hard to use...
Okay, Dad, shut the door now. This isn't funny anymore!
HA! HA! HA!
SLAP
SLAP SLAP

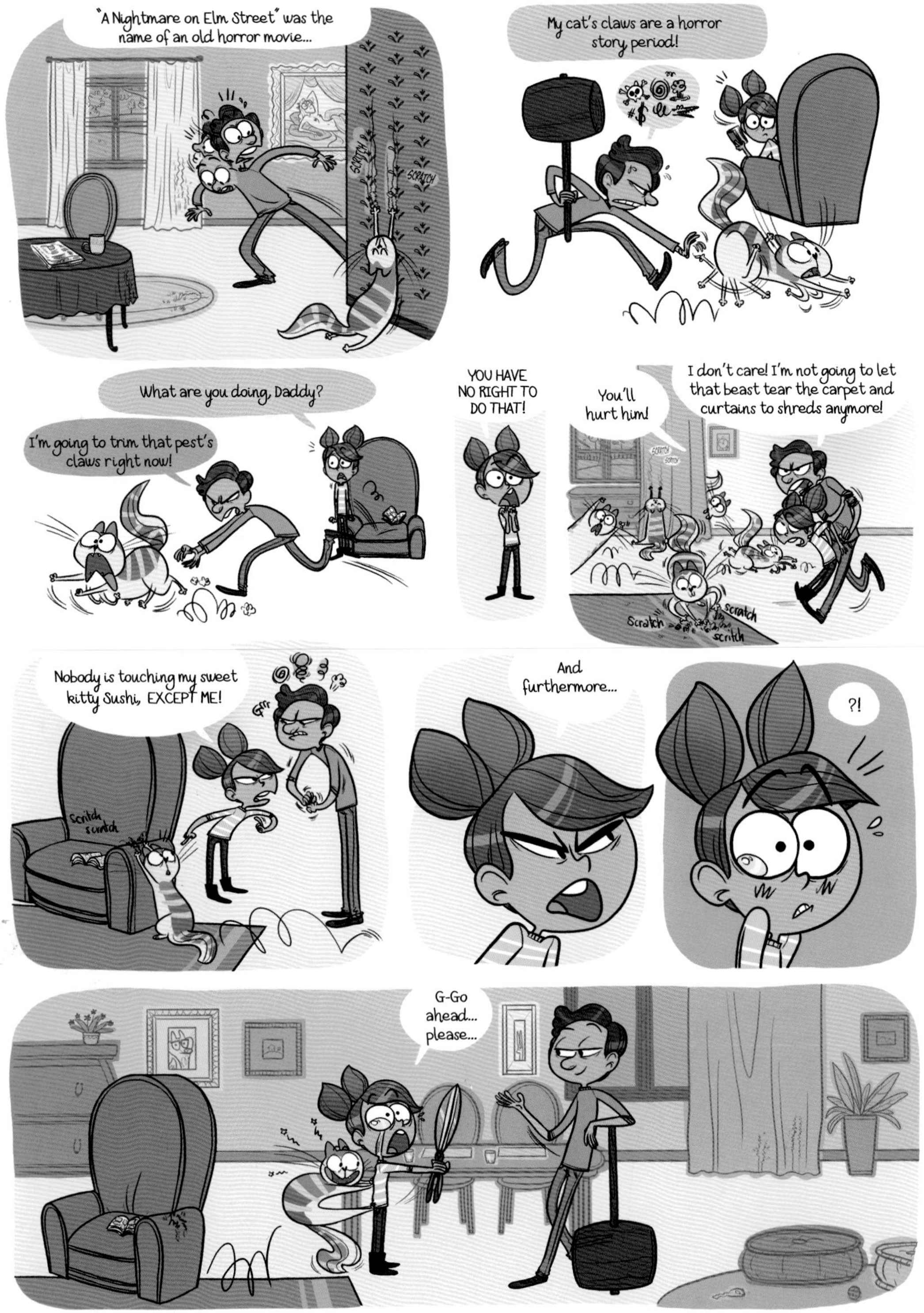
"A Nightmare on Elm Street" was the name of an old horror movie...
SCRATCH
SCRATCH
My cat's claws are a horror story, period!
#$
What are you doing, Daddy?
I'm going to trim that pest's claws right now!
YOU HAVE NO RIGHT TO DO THAT!
You'll hurt him!
I don't care! I'm not going to let that beast tear the carpet and curtains to shreds anymore!
Scratch
scratch
scritch
Nobody is touching my sweet kitty Sushi, EXCEPT ME!
Grrr
Scritch scratch
And furthermore...
?!
G-Go ahead... please...

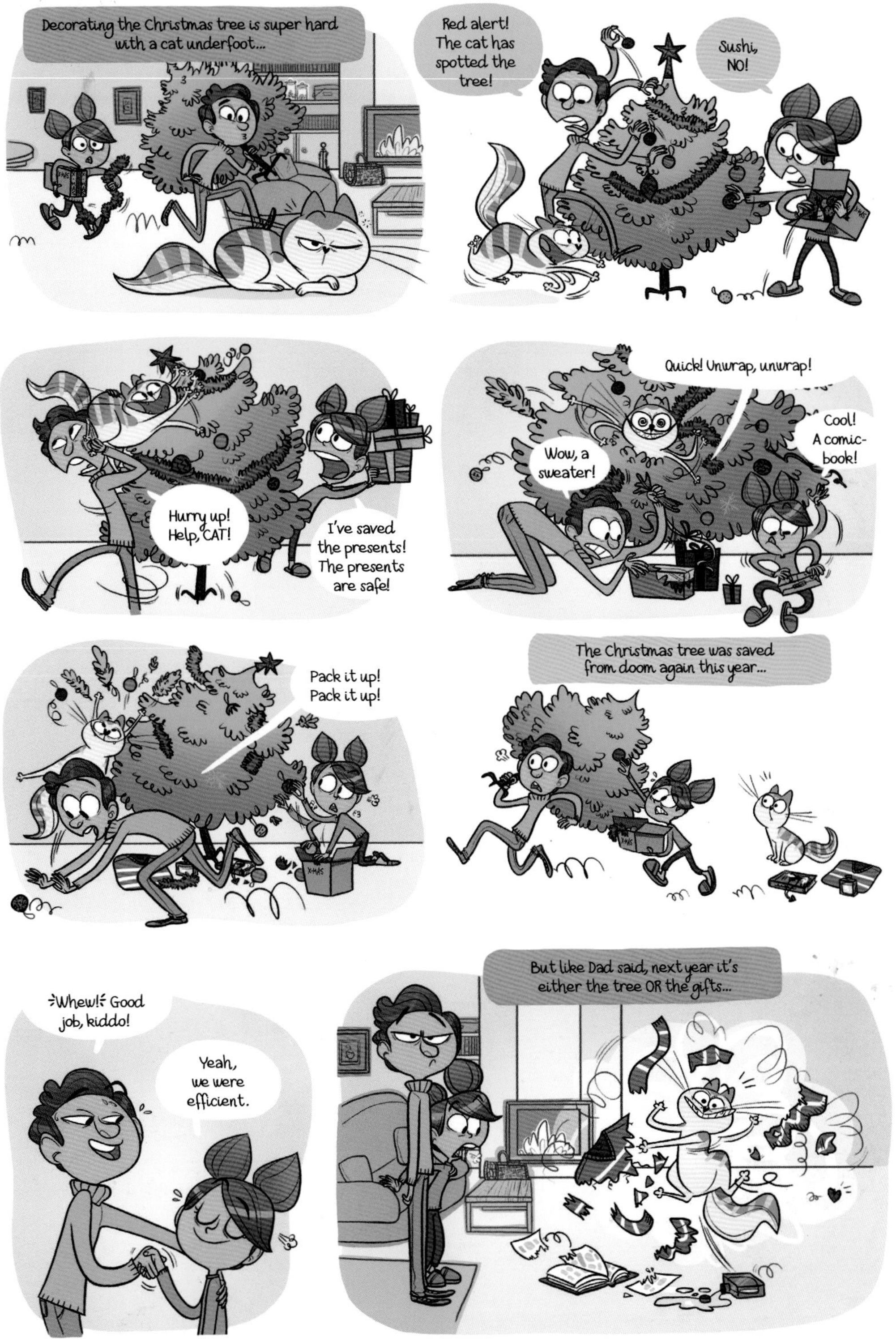
Decorating the Christmas tree is super hard with a cat underfoot...
Red alert! The cat has spotted the tree!
Sushi, NO!
Hurry up! Help, CAT!
I've saved the presents! The presents are safe!
Quick! Unwrap, unwrap!
Wow, a sweater!
Cool! A comic-book!
Pack it up! Pack it up!
The Christmas tree was saved from doom again this year...
Whew! Good job, kiddo!
Yeah, we were efficient.
But like Dad said, next year it's either the tree OR the gifts...

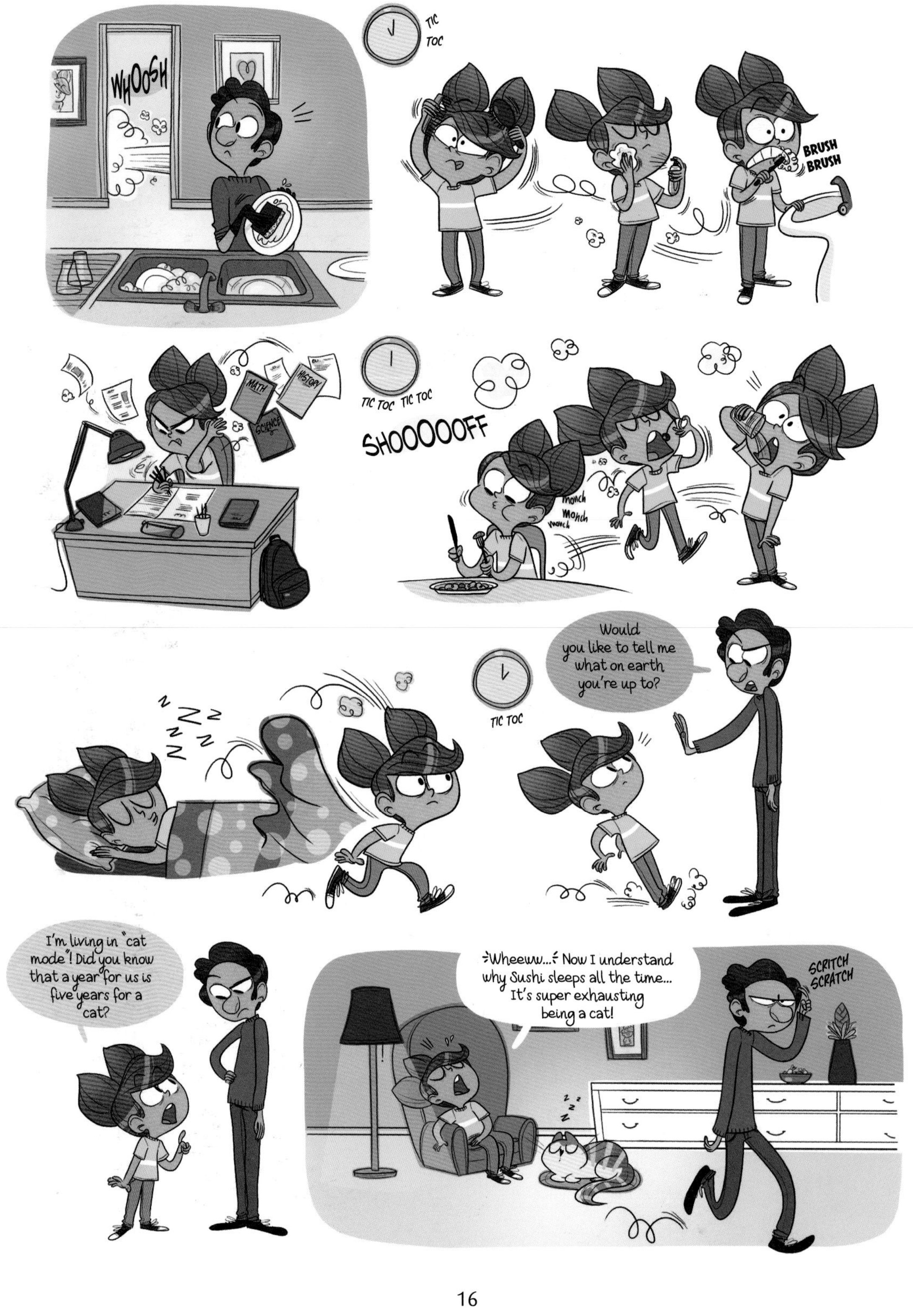
WHOOSH
TIC
TOC
BRUSH
BRUSH
MATH
HISTORY
SCIENCE
TIC TOC TIC TOC
SHOOOOOFF
monch
monch
monch
Z Z Z
Z Z
TIC TOC
Would you like to tell me what on earth you're up to?
I'm living in "cat mode"! Did you know that a year for us is five years for a cat?
Wheeuw... Now I understand why Sushi sleeps all the time... It's super exhausting being a cat!
SCRITCH
SCRATCH

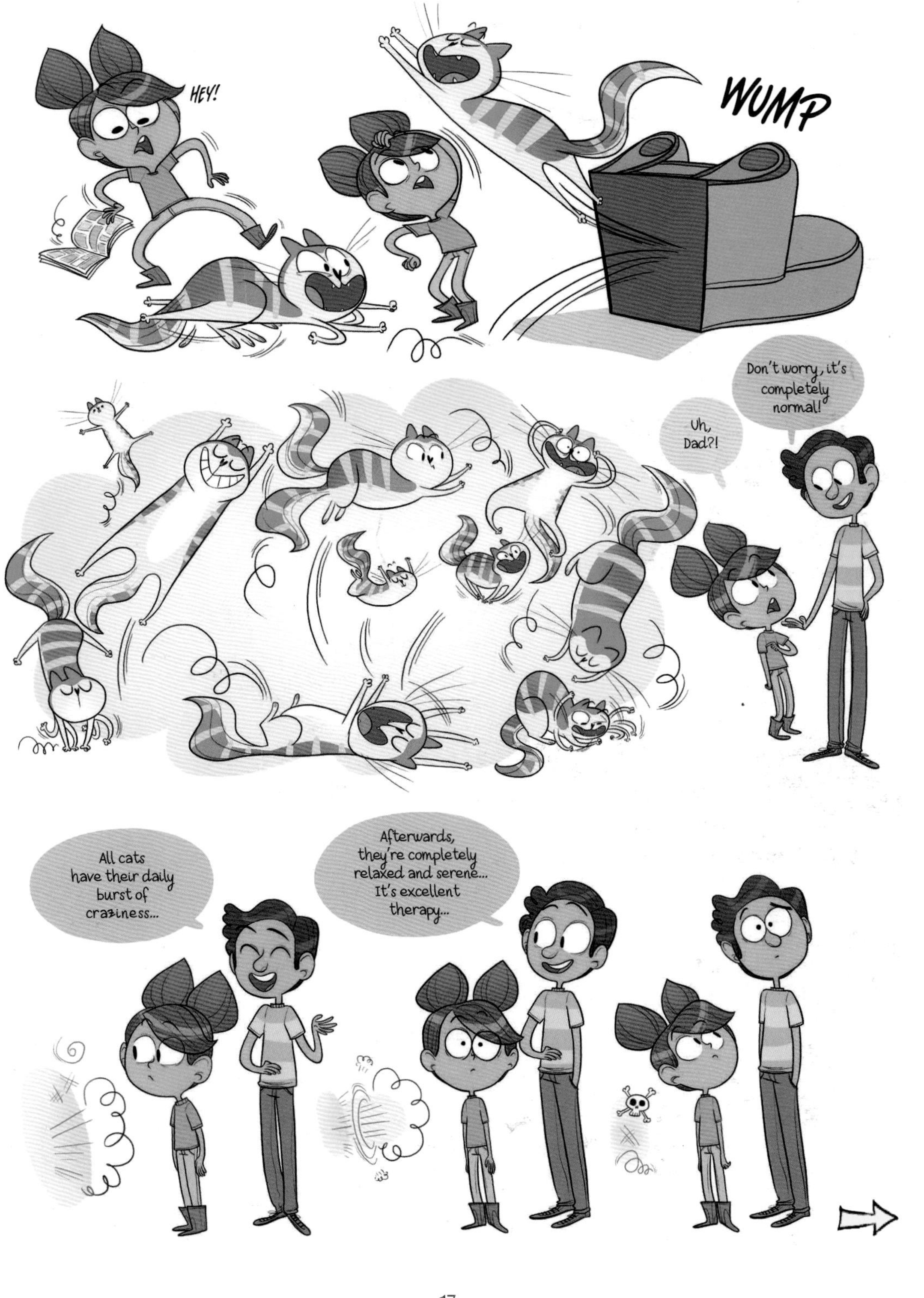
HEY!
WUMP
Uh, Dad?!
Don't worry, it's completely normal!
All cats have their daily burst of craziness...
Afterwards, they're completely relaxed and serene... It's excellent therapy...

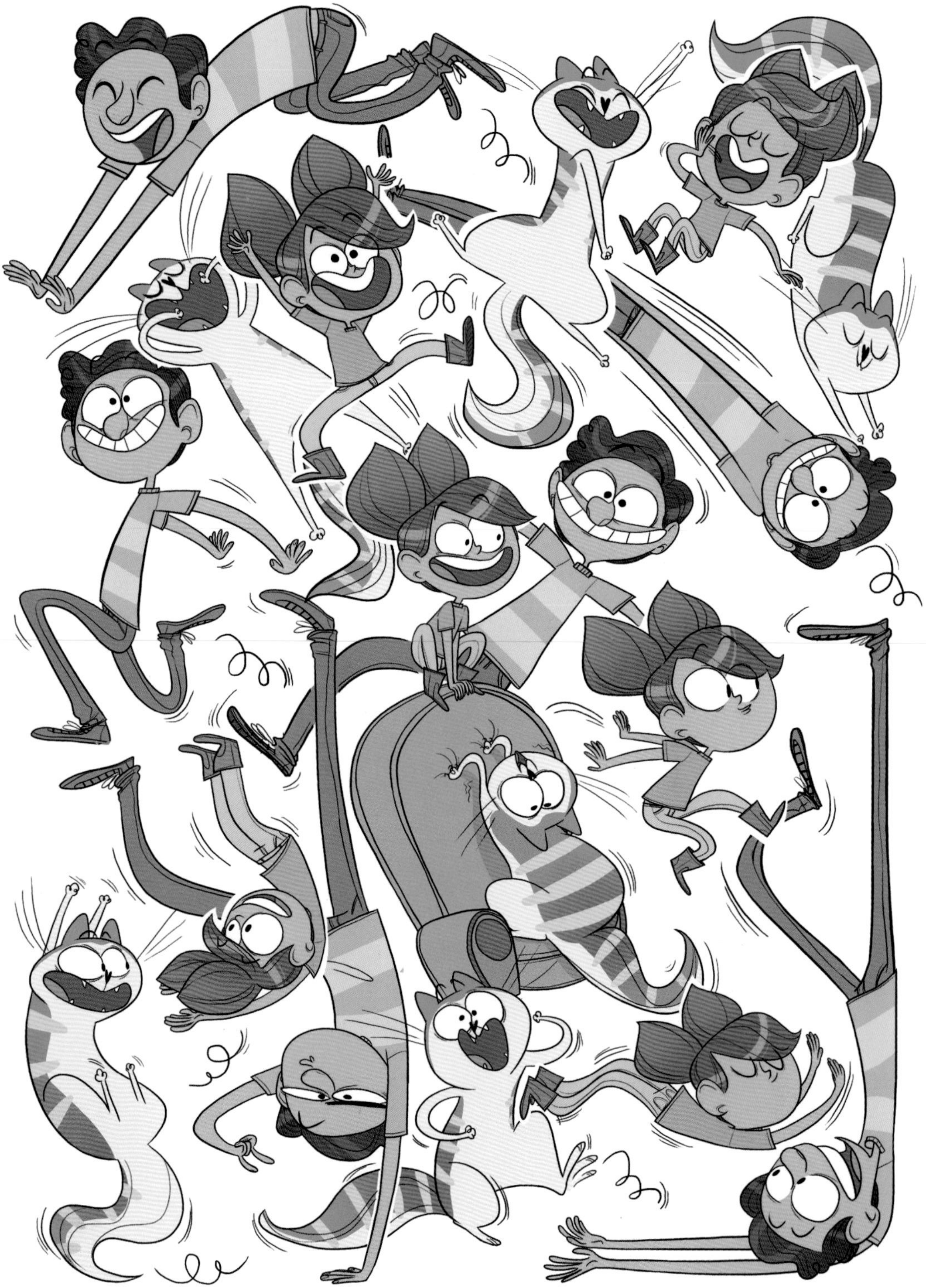

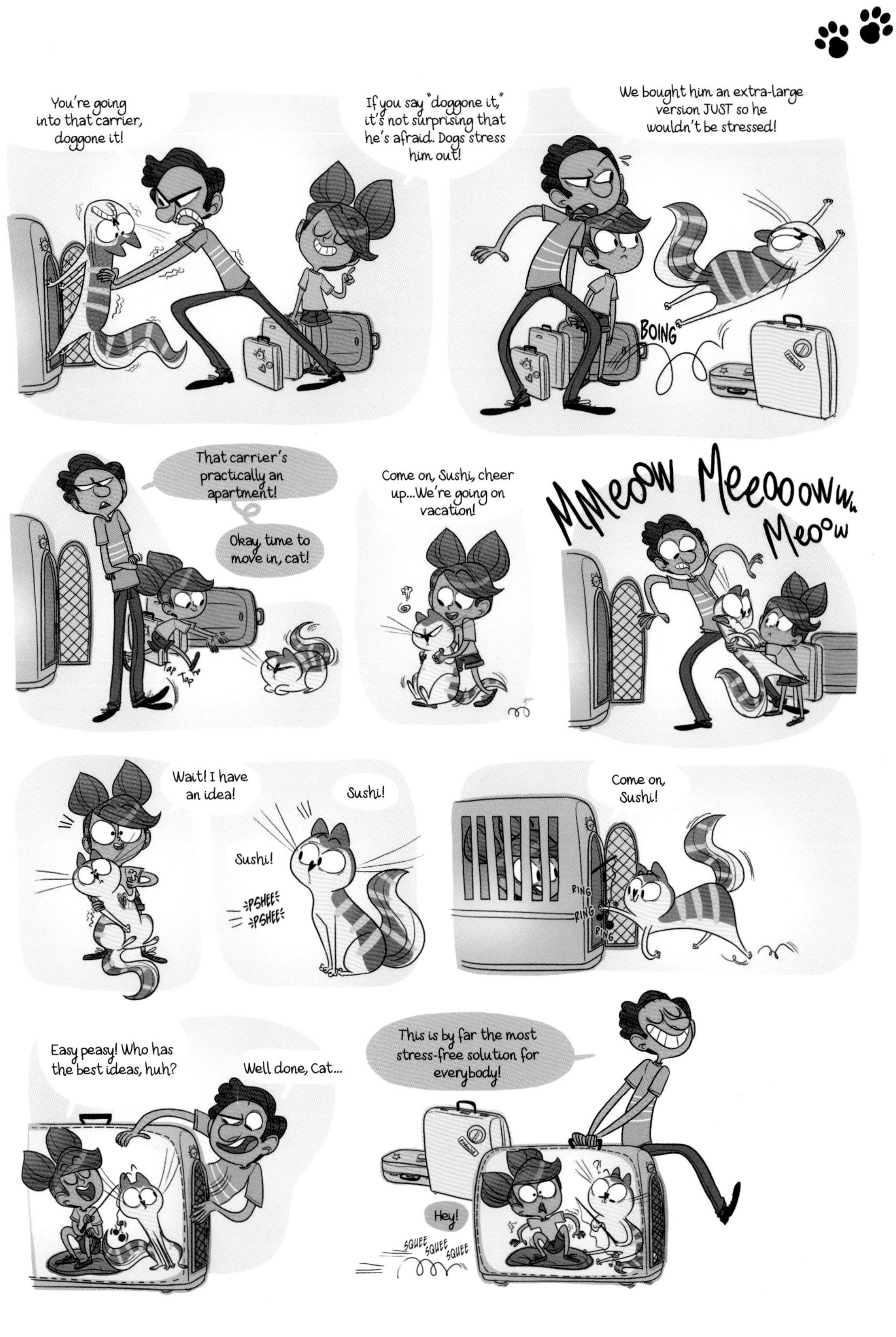

You're going into that carrier, doggone it!
If you say "doggone it," it's not surprising that he's afraid. Dogs stress him out!
We bought him an extra-large version JUST so he wouldn't be stressed!
BOING
That carrier's practically an apartment!
Okay, time to move in, cat!
Come on, Sushi, cheer up...We're going on vacation!
MMeow Meeooowww Meow
Wait! I have an idea!
Sushi!
Sushi!
PSHEE
PSHEE
Come on, Sushi!
RING
RING
RING
Easy peasy! Who has the best ideas, huh?
Well done, Cat...
This is by far the most stress-free solution for everybody!
Hey!
SQUEE SQUEE SQUEE

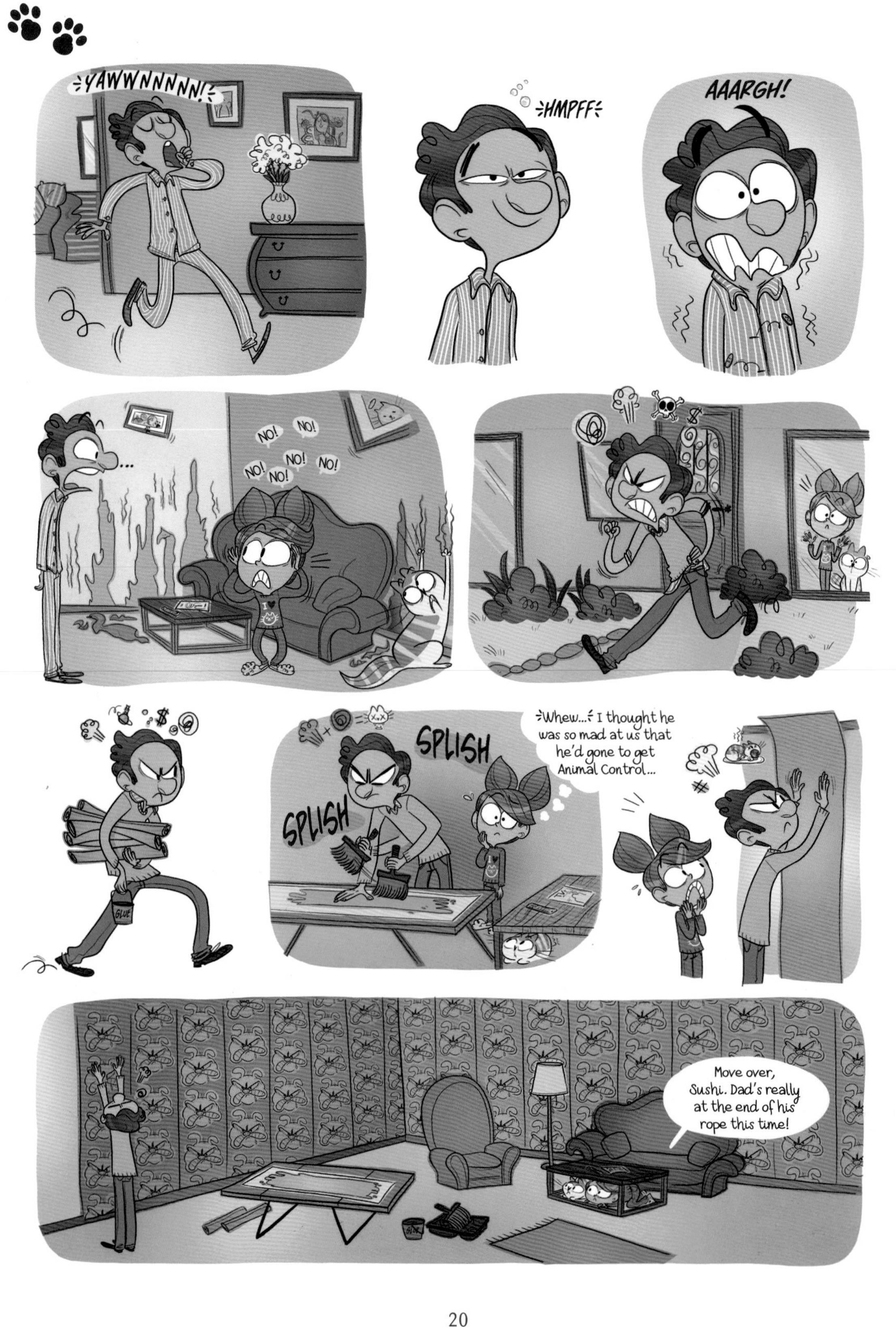
YAWWNNNNN!
HMPFF
AAARGH!
NO!
NO!
NO!
NO!
NO!
SPLISH
SPLISH
Whew... I thought he was so mad at us that he'd gone to get Animal Control...
GLUE
Move over, Sushi. Dad's really at the end of his rope this time!

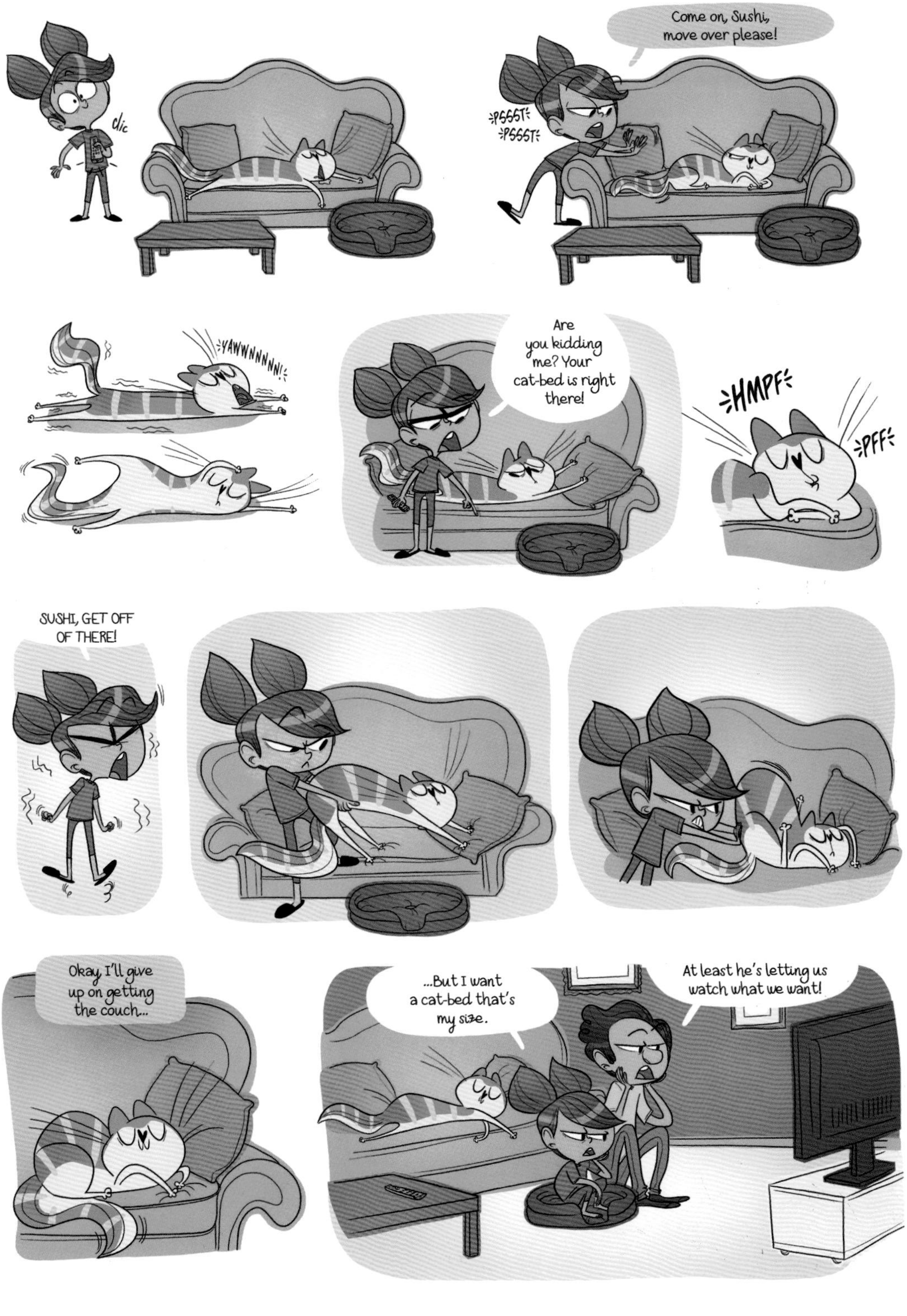

clic
Come on, Sushi, move over please!
PSSST PSSST
YAWWNNNNN!
Are you kidding me? Your cat-bed is right there!
HMPF
PFF
SUSHI, GET OFF OF THERE!
Okay, I'll give up on getting the couch...
...But I want a cat-bed that's my size.
At least he's letting us watch what we want!

People saying that cats have nine lives is no joke!

I ought to know...

BOOOM

The first time, I stupidly bit the dust while crossing the street...

BOOOM

SPLOTCH

...and back then, they didn't care about right-of-way!

BOOM BOOM BOOM

The second time was in Egypt...

This is all very fancy but they forgot my cat food...

...Locked up with my master the Pharaoh.

Meow!?

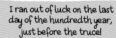

I lost my third life during the Hundred Years War...

Charge!

I ran out of luck on the last day of the hundredth year, just before the truce!

Run!

ZoOOM

⇨

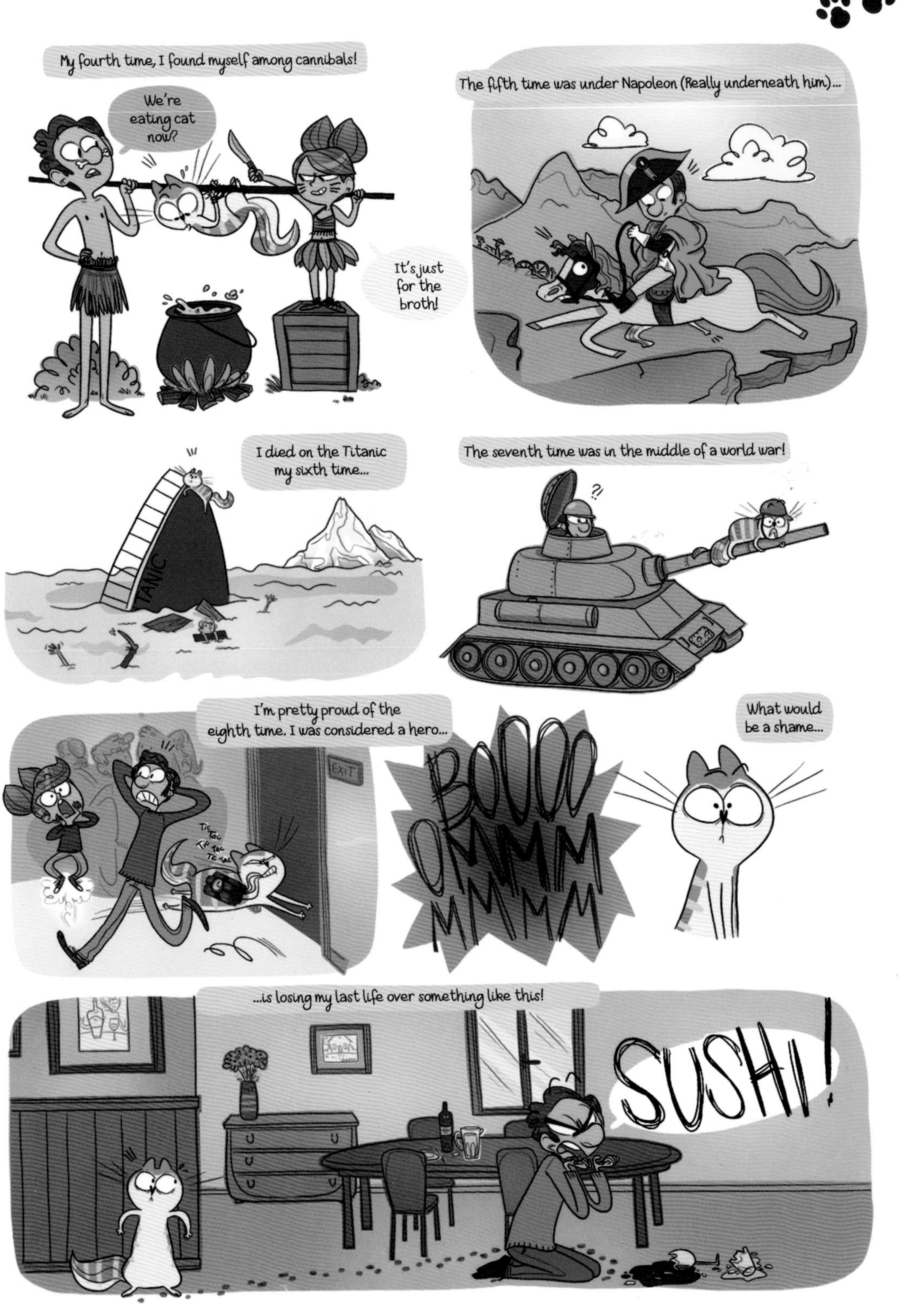
My fourth time, I found myself among cannibals!
We're eating cat now?
It's just for the broth!
The fifth time was under Napoleon (Really underneath him)...
I died on the Titanic my sixth time...
TANIC
The seventh time was in the middle of a world war!
I'm pretty proud of the eighth time. I was considered a hero...
EXIT
BOOOOOMMMMMMMM
What would be a shame...
...is losing my last life over something like this!
SUSHI!

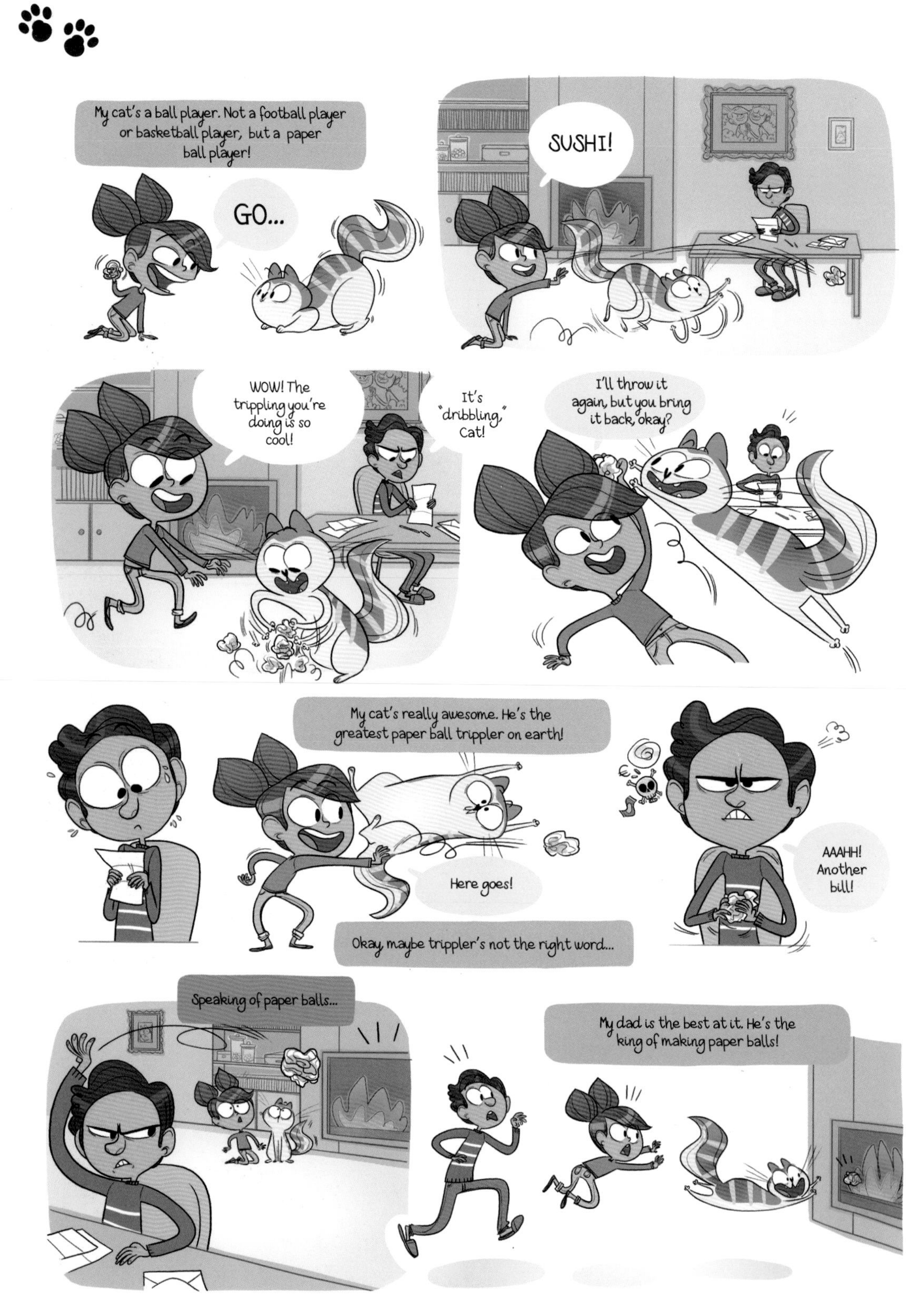
My cat's a ball player. Not a football player or basketball player, but a paper ball player!
GO...
SUSHI!
WOW! The trippling you're doing is so cool!
It's "dribbling," Cat!
I'll throw it again, but you bring it back, okay?
My cat's really awesome. He's the greatest paper ball trippler on earth!
Here goes!
Okay, maybe trippler's not the right word...
AAAHH! Another bill!
Speaking of paper balls...
My dad is the best at it. He's the king of making paper balls!

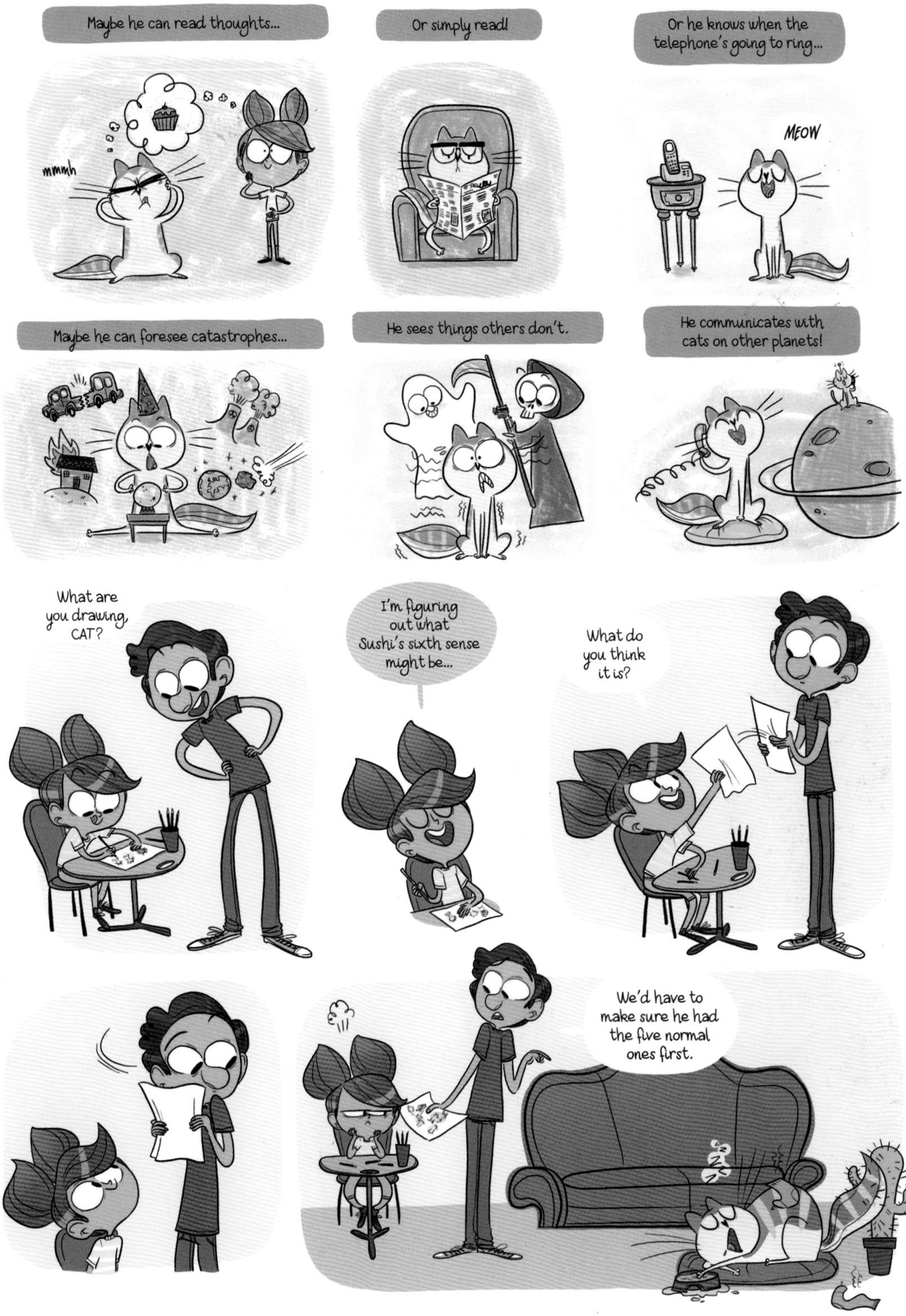

Maybe he can read thoughts...
mmmh
Or simply read!
Or he knows when the telephone's going to ring...
MEOW
Maybe he can foresee catastrophes...
He sees things others don't.
He communicates with cats on other planets!
What are you drawing, CAT?
I'm figuring out what Sushi's sixth sense might be...
What do you think it is?
We'd have to make sure he had the five normal ones first.

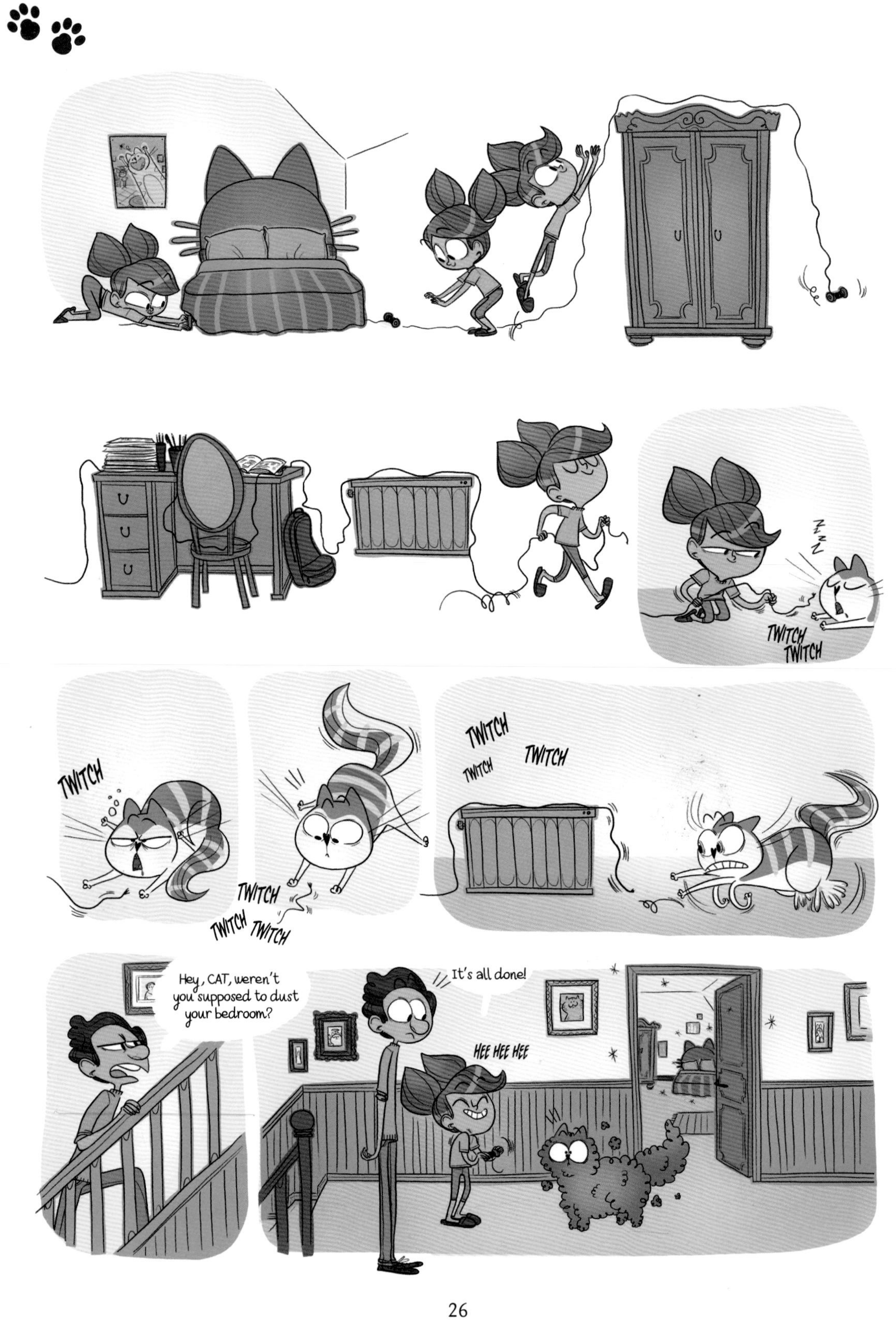

Z Z Z
TWITCH
TWITCH
TWITCH
TWITCH
TWITCH
TWITCH
TWITCH
TWITCH
TWITCH
Hey, CAT, weren't you supposed to dust your bedroom?
It's all done!
HEE HEE HEE

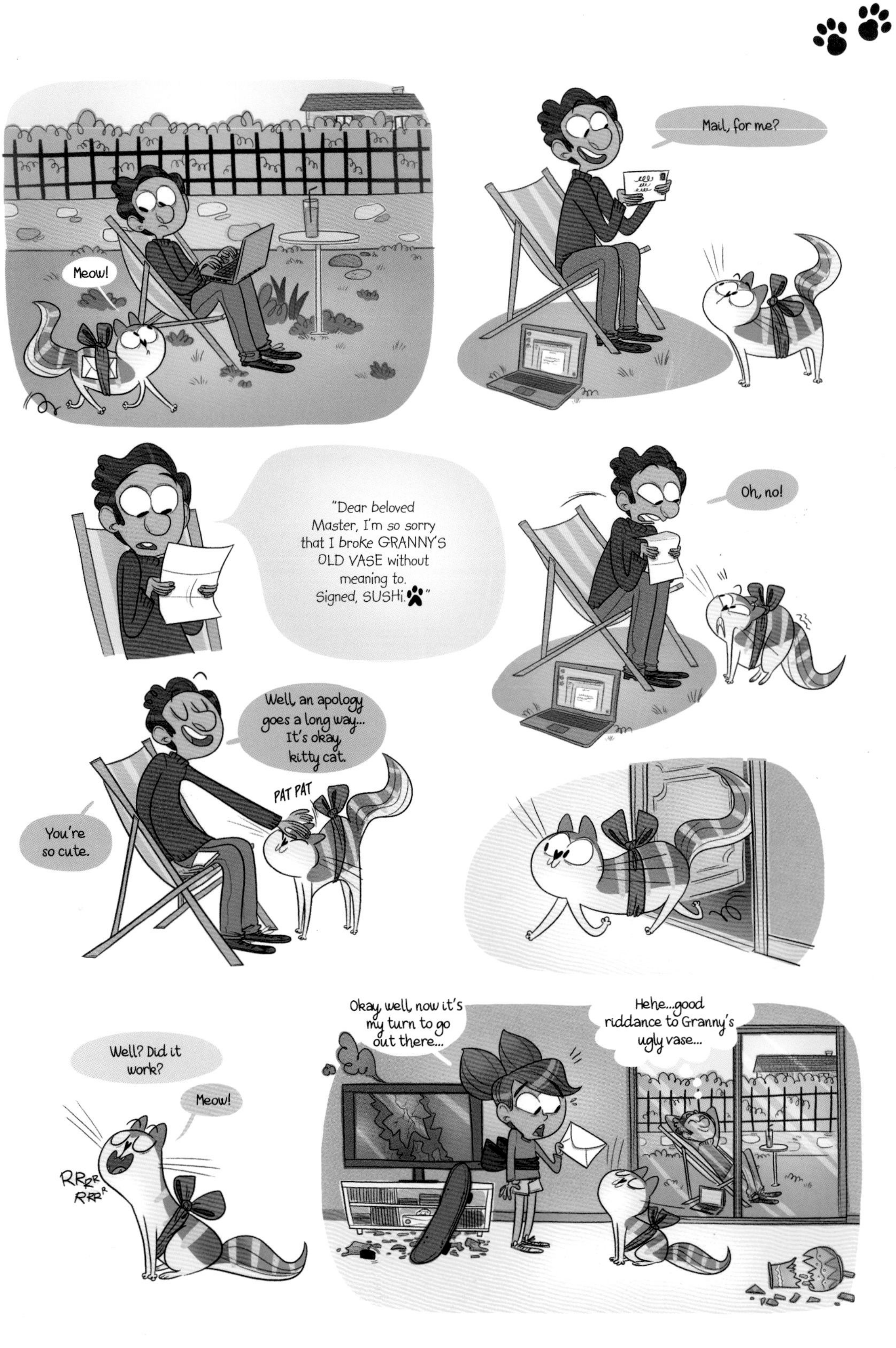

Meow!
Mail, for me?
"Dear beloved Master, I'm so sorry that I broke GRANNY'S OLD VASE without meaning to. Signed, SUSHi."
Oh, no!
Well, an apology goes a long way... It's okay, kitty cat.
PAT PAT
You're so cute.
Well? Did it work?
Meow!
RRRR RRRR
Okay, well, now it's my turn to go out there...
Hehe...good riddance to Granny's ugly vase...

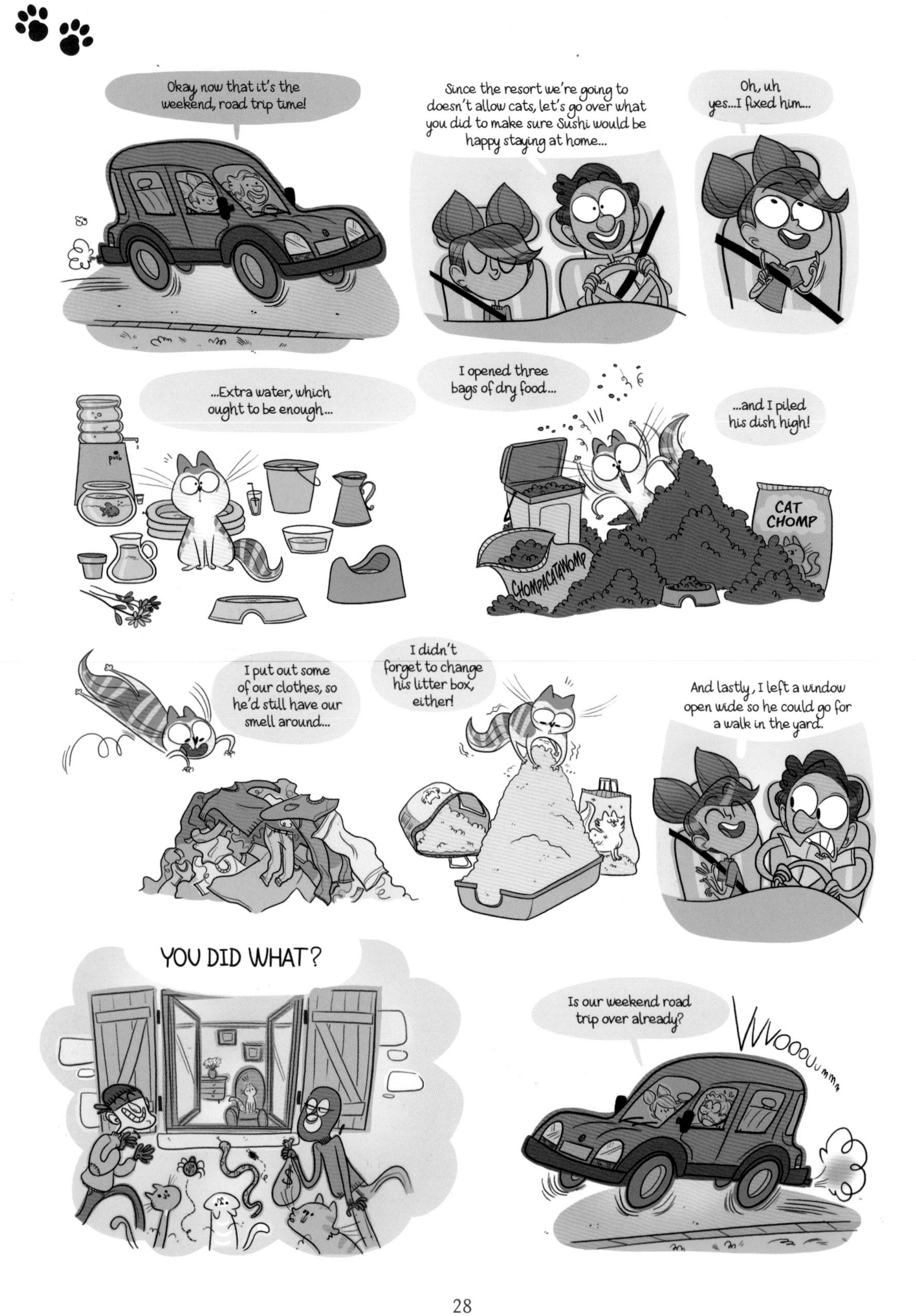
Okay, now that it's the weekend, road trip time!
Since the resort we're going to doesn't allow cats, let's go over what you did to make sure Sushi would be happy staying at home...
Oh, uh yes...I fixed him...
...Extra water, which ought to be enough...
I opened three bags of dry food...
...and I piled his dish high!
CAT CHOMP
CHOMPACATAVOMP
I put out some of our clothes, so he'd still have our smell around...
I didn't forget to change his litter box, either!
And lastly, I left a window open wide so he could go for a walk in the yard.
YOU DID WHAT?
Is our weekend road trip over already?
VVVOOOUUmmm

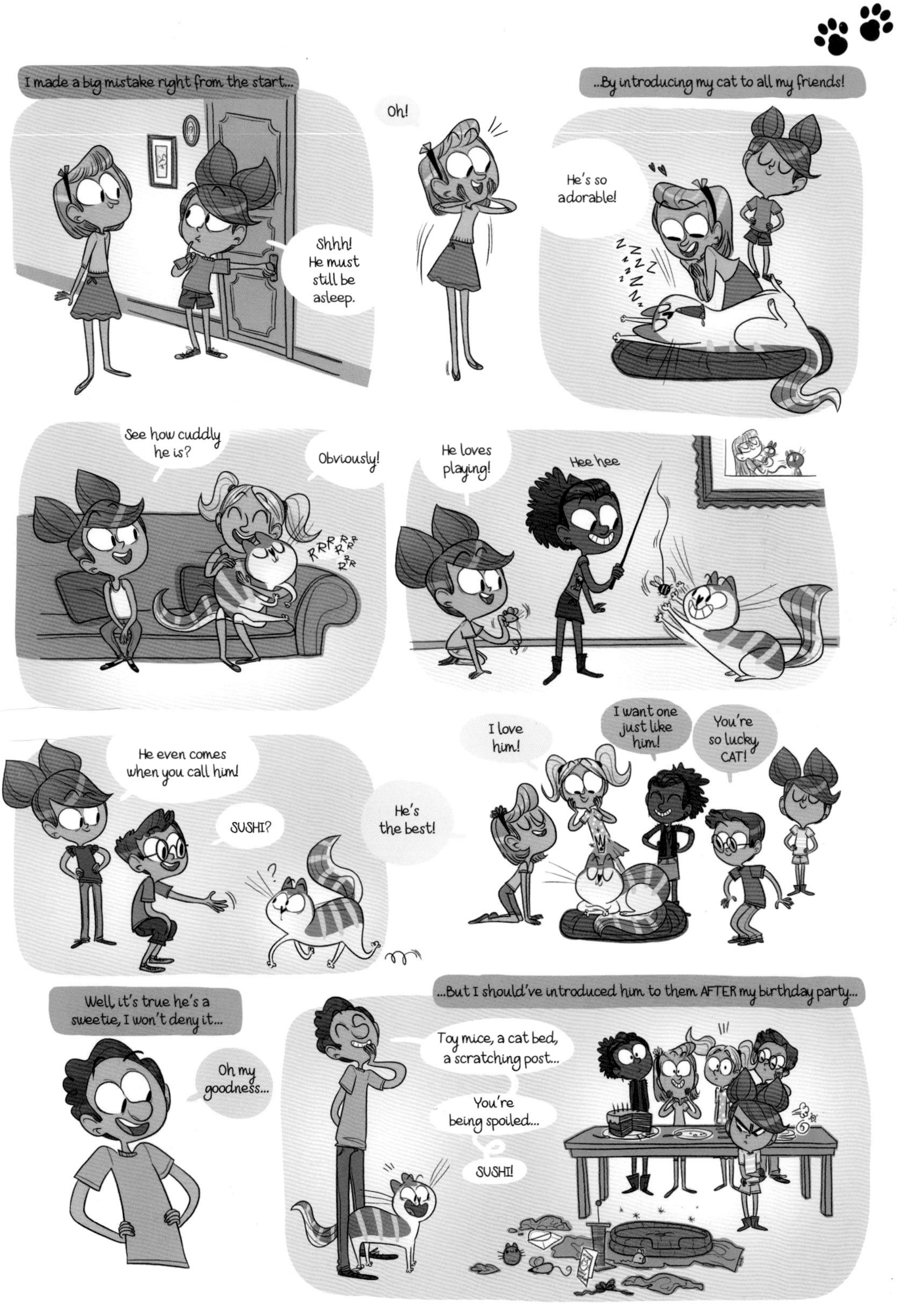

I made a big mistake right from the start...
Shhh! He must still be asleep.
Oh!
...By introducing my cat to all my friends!
He's so adorable!
ZZZZZ
See how cuddly he is?
Obviously!
RRRRR
He loves playing!
Hee hee
He even comes when you call him!
SUSHI?
?
He's the best!
I love him!
I want one just like him!
You're so lucky CAT!
Well, it's true he's a sweetie, I won't deny it...
Oh my goodness...
...But I should've introduced him to them AFTER my birthday party...
Toy mice, a cat bed, a scratching post...
You're being spoiled...
SUSHI!

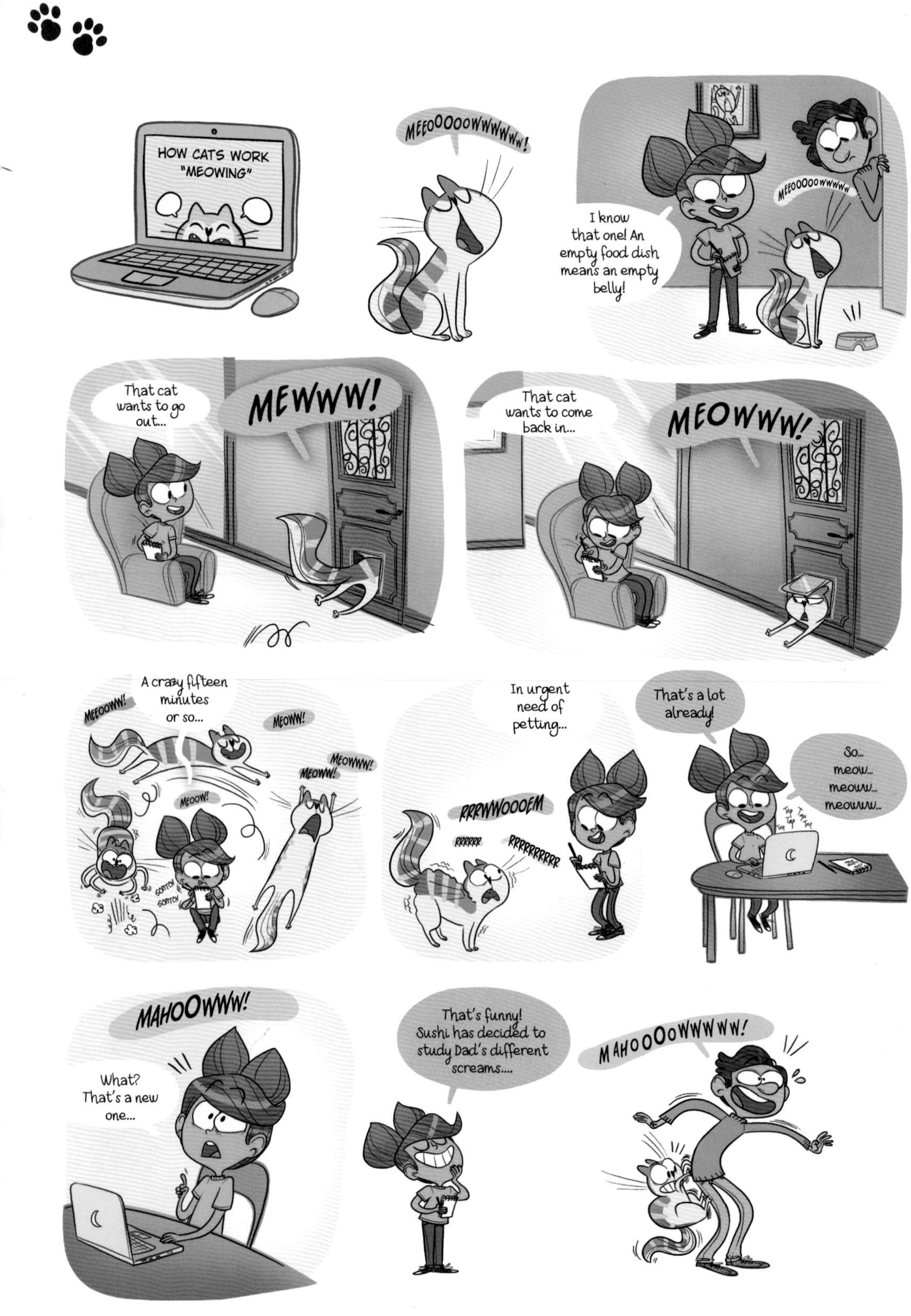
HOW CATS WORK
"MEOWING"
MEEOOOOOWWWWWw!
I know that one! An empty food dish means an empty belly!
MEEOOOOOWWWWW
That cat wants to go out...
MEWWW!
That cat wants to come back in...
MEOWWW!
A crazy fifteen minutes or so...
MEEOOWW!
MEOWW!
MEOWWW!
MEOWW!
MEOOW!
SCRITCH
SCRITCH
In urgent need of petting...
RRRWWOOOEM
RRRRRR
RRRRRRRRRR
That's a lot already!
So... meow... meouw... meouuw...
MAHOOWWW!
What? That's a new one...
That's funny! Sushi has decided to study Dad's different screams....
MAHOOOOOWWWWW!

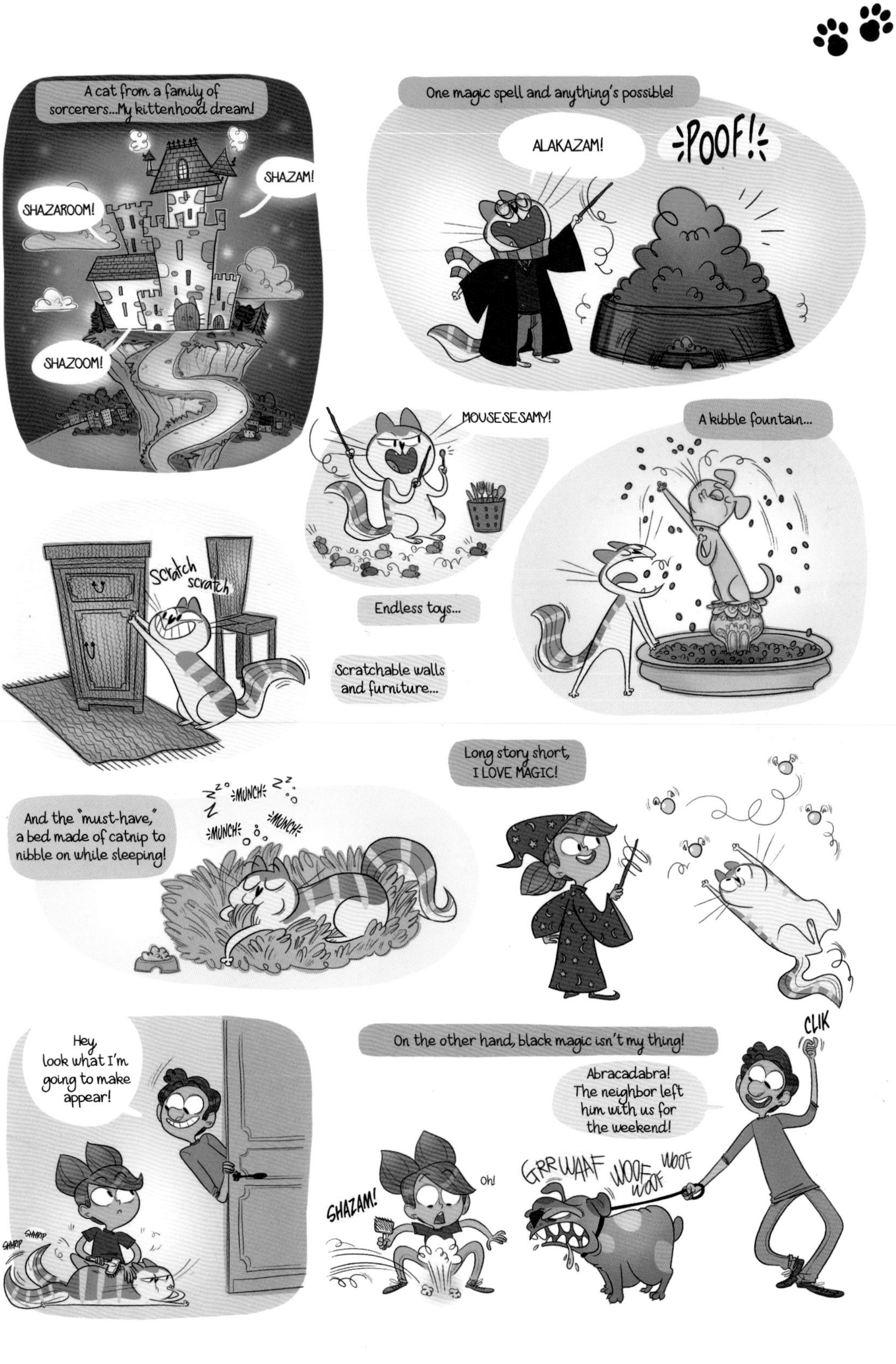
A cat from a family of sorcerers...My kittenhood dream!
SHAZAROOM!
SHAZAM!
SHAZOOM!
One magic spell and anything's possible!
ALAKAZAM!
POOF!
MOUSESESAMY!
A kibble fountain...
Scratch scratch
Endless toys...
Scratchable walls and furniture...
Long story short, I LOVE MAGIC!
And the "must-have," a bed made of catnip to nibble on while sleeping!
MUNCH
MUNCH
MUNCH
Hey, look what I'm going to make appear!
SHHRIP
SHHRIP
On the other hand, black magic isn't my thing!
CLIK
Abracadabra! The neighbor left him with us for the weekend!
GRRWAAF
WOOF
WOOF
WOOF
SHAZAM!
Oh!

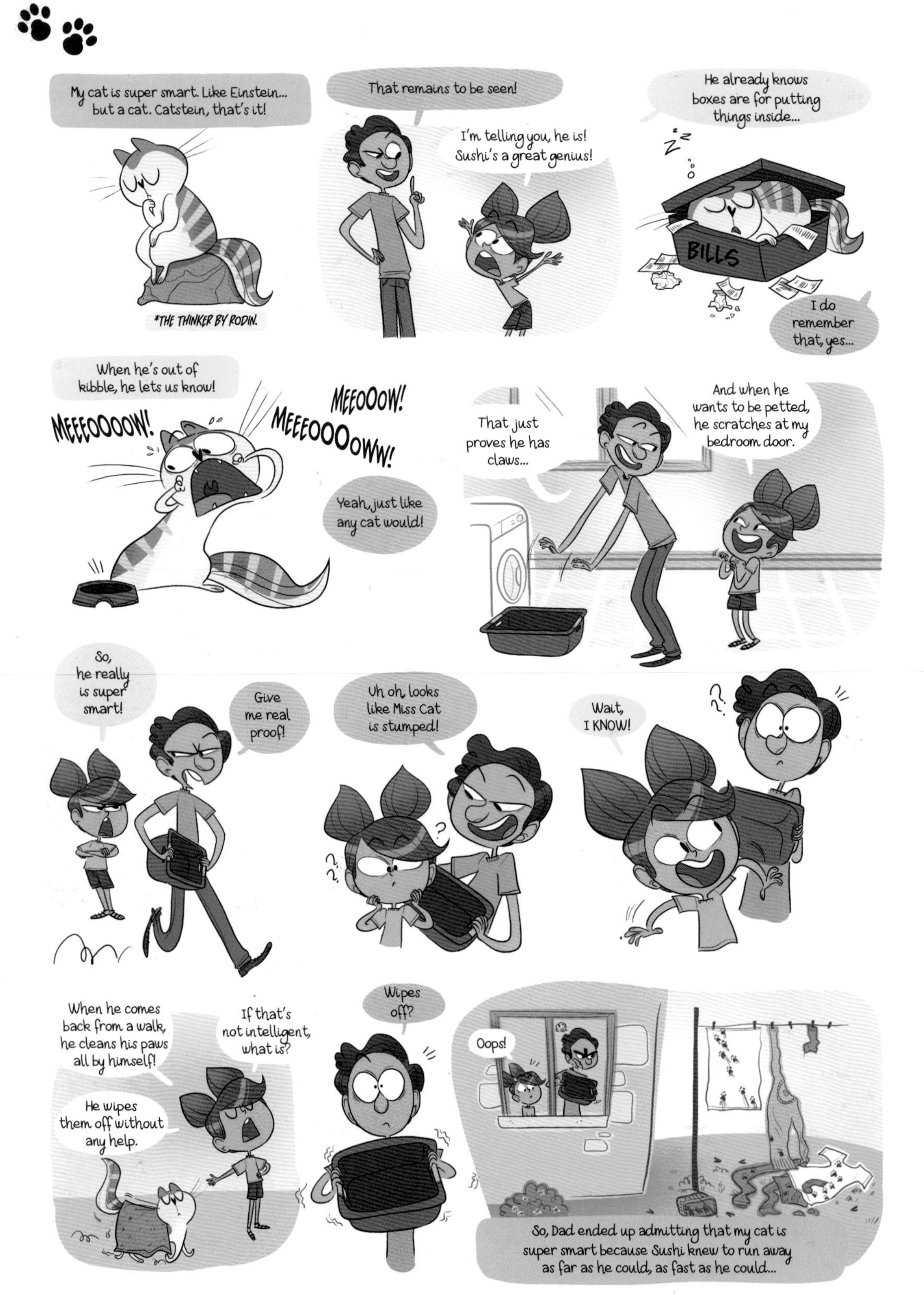
My cat is super smart. Like Einstein... but a cat. Catstein, that's it!
*THE THINKER BY RODIN.
That remains to be seen!
I'm telling you, he is! Sushi's a great genius!
He already knows boxes are for putting things inside...
BILLS
I do remember that, yes...
When he's out of kibble, he lets us know!
MEEEOOOOW!
MEEOOOW!
MEEEOOOOoWW!
Yeah, just like any cat would!
That just proves he has claws...
And when he wants to be petted, he scratches at my bedroom door.
So, he really is super smart!
Give me real proof!
Uh oh, looks like Miss Cat is stumped!
Wait, I KNOW!
When he comes back from a walk, he cleans his paws all by himself!
If that's not intelligent, what is?
He wipes them off without any help.
Wipes off?
Oops!
So, Dad ended up admitting that my cat is super smart because Sushi knew to run away as far as he could, as fast as he could...

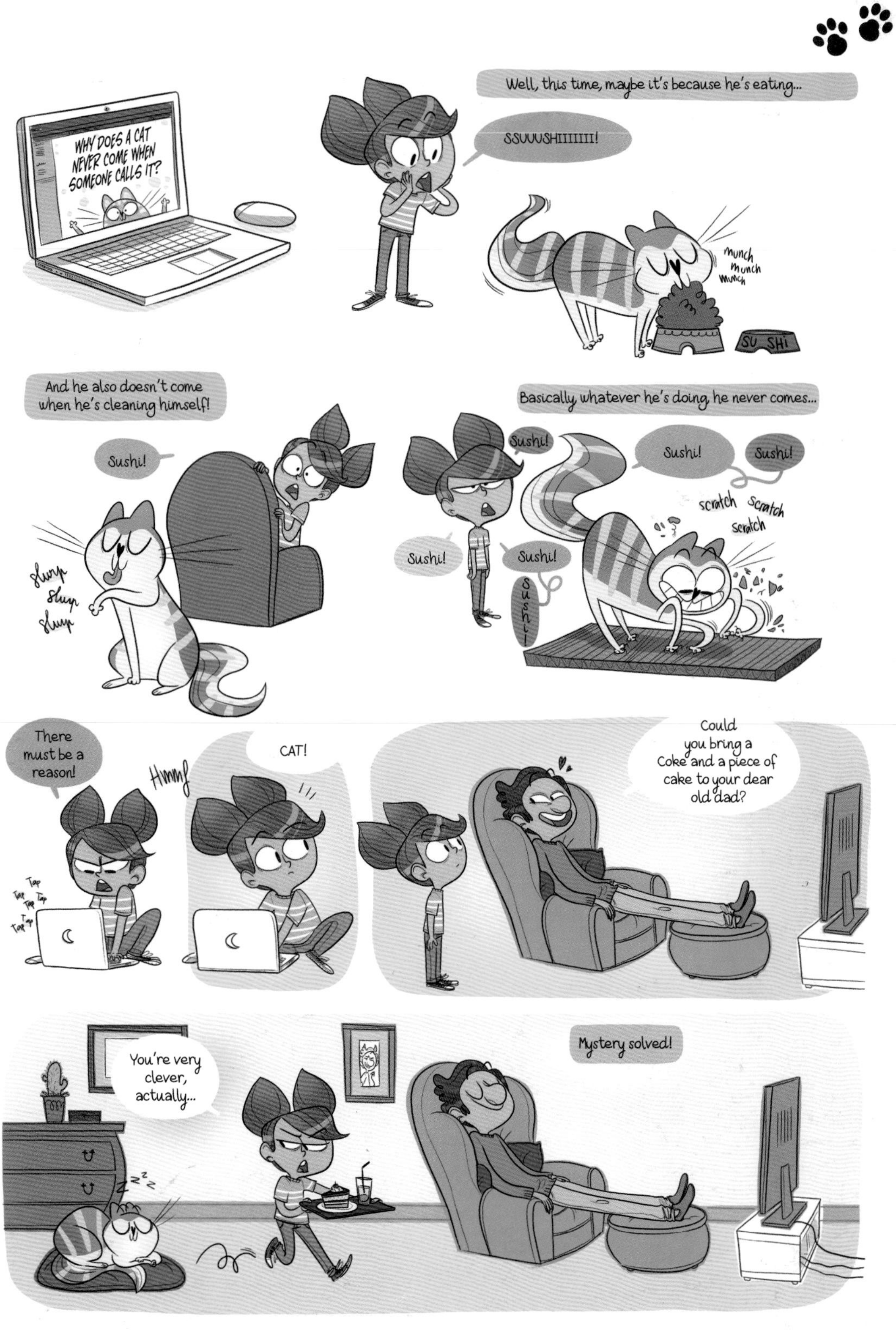
WHY DOES A CAT NEVER COME WHEN SOMEONE CALLS IT?
Well, this time, maybe it's because he's eating...
SSUUUSHIIIIIII!
munch munch munch
SU SHI
And he also doesn't come when he's cleaning himself!
Sushi!
slurp slurp slurp
Basically, whatever he's doing, he never comes...
Sushi!
Sushi!
Sushi!
Sushi!
Sushi!
Sushi!
scratch scratch scratch
There must be a reason!
Hmmf
Tap Tap Tap Tap Tap Tap
CAT!
Could you bring a Coke and a piece of cake to your dear old dad?
You're very clever, actually...
Mystery solved!

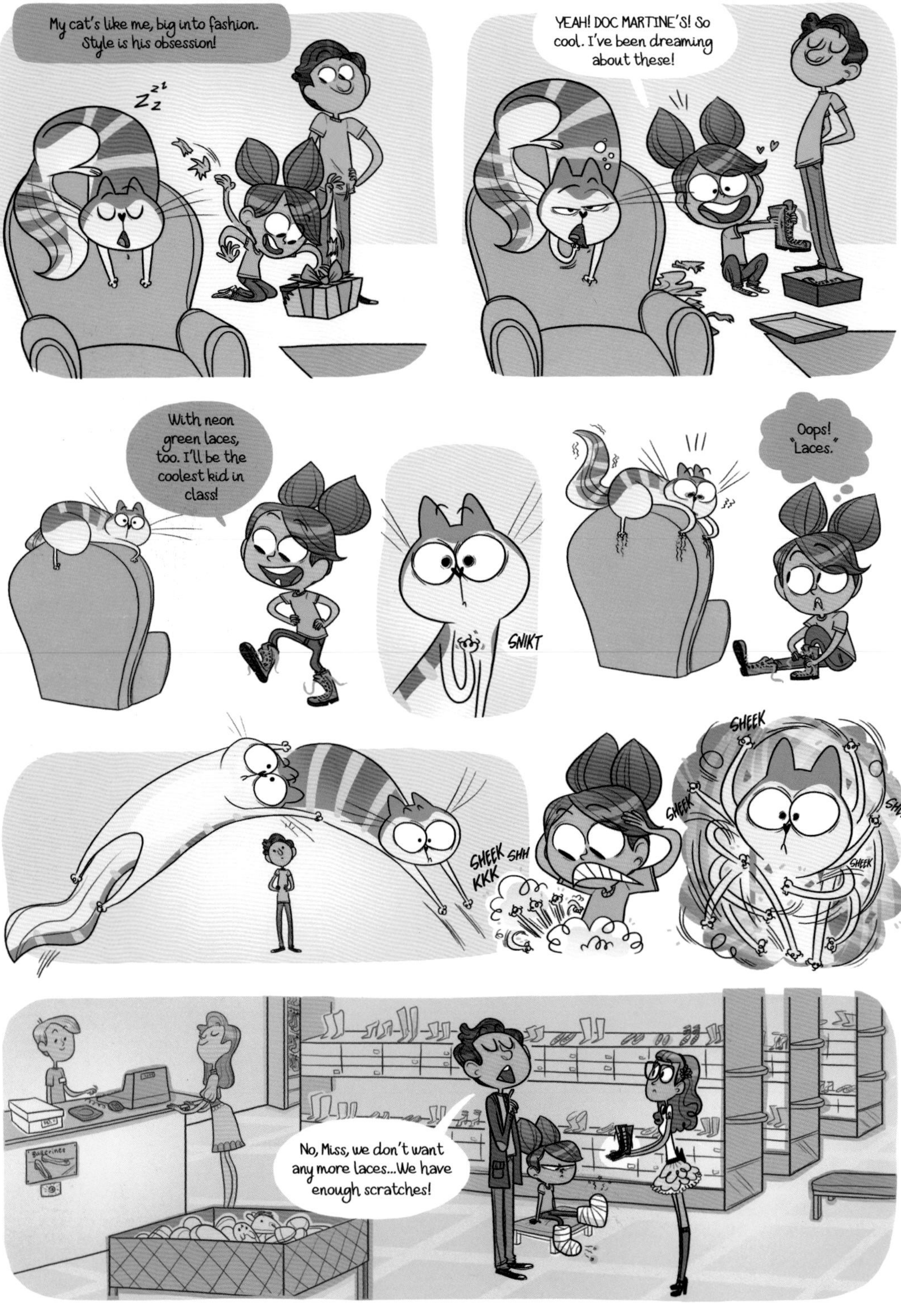
My cat's like me, big into fashion. Style is his obsession!
Zzz
YEAH! DOC MARTINE'S! So cool. I've been dreaming about these!
With neon green laces, too. I'll be the coolest kid in class!
SNIKT
Oops! "Laces."
SHEEK SHH KKK
SHEEK
SHEEK
SHEEK
SHEEK
No, Miss, we don't want any more laces...We have enough scratches!

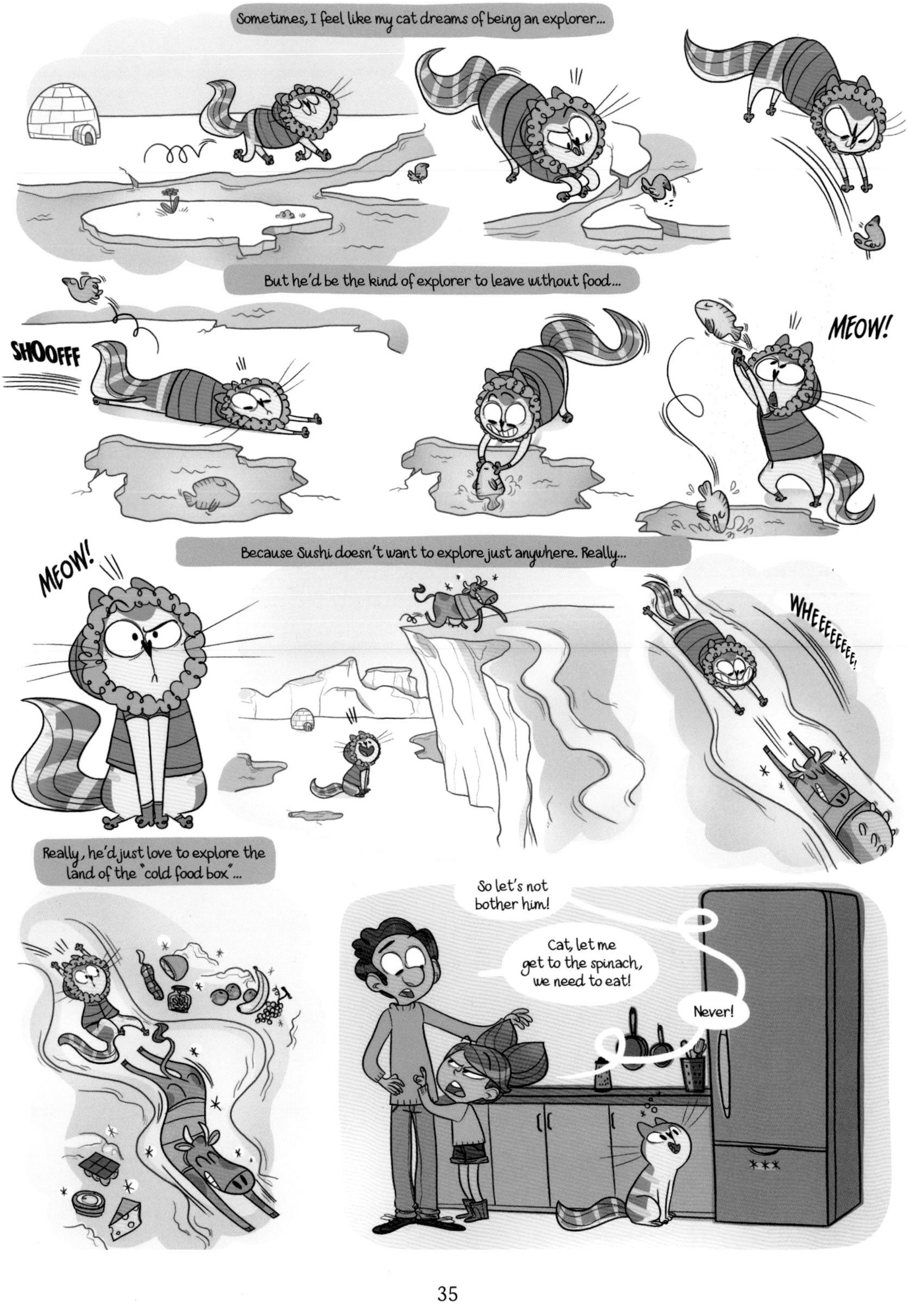
Sometimes, I feel like my cat dreams of being an explorer...
But he'd be the kind of explorer to leave without food...
SHOOFFF
MEOW!
Because Sushi doesn't want to explore just anywhere. Really...
MEOW!
WHEEEEEEEE!
Really, he'd just love to explore the land of the "cold food box"...
So let's not bother him!
Cat, let me get to the spinach, we need to eat!
Never!

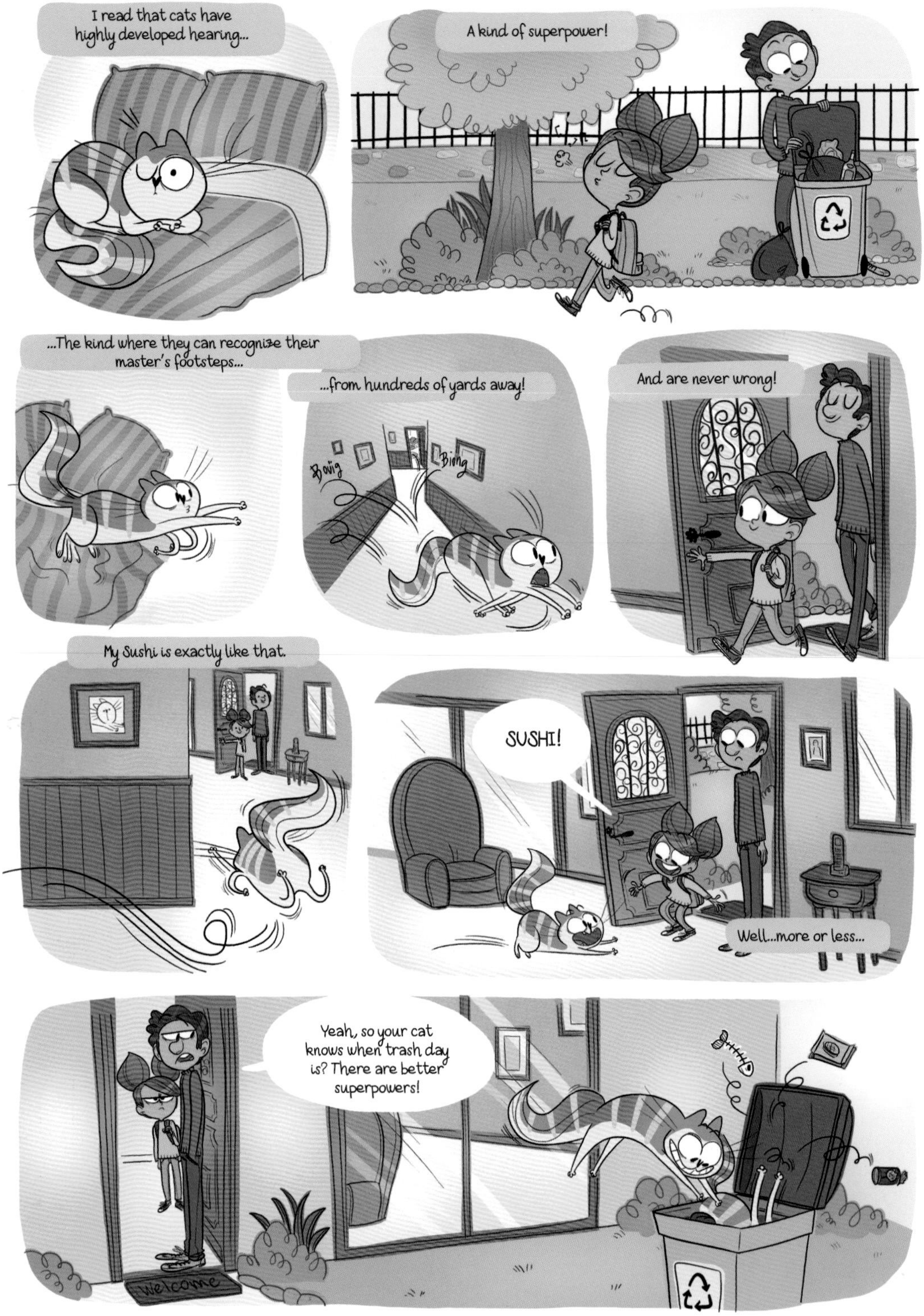
I read that cats have highly developed hearing...
A kind of superpower!
...The kind where they can recognize their master's footsteps...
...from hundreds of yards away!
And are never wrong!
My Sushi is exactly like that.
SUSHI!
Well...more or less...
Yeah, so your cat knows when trash day is? There are better superpowers!
Welcome

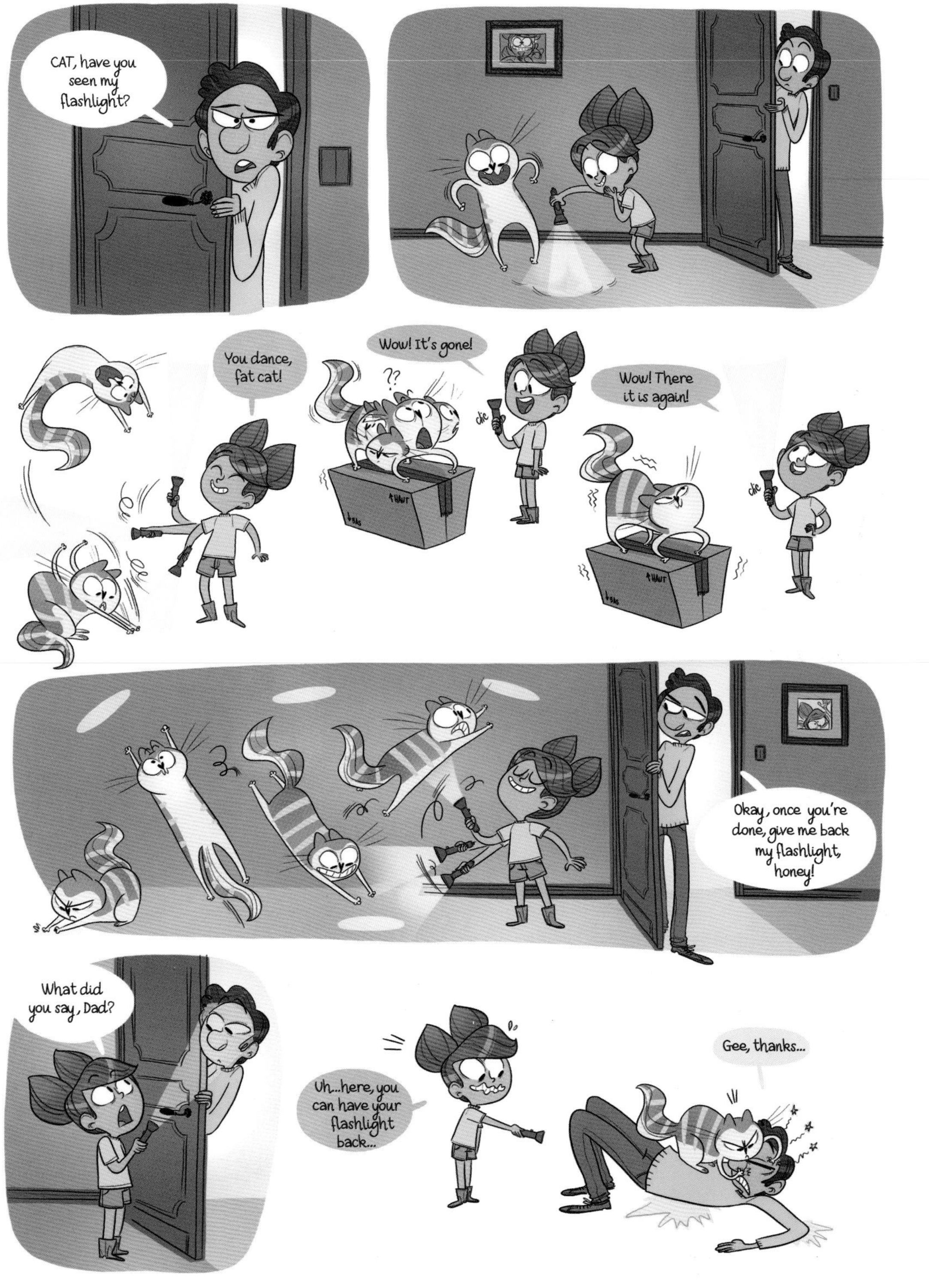
CAT, have you seen my flashlight?
You dance, fat cat!
Wow! It's gone!
??
clic
Wow! There it is again!
clic
HAUT
BAS
Okay, once you're done, give me back my flashlight, honey!
What did you say, Dad?
Uh...here, you can have your flashlight back...
Gee, thanks...

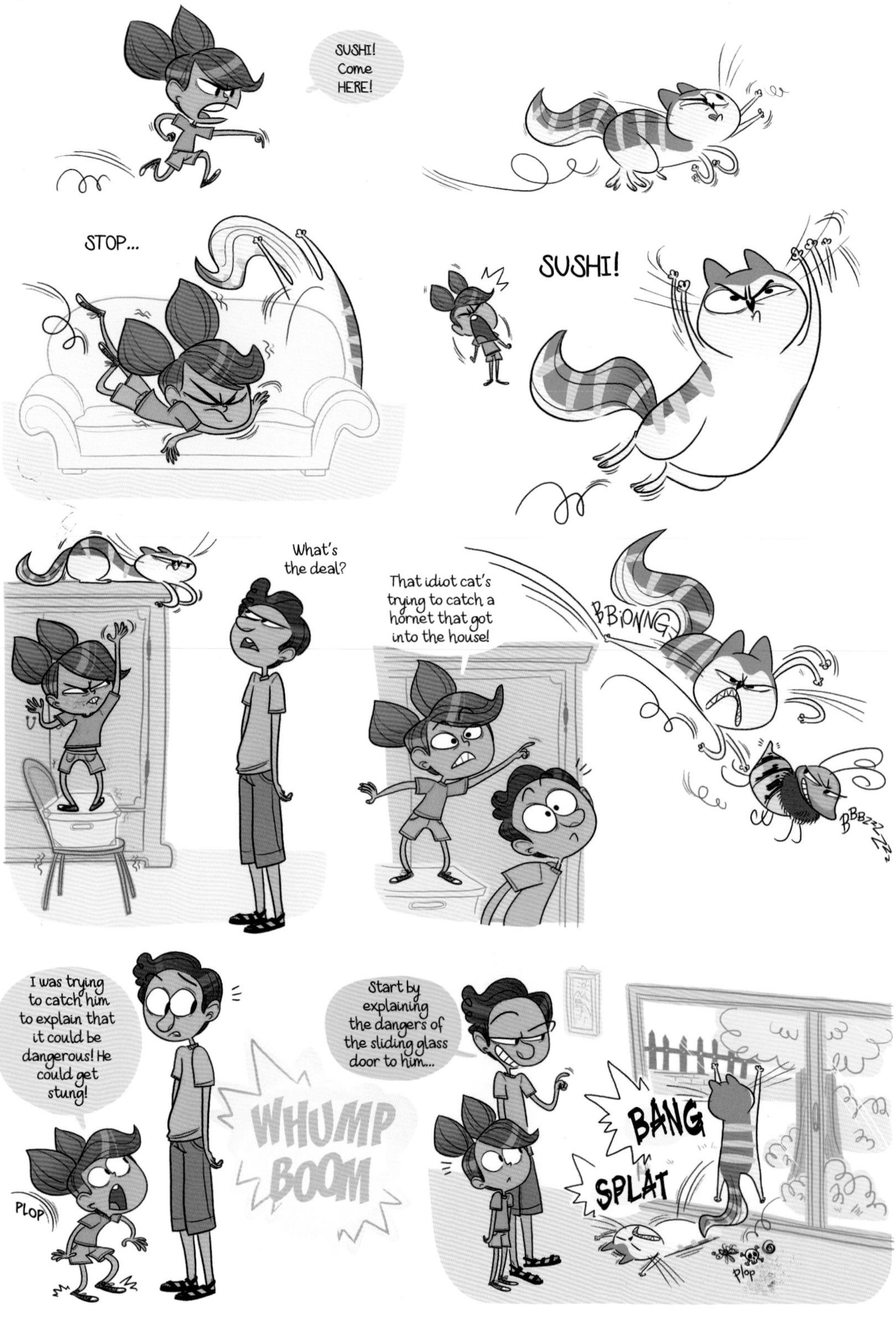
SUSHI! Come HERE!
STOP...
SUSHI!
What's the deal?
That idiot cat's trying to catch a hornet that got into the house!
BBIONNG
BBZZZ
I was trying to catch him to explain that it could be dangerous! He could get stung!
WHUMP BOOM
PLOP
Start by explaining the dangers of the sliding glass door to him...
BANG
SPLAT
plop

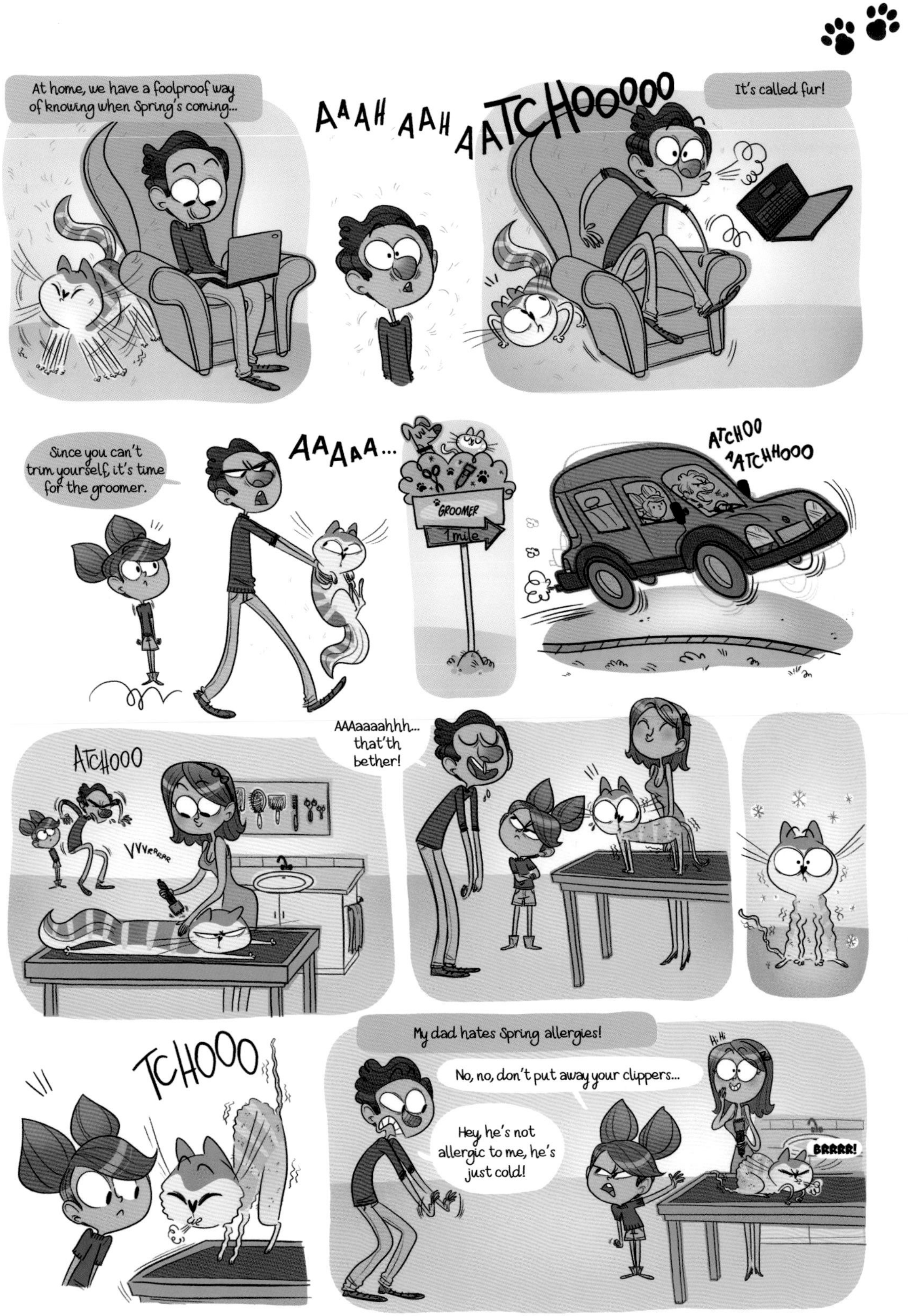

At home, we have a foolproof way of knowing when Spring's coming...
AAAH AAH AATCHOOOOO
It's called fur!
Since you can't trim yourself, it's time for the groomer.
AAAAA...
GROOMER
1 mile
ATCHOO AATCHHOOO
ATCHOOO
VVVRRRRR
AAAaaaahhh... that'th bether!
TCHOOO
My dad hates Spring allergies!
No, no, don't put away your clippers...
Hey, he's not allergic to me, he's just cold!
BRRRR!

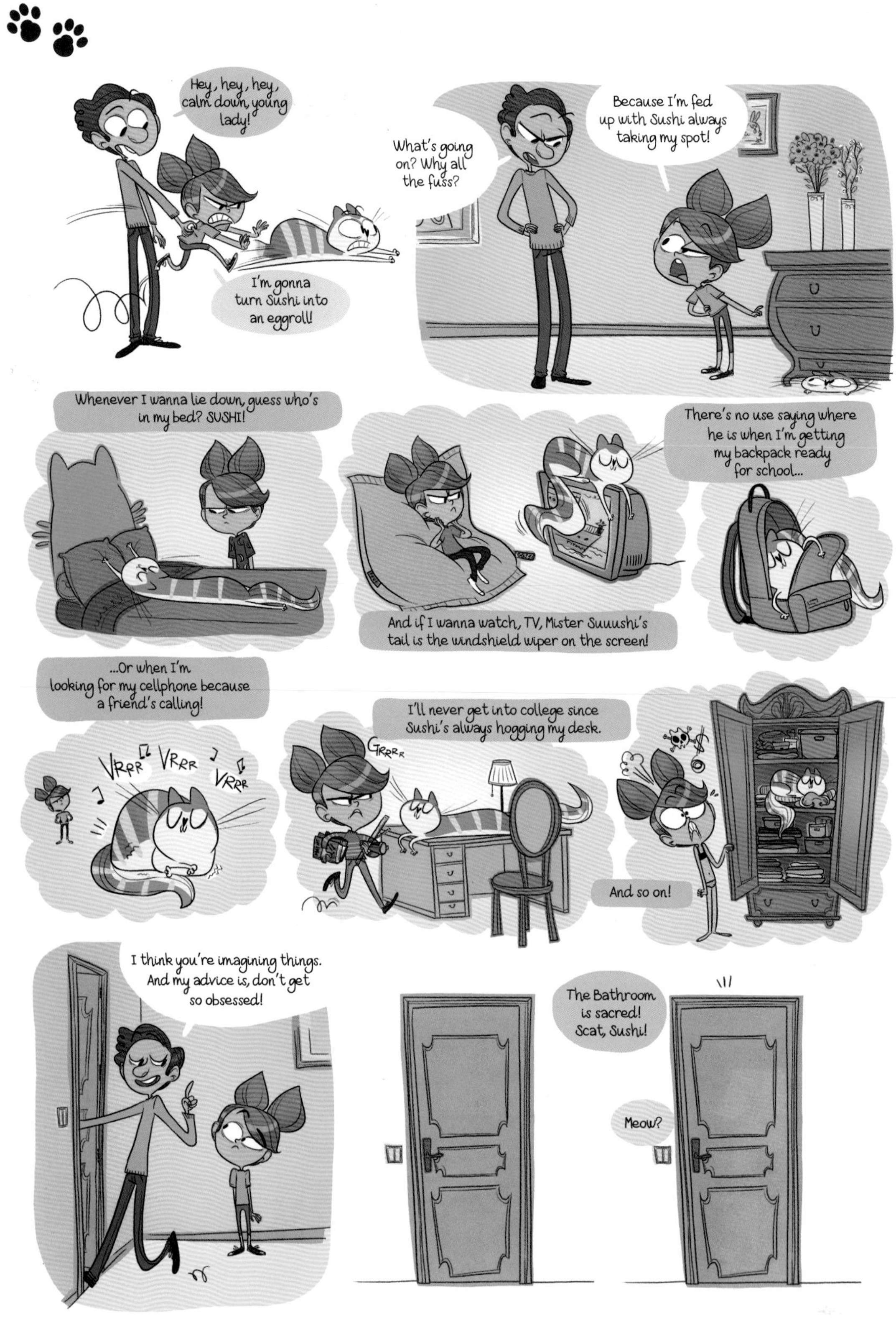
Hey, hey, hey, calm down, young lady!
I'm gonna turn Sushi into an eggroll!
What's going on? Why all the fuss?
Because I'm fed up with Sushi always taking my spot!
Whenever I wanna lie down, guess who's in my bed? SUSHI!
And if I wanna watch, TV, Mister Suuushi's tail is the windshield wiper on the screen!
There's no use saying where he is when I'm getting my backpack ready for school...
...Or when I'm looking for my cellphone because a friend's calling!
VRRR VRRR VRRR
I'll never get into college since Sushi's always hogging my desk.
GRRRR
And so on!
I think you're imagining things. And my advice is, don't get so obsessed!
The Bathroom is sacred! Scat, Sushi!
Meow?

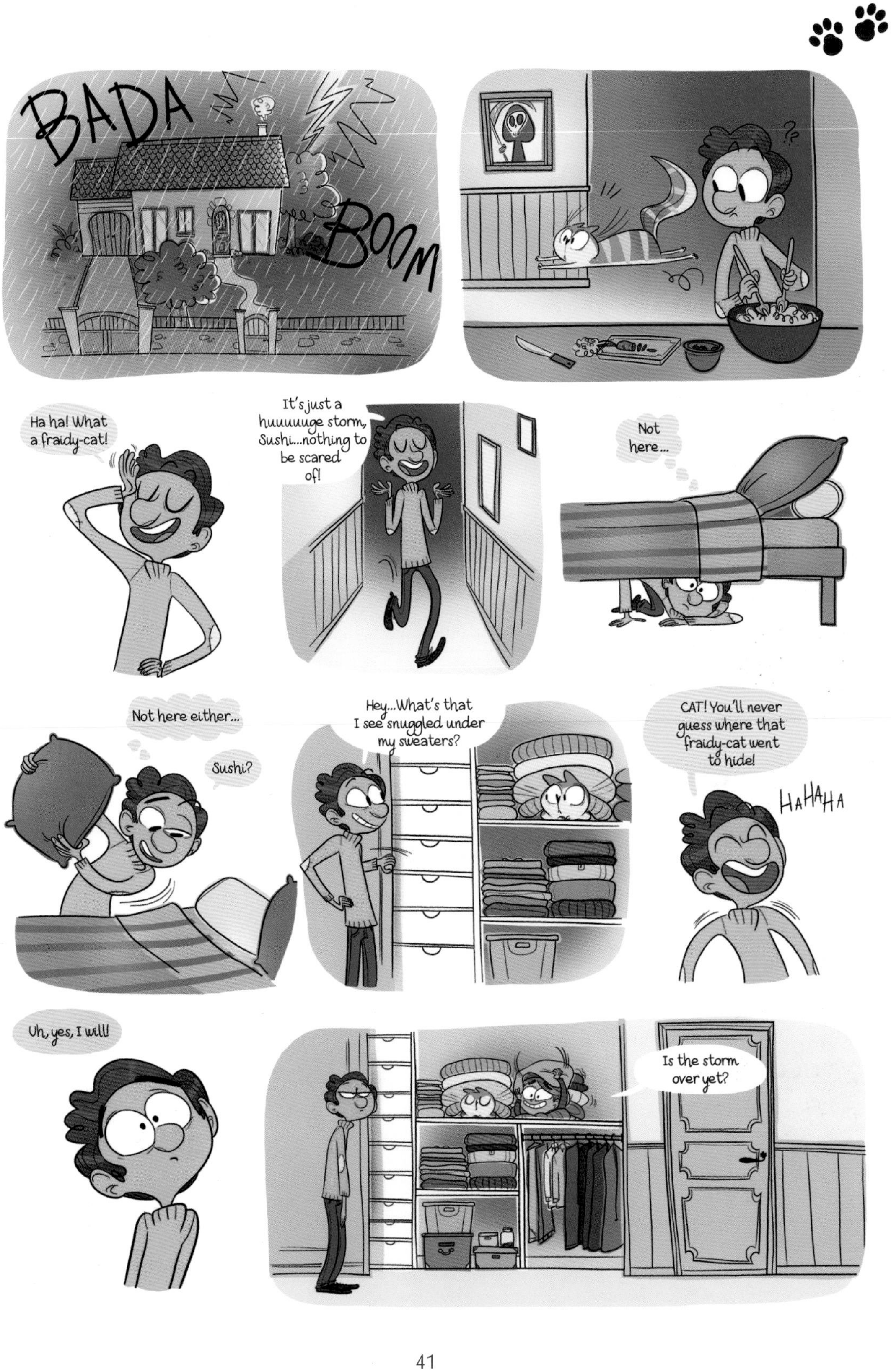
BADA
BOOM
?
Ha ha! What a fraidy-cat!
It's just a huuuuuge storm, Sushi...nothing to be scared of!
Not here...
Not here either...
Sushi?
Hey...What's that I see snuggled under my sweaters?
CAT! You'll never guess where that fraidy-cat went to hide!
HAHAHA
Uh, yes, I will!
Is the storm over yet?

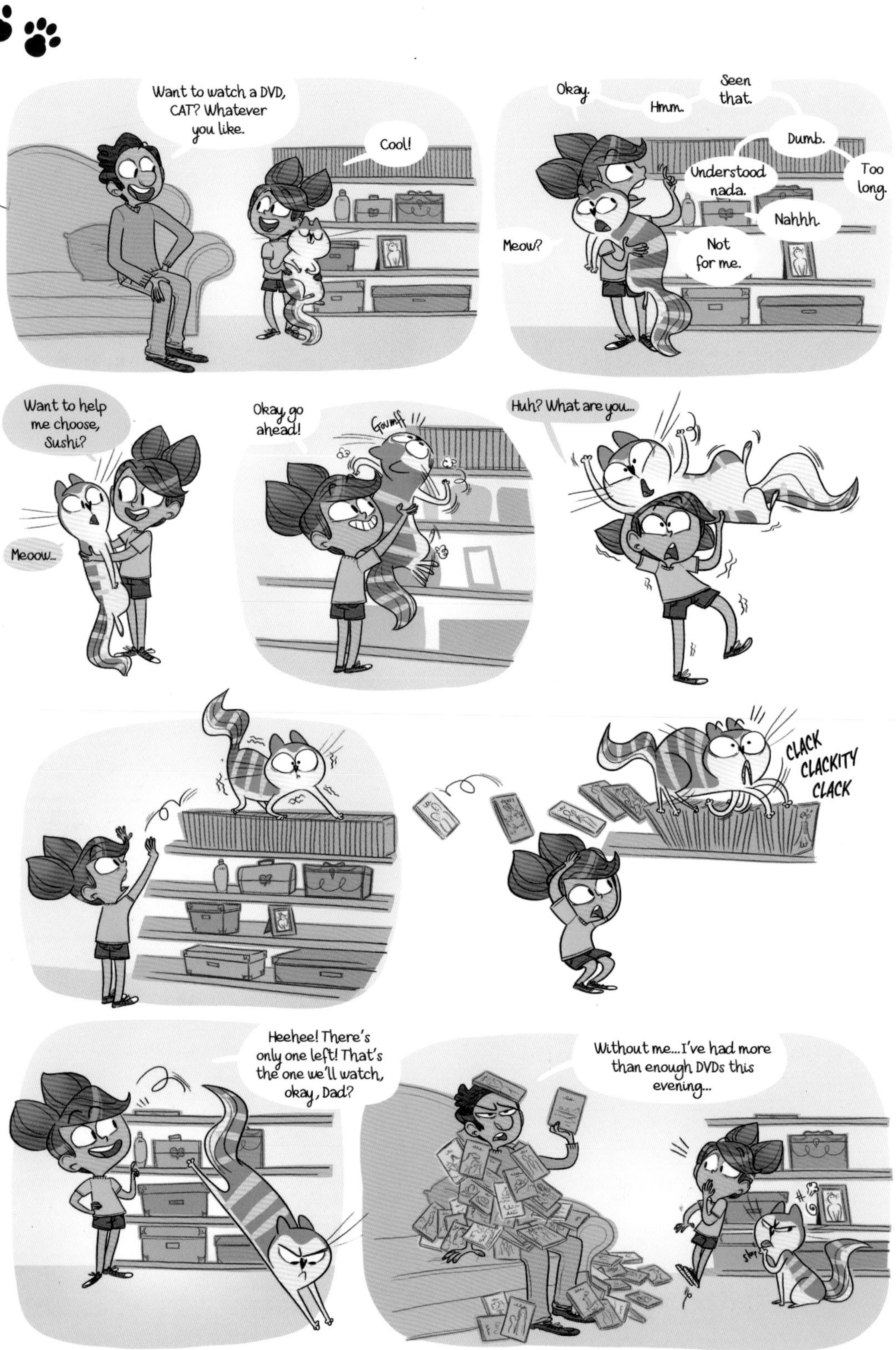

Want to watch a DVD, CAT? Whatever you like.
Cool!
Okay.
Hmm.
Seen that.
Dumb.
Too long.
Understood nada.
Nahhh.
Not for me.
Meow?
Want to help me choose, Sushi?
Meoow...
Okay, go ahead!
Goumf
Huh? What are you...
CLACK
CLACKITY
CLACK
Heehee! There's only one left! That's the one we'll watch, okay, Dad?
Without me...I've had more than enough DVDs this evening...

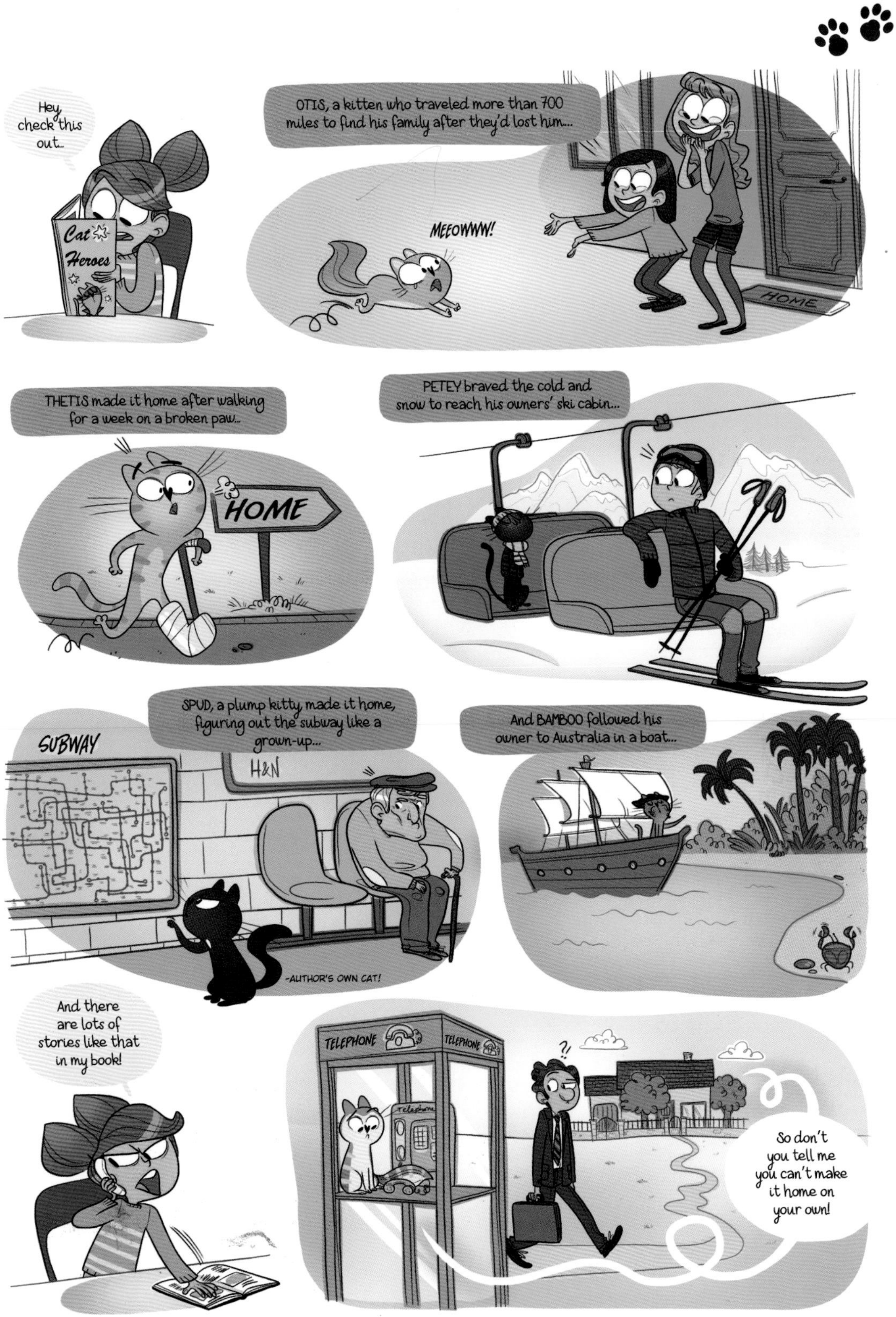
Hey, check this out...
Cat Heroes
OTIS, a kitten who traveled more than 700 miles to find his family after they'd lost him...
MEEOWWW!
HOME
THETIS made it home after walking for a week on a broken paw...
HOME
PETEY braved the cold and snow to reach his owners' ski cabin...
SUBWAY
SPUD, a plump kitty, made it home, figuring out the subway like a grown-up...
H&N
-AUTHOR'S OWN CAT!
And BAMBOO followed his owner to Australia in a boat...
And there are lots of stories like that in my book!
TELEPHONE
TELEPHONE
So don't you tell me you can't make it home on your own!

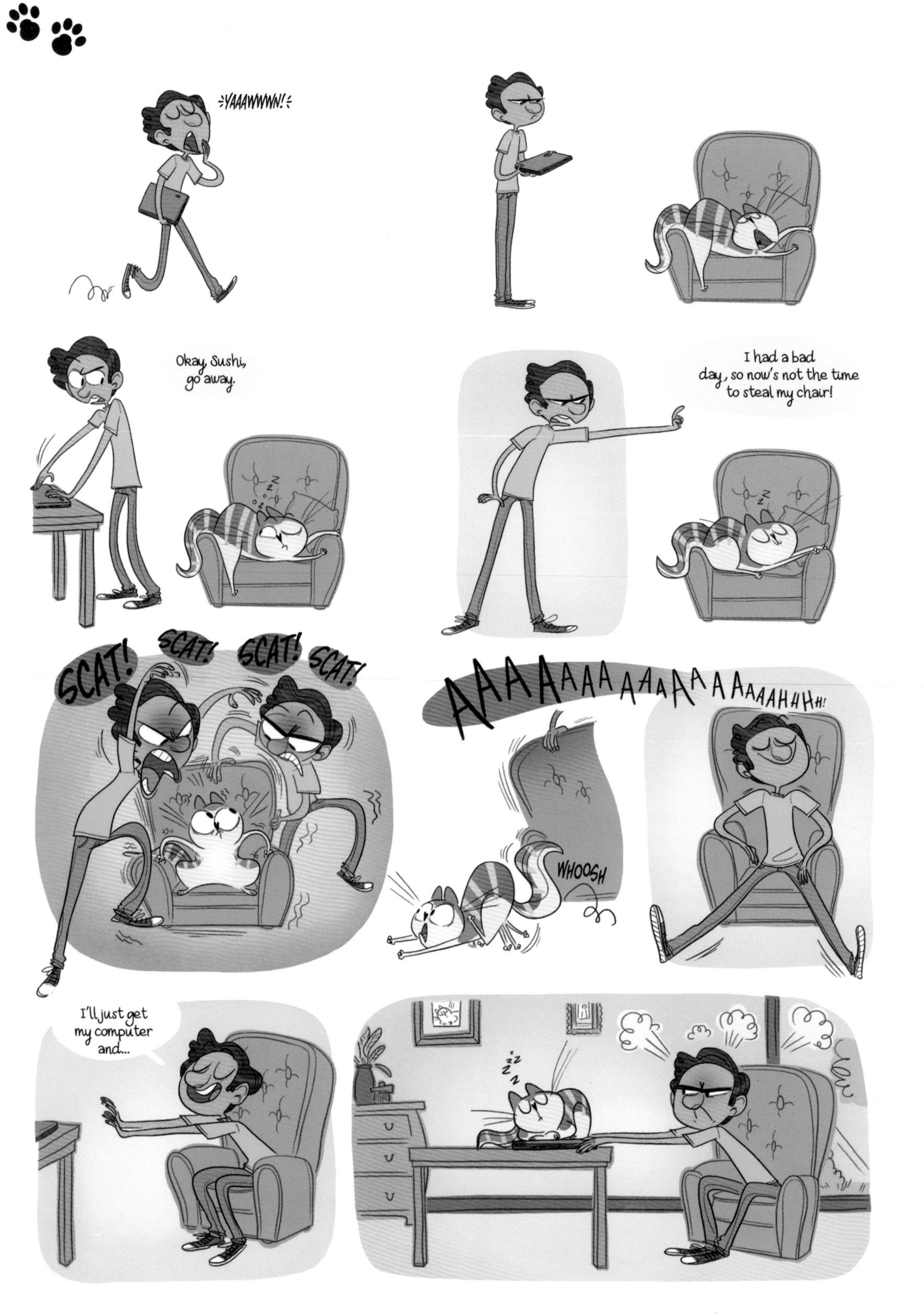
YAAAWWWN!
Okay, Sushi, go away.
I had a bad day, so now's not the time to steal my chair!
SCAT! SCAT! SCAT! SCAT!
AAAAAAAAAAAAAAAAAAHHHH!
WHOOSH
I'll just get my computer and...

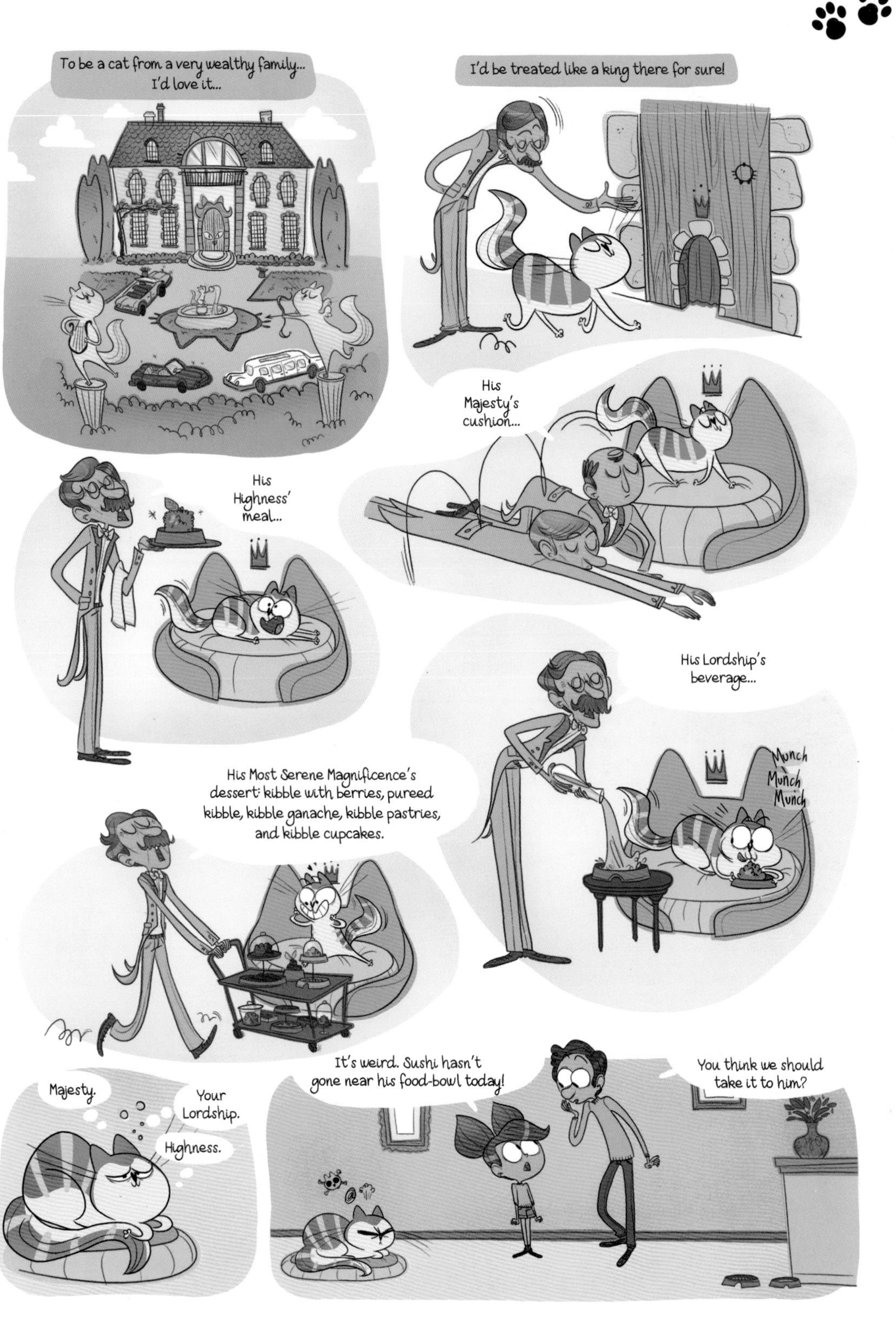

To be a cat from a very wealthy family... I'd love it...
I'd be treated like a king there for sure!
His Majesty's cushion...
His Highness' meal...
His Lordship's beverage...
Munch
Munch
Munch
His Most Serene Magnificence's dessert: kibble with berries, pureed kibble, kibble ganache, kibble pastries, and kibble cupcakes.
Majesty.
Your Lordship.
Highness.
It's weird. Sushi hasn't gone near his food-bowl today!
You think we should take it to him?

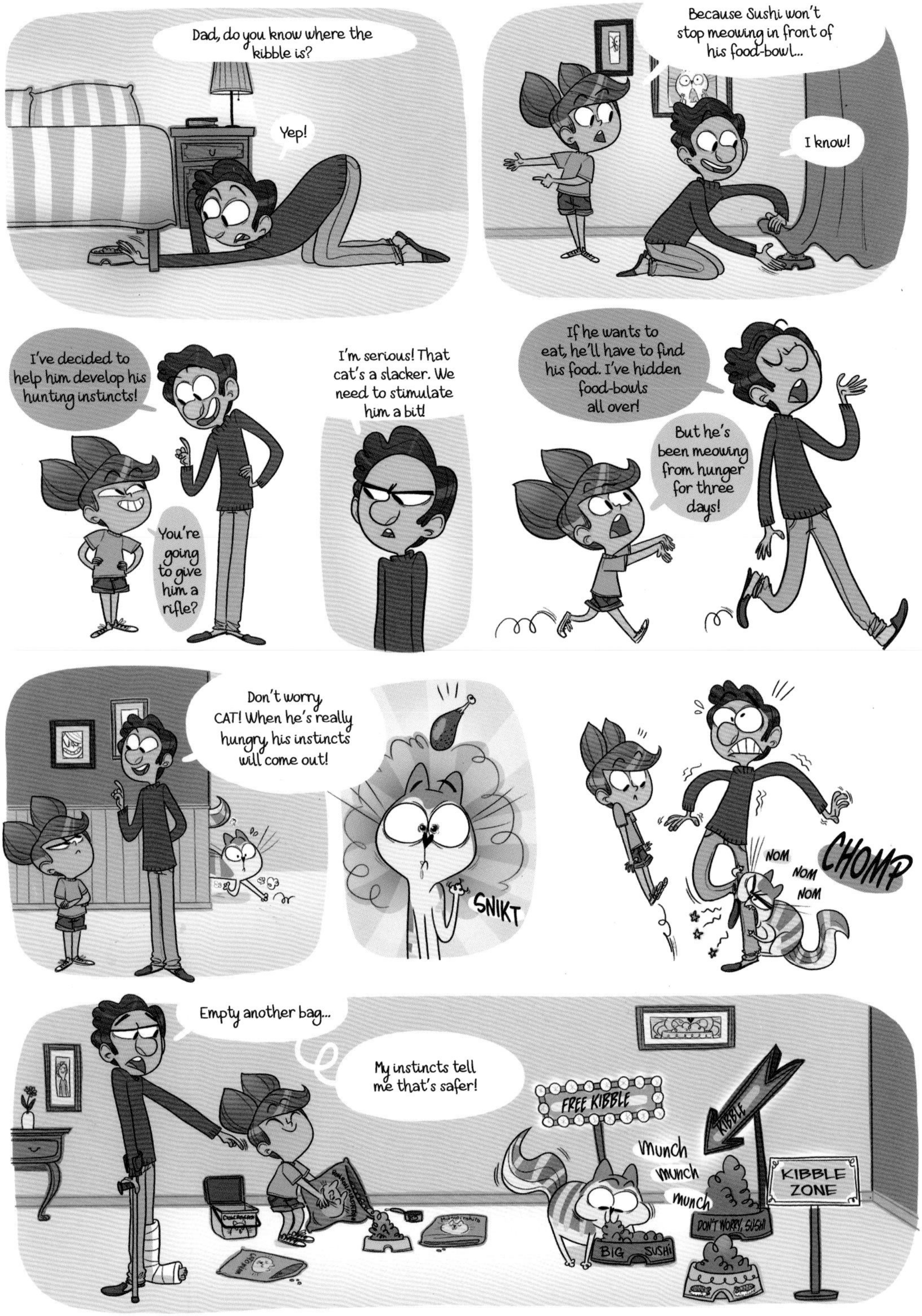
Dad, do you know where the kibble is?
Yep!
Because Sushi won't stop meowing in front of his food-bowl...
I know!
I've decided to help him develop his hunting instincts!
You're going to give him a rifle?
I'm serious! That cat's a slacker. We need to stimulate him a bit!
If he wants to eat, he'll have to find his food. I've hidden food-bowls all over!
But he's been meowing from hunger for three days!
Don't worry, CAT! When he's really hungry, his instincts will come out!
SNIKT
NOM
NOM
NOM
CHOMP
Empty another bag...
My instincts tell me that's safer!
FREE KIBBLE
KIBBLE
munch
munch
munch
KIBBLE ZONE
DON'T WORRY, SUSHI
BIG SUSHI

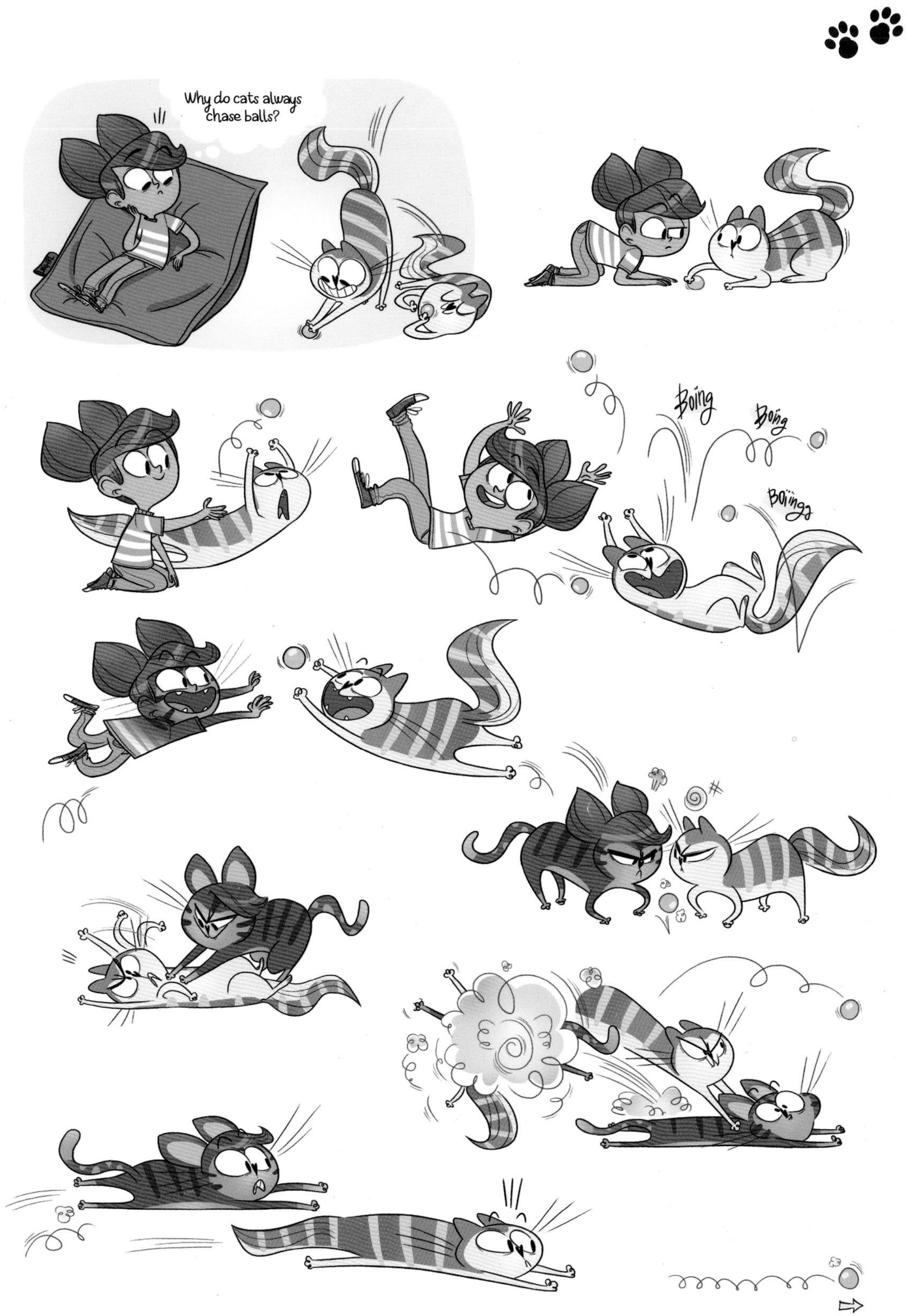
Why do cats always chase balls?
Boing
Boing
Boinga

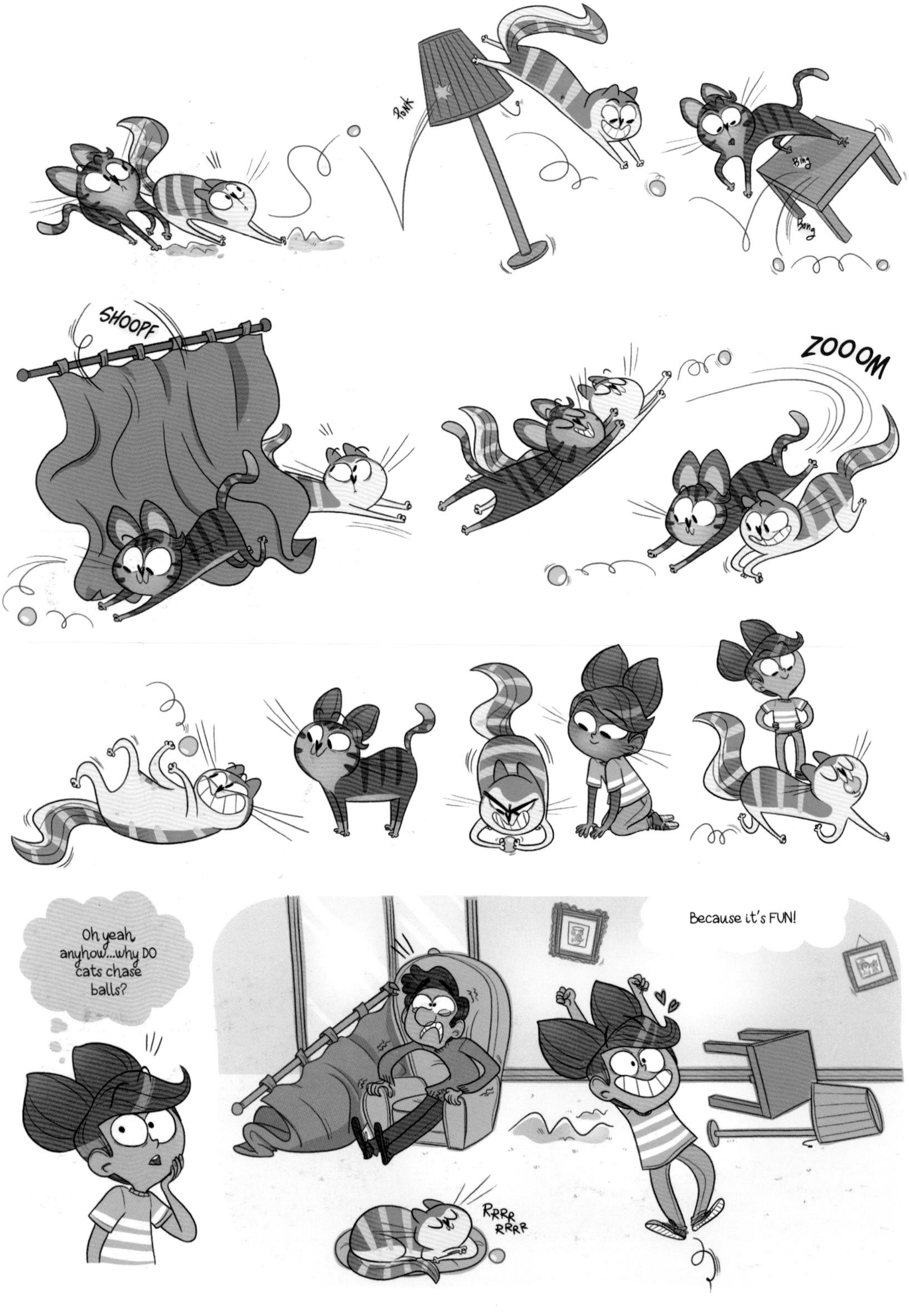
Ponk
Bing
Bang
SHOOPF
ZOOOM
Oh yeah, anyhow...why DO cats chase balls?
Because it's FUN!
RRRR RRRR

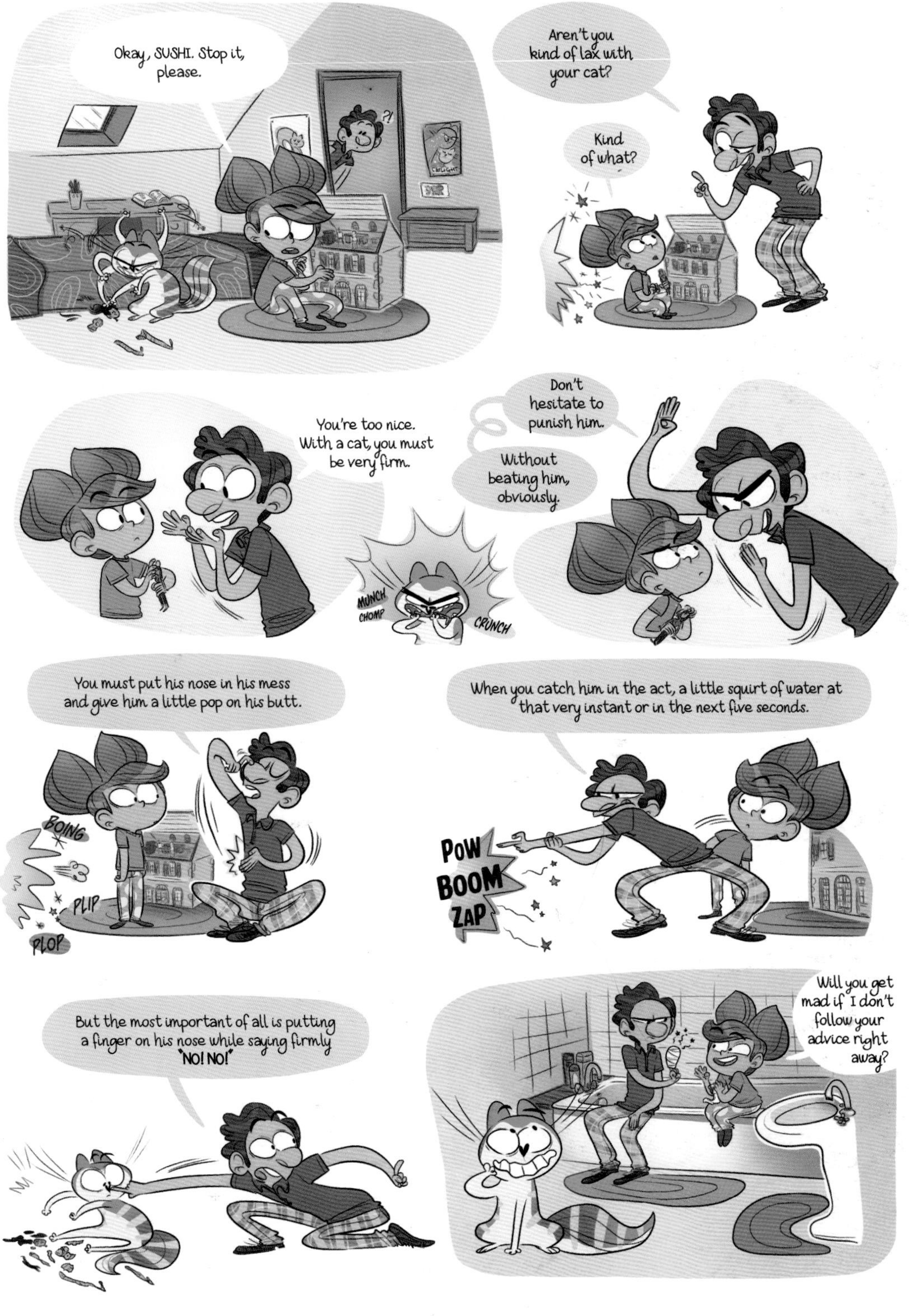
Okay, SUSHI. Stop it, please.
Aren't you kind of lax with your cat?
Kind of what?
You're too nice. With a cat, you must be very firm.
MUNCH
CHOMP
CRUNCH
Don't hesitate to punish him.
Without beating him, obviously.
You must put his nose in his mess and give him a little pop on his butt.
BOING
PLIP
PLOP
When you catch him in the act, a little squirt of water at that very instant or in the next five seconds.
POW
BOOM
ZAP
But the most important of all is putting a finger on his nose while saying firmly "NO! NO!"
Will you get mad if I don't follow your advice right away?

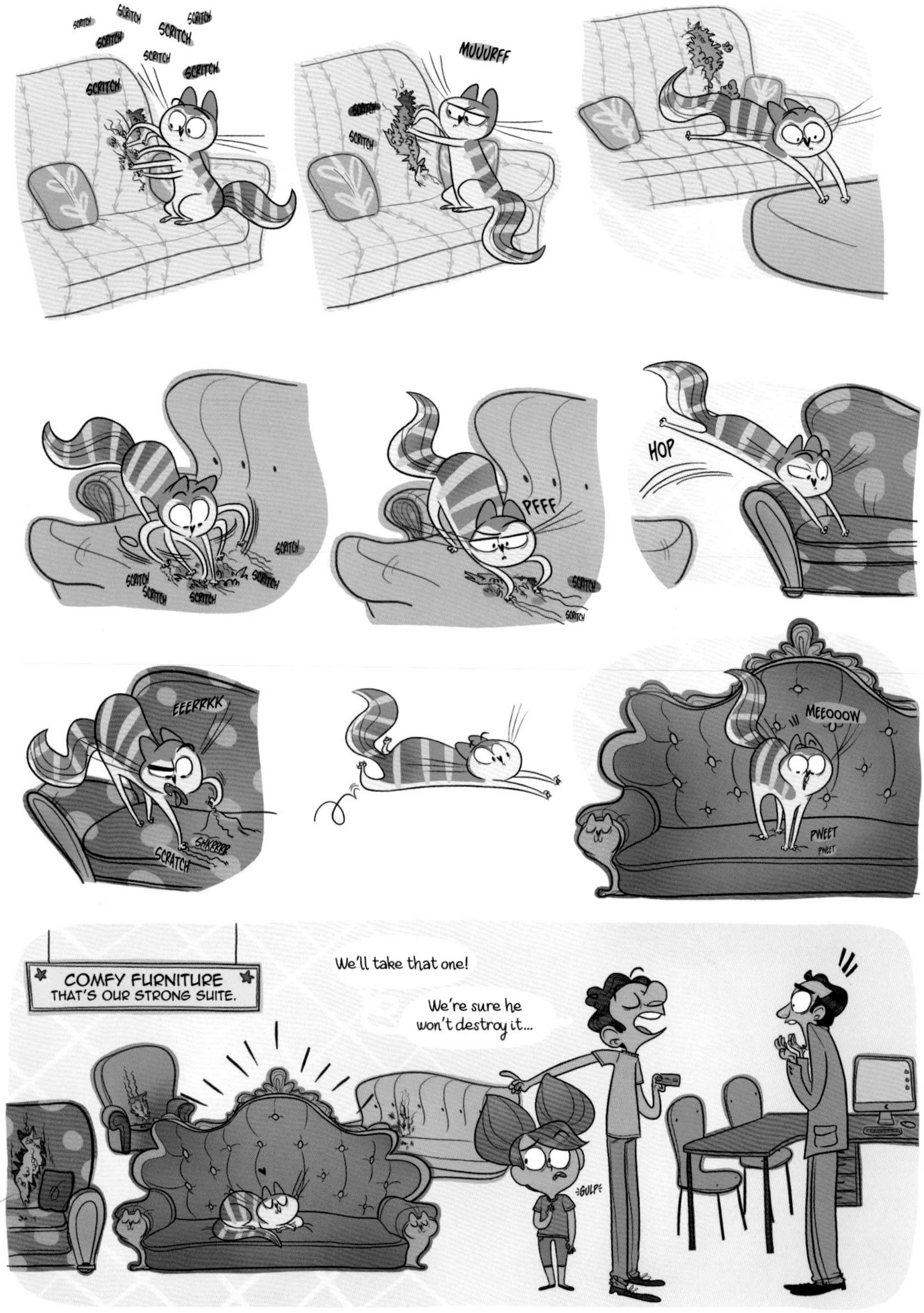
SCRITCH
SCRITCH
SCRITCH
SCRITCH
SCRITCH
SCRITCH
SCRITCH
SCRITCH
MUUURFF
SCRITCH
SCRITCH
SCRITCH
SCRITCH
SCRITCH
SCRITCH
SCRITCH
PFFF
SCRITCH
SCRITCH
HOP
EEERRKK
SHKRRRR
SCRATCH
MEEOOOW
PWEET
PWEET
COMFY FURNITURE
THAT'S OUR STRONG SUITE.
We'll take that one!
We're sure he won't destroy it...
GULP

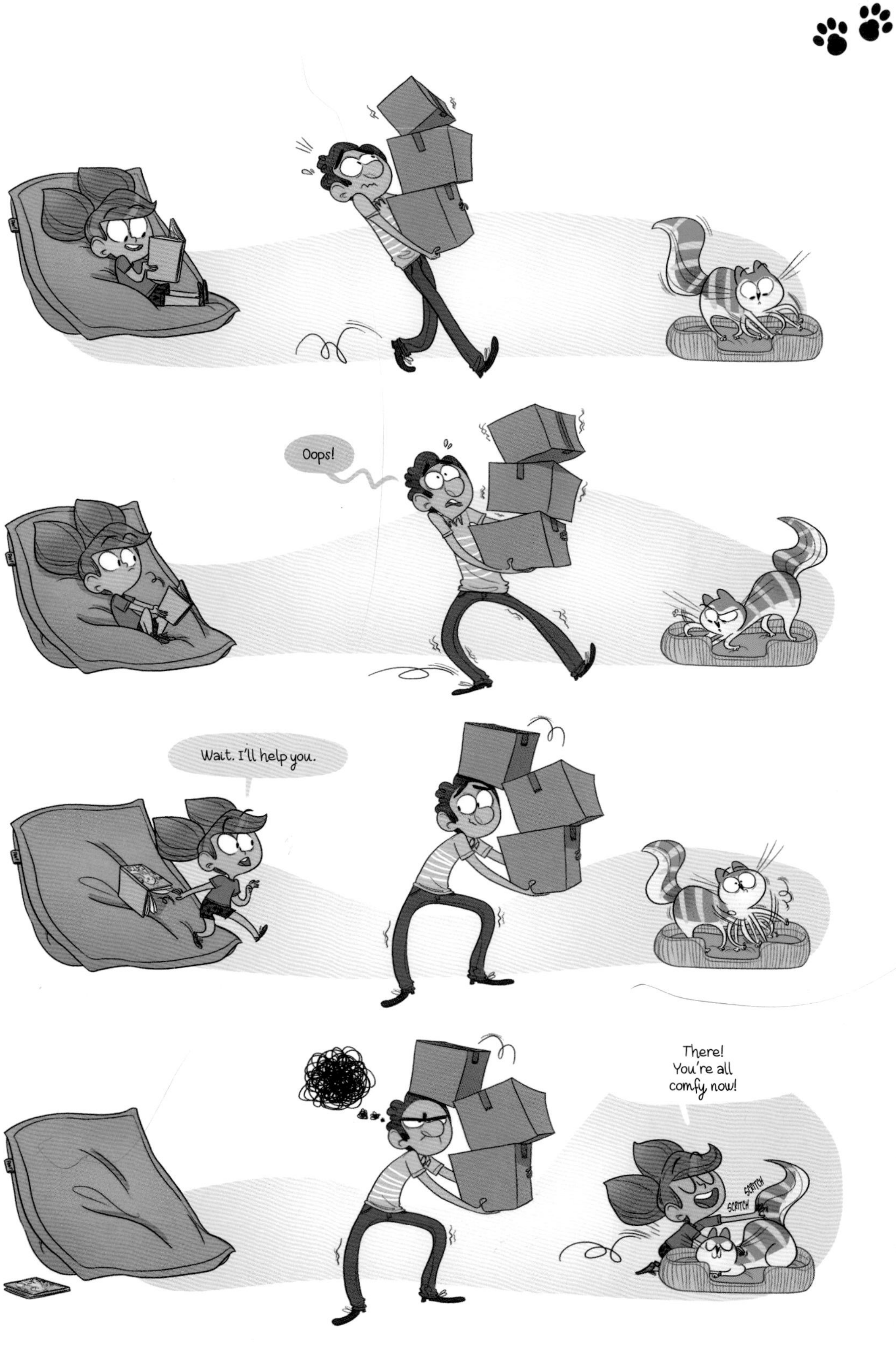
Oops!
Wait. I'll help you.
There! You're all comfy now!
SCRITCH
SCRITCH

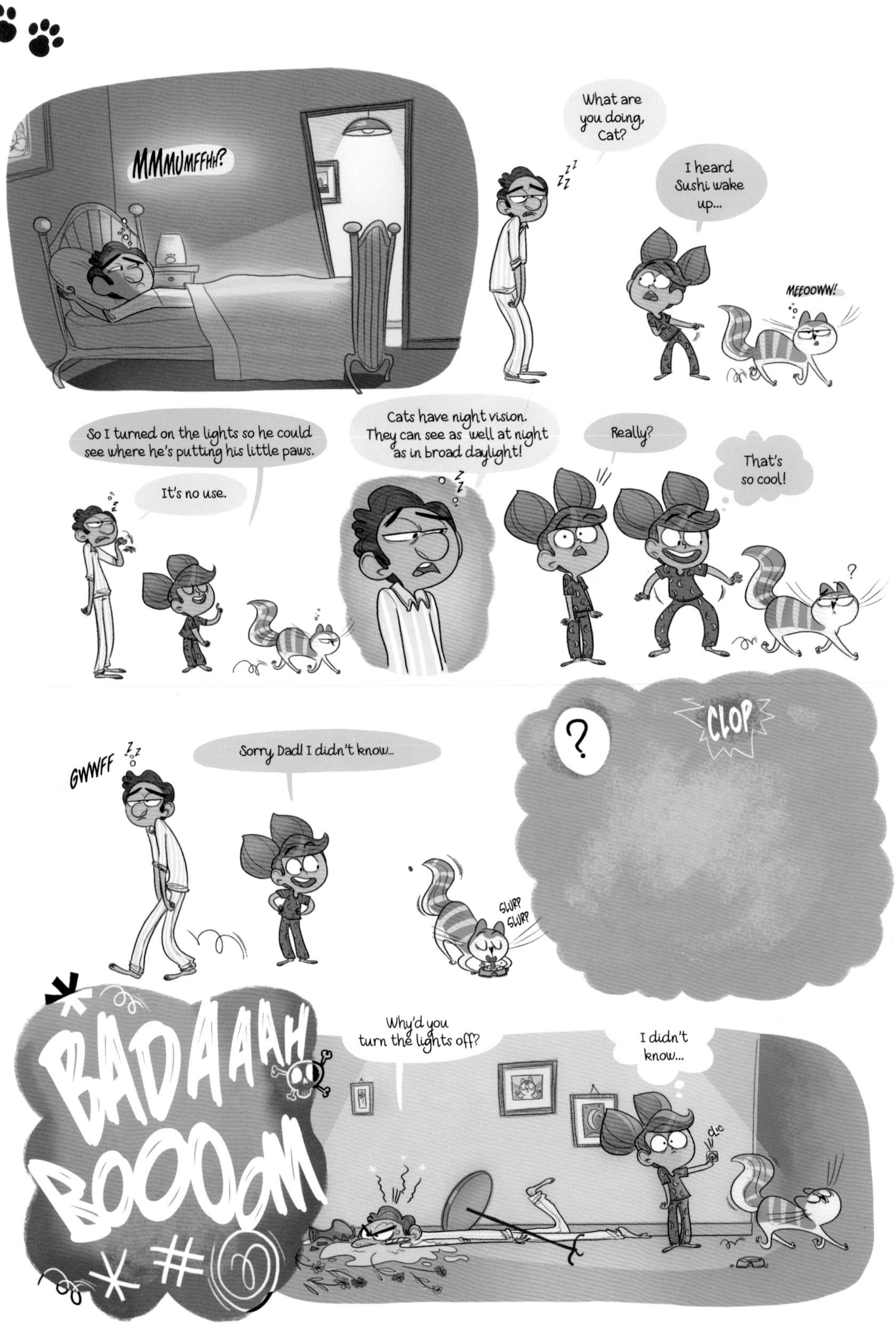
MMMUMFFHH?
What are you doing, Cat?
I heard Sushi wake up...
MEEOOWW!
So I turned on the lights so he could see where he's putting his little paws.
It's no use.
Cats have night vision. They can see as well at night as in broad daylight!
Really?
That's so cool!
GWWFF
Sorry, Dad! I didn't know...
SLURP SLURP
?
CLOP
BADAAAH BOOOOM
Why'd you turn the lights off?
I didn't know...
CLIC

In a house, when you have a cat, you must think about its freedom.

MEEEOOWWW

Come in...

That's why Dad decided to install a cat door.

Unfortunately, our cat door squeaks.

SQUEEEE

And at night, a cat goes in and out every four minutes or so...

SQUEEEE

SQUEEEE

SQUEEEE

SQUEEE

SQUEE

...a cat door gets stuck sometimes, too.

MEEEOOOWWW

MEOW

MEEOOW

OO OOOMMM

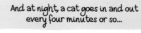

And once you get it unstuck...

...you'd better have put away all your papers.

Z

CRAK

That's why Dad put a lock on the cat door.

WOOEE

WOOOOEEE

WVV

VOOOOEE

VVEE

MEEOOW?!

Because in a house, when you have a cat, you also need to think about YOUR freedom.

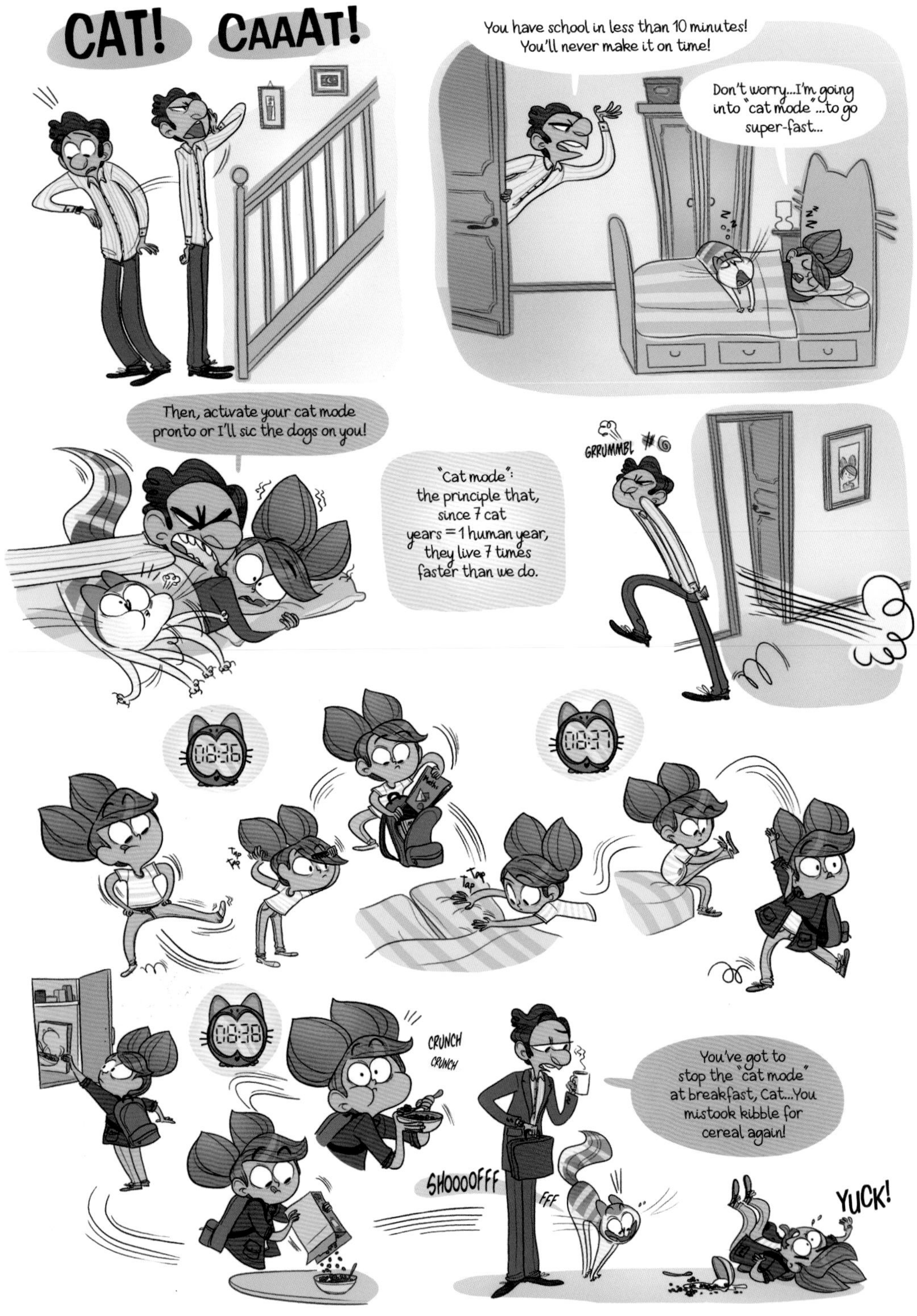

CAT! CAAAT!
You have school in less than 10 minutes! You'll never make it on time!
Don't worry...I'm going into "cat mode"...to go super-fast...
Then, activate your cat mode pronto or I'll sic the dogs on you!
"Cat mode": the principle that, since 7 cat years = 1 human year, they live 7 times faster than we do.
GRRUMMBL
08:36
Tap Tap
08:37
Tap Tap
08:38
CRUNCH CRUNCH
You've got to stop the "cat mode" at breakfast, Cat...You mistook kibble for cereal again!
SHOOOOFFF
FFF
YUCK!

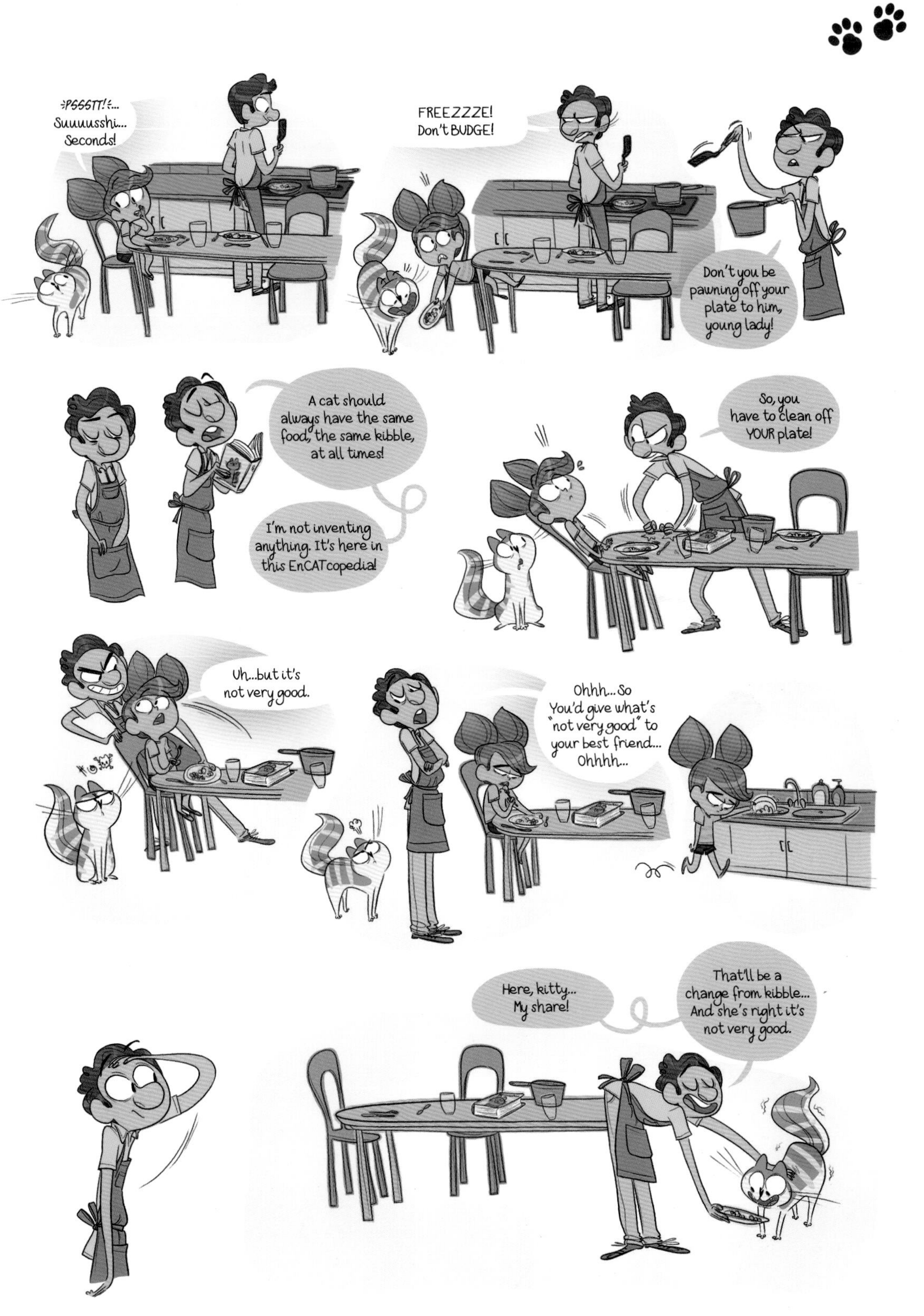
PSSSTT!... Suuuusshi... Seconds!
FREEZZZE! Don't BUDGE!
Don't you be pawning off your plate to him, young lady!
A cat should always have the same food, the same kibble, at all times!
I'm not inventing anything. It's here in this EnCATcopedia!
So, you have to clean off YOUR plate!
Uh...but it's not very good.
Ohhh...So You'd give what's "not very good" to your best friend... Ohhhh...
Here, kitty... My share!
That'll be a change from kibble... And she's right it's not very good.

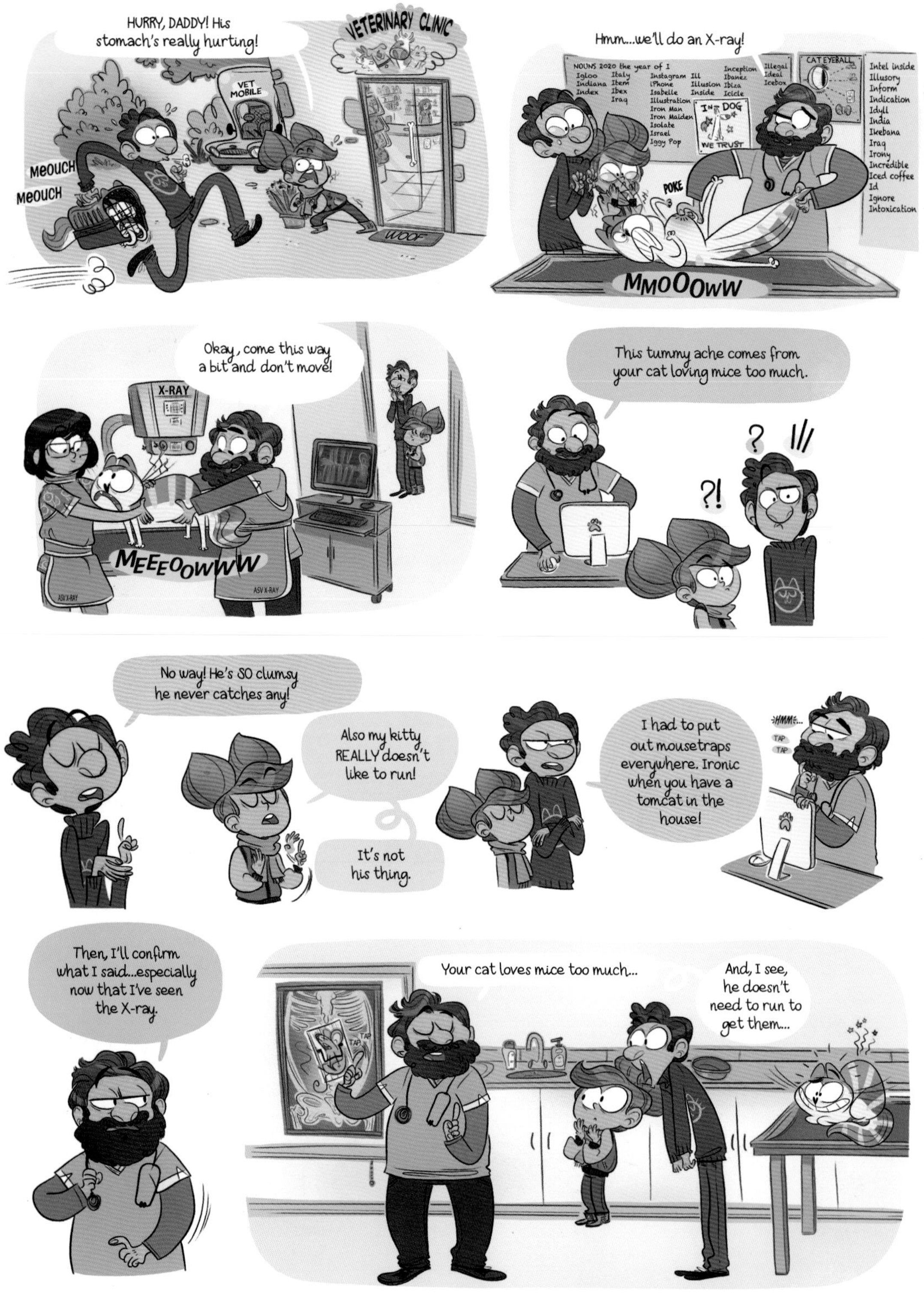

HURRY, DADDY! His stomach's really hurting!
VETERINARY CLINIC
VET MOBILE
MEOUCH
MEOUCH
WOOF
Hmm...we'll do an X-ray!
NOUNS 2020 the year of I
Igloo Indiana Index
Italy Item Ibex Iraq
Instagram iPhone Isabelle Illustration Iron Man Iron Maiden Isolate Israel Iggy Pop
Ill Illusion Inside
Inception Ibanez Ibiza Icicle
Illegal Ideal Icebox
IN DOG WE TRUST
CAT EYEBALL
Intel inside Illusory Inform Indication Idyll India Ikebana Iraq Irony Incredible Iced coffee Id Ignore Intoxication
POKE
MMOOOWW
Okay, come this way a bit and don't move!
X-RAY
MEEEOOWWW
ASV X-RAY
ASV X-RAY
This tummy ache comes from your cat loving mice too much.
?
?!
No way! He's SO clumsy he never catches any!
Also my kitty REALLY doesn't like to run!
It's not his thing.
I had to put out mousetraps everywhere. Ironic when you have a tomcat in the house!
HMM...
TAP
TAP
Then, I'll confirm what I said...especially now that I've seen the X-ray.
Your cat loves mice too much...
TAP
TAP
And, I see, he doesn't need to run to get them...

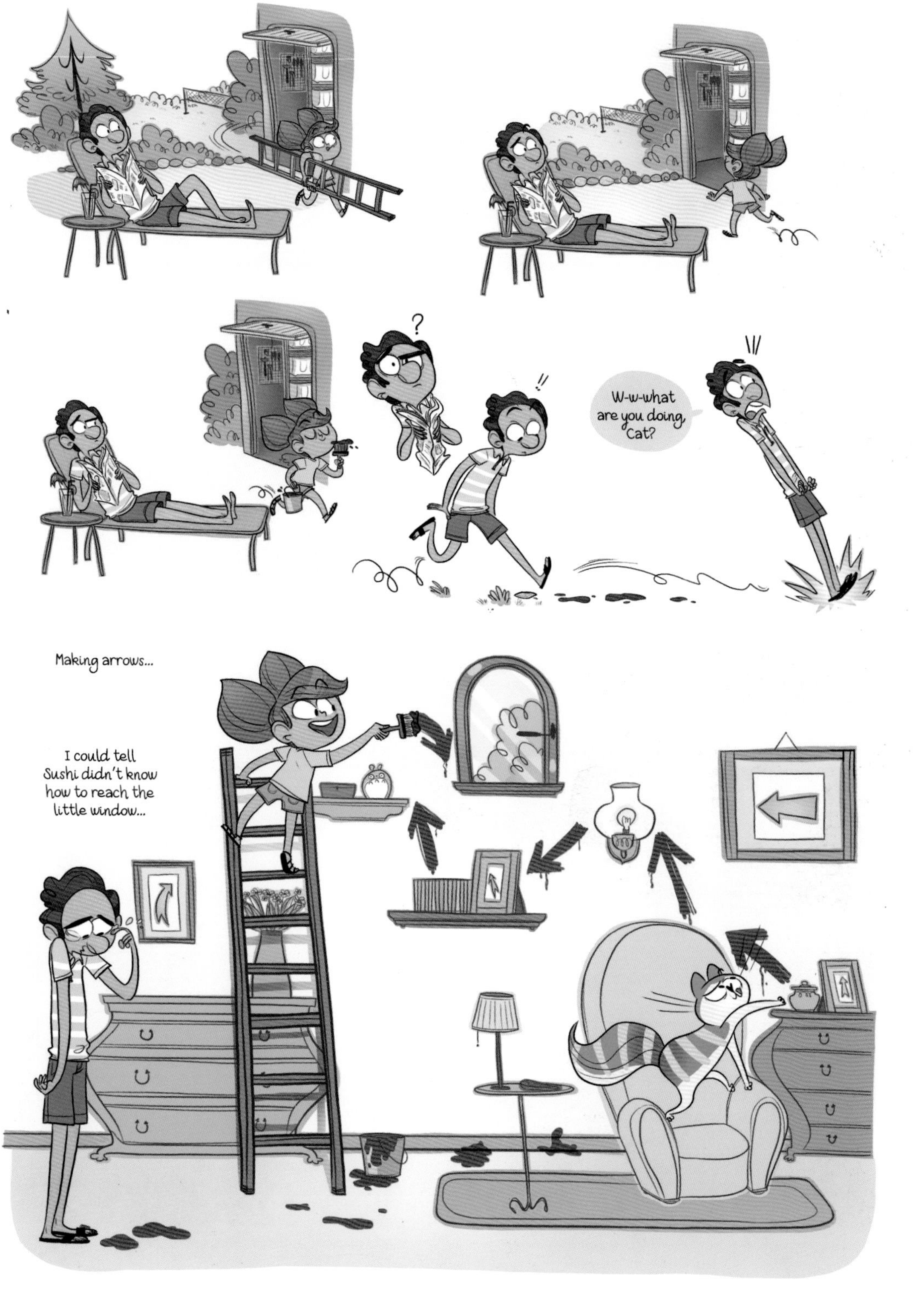
?
!!
W-w-what are you doing, Cat?
!!!
Making arrows...
I could tell Sushi didn't know how to reach the little window...

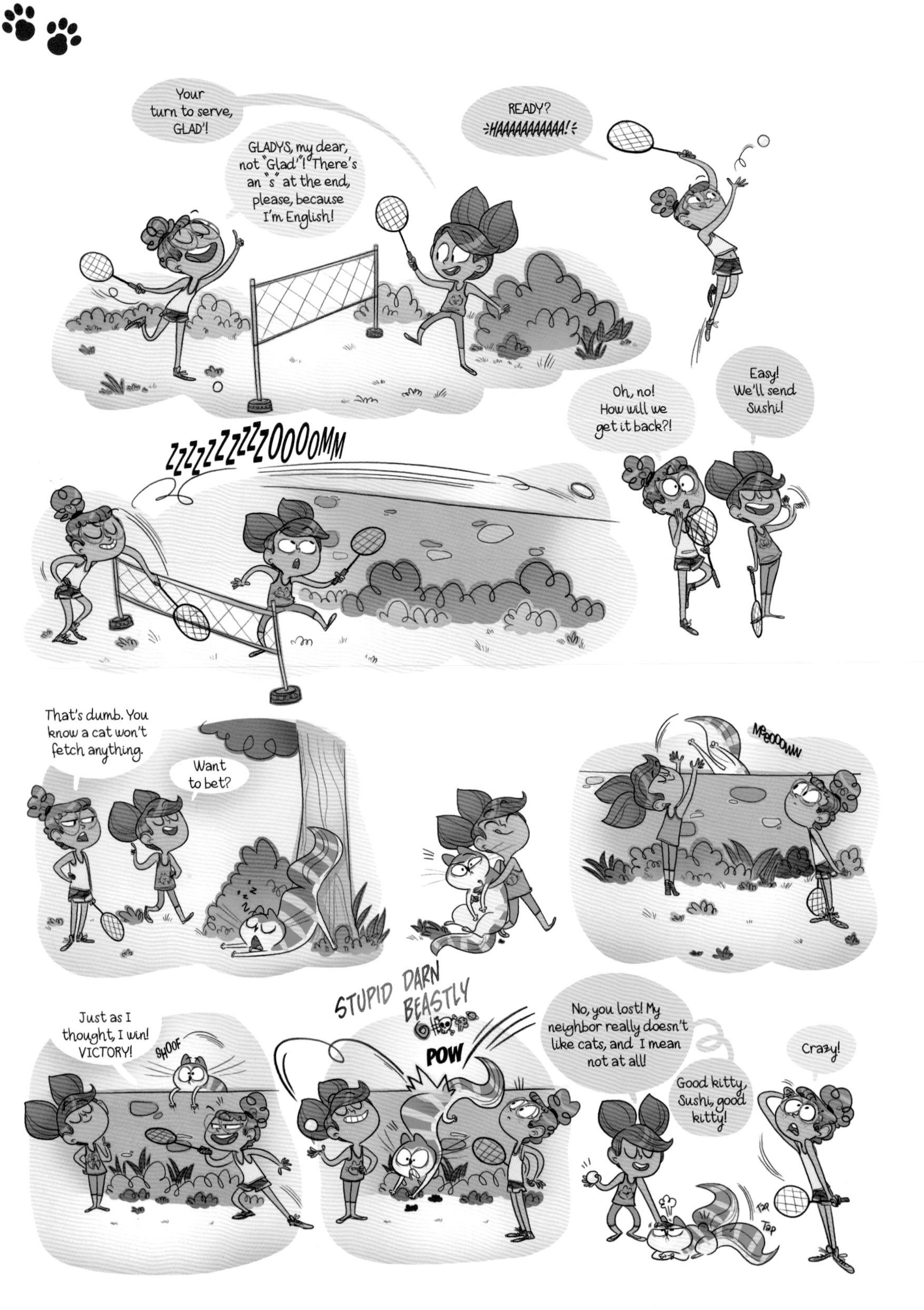
Your turn to serve, GLAD'!
GLADYS, my dear, not "Glad'"! There's an "s" at the end, please, because I'm English!
READY? HAAAAAAAAAAA!
ZZZZZZZZZZOOOOMM
Oh, no! How will we get it back?!
Easy! We'll send Sushi!
That's dumb. You know a cat won't fetch anything.
Want to bet?
MREOOOWW
Just as I thought, I win! VICTORY!
SHOOF
STUPID DARN BEASTLY
POW
No, you lost! My neighbor really doesn't like cats, and I mean not at all!
Good kitty, Sushi, good kitty!
Crazy!
TAP
TAP

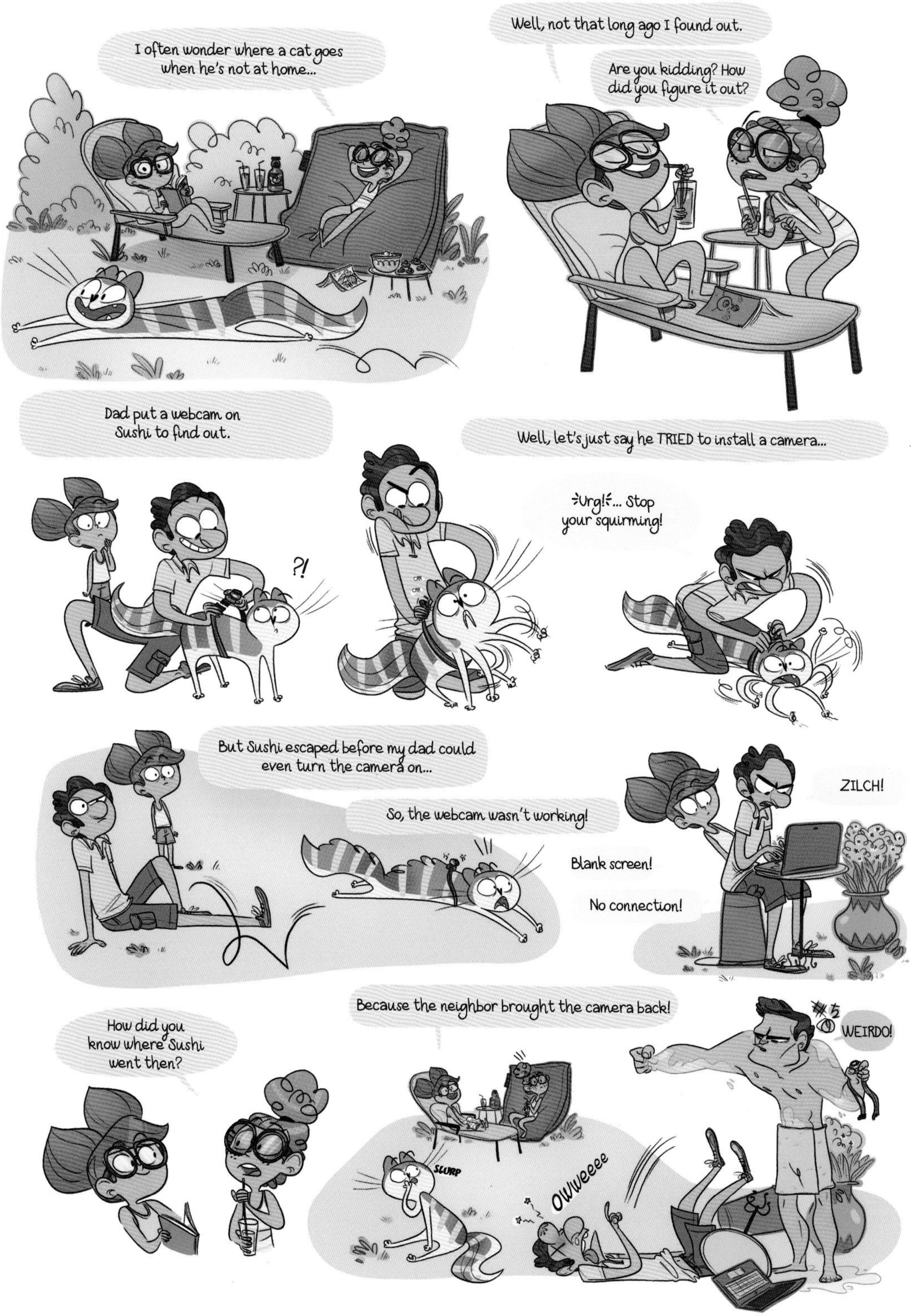
I often wonder where a cat goes when he's not at home...
Well, not that long ago I found out.
Are you kidding? How did you figure it out?
Dad put a webcam on Sushi to find out.
Well, let's just say he TRIED to install a camera...
?!
Urg!... Stop your squirming!
But Sushi escaped before my dad could even turn the camera on...
So, the webcam wasn't working!
Blank screen!
No connection!
ZILCH!
How did you know where Sushi went then?
Because the neighbor brought the camera back!
SLURP
OWWeeee
WEIRDO!

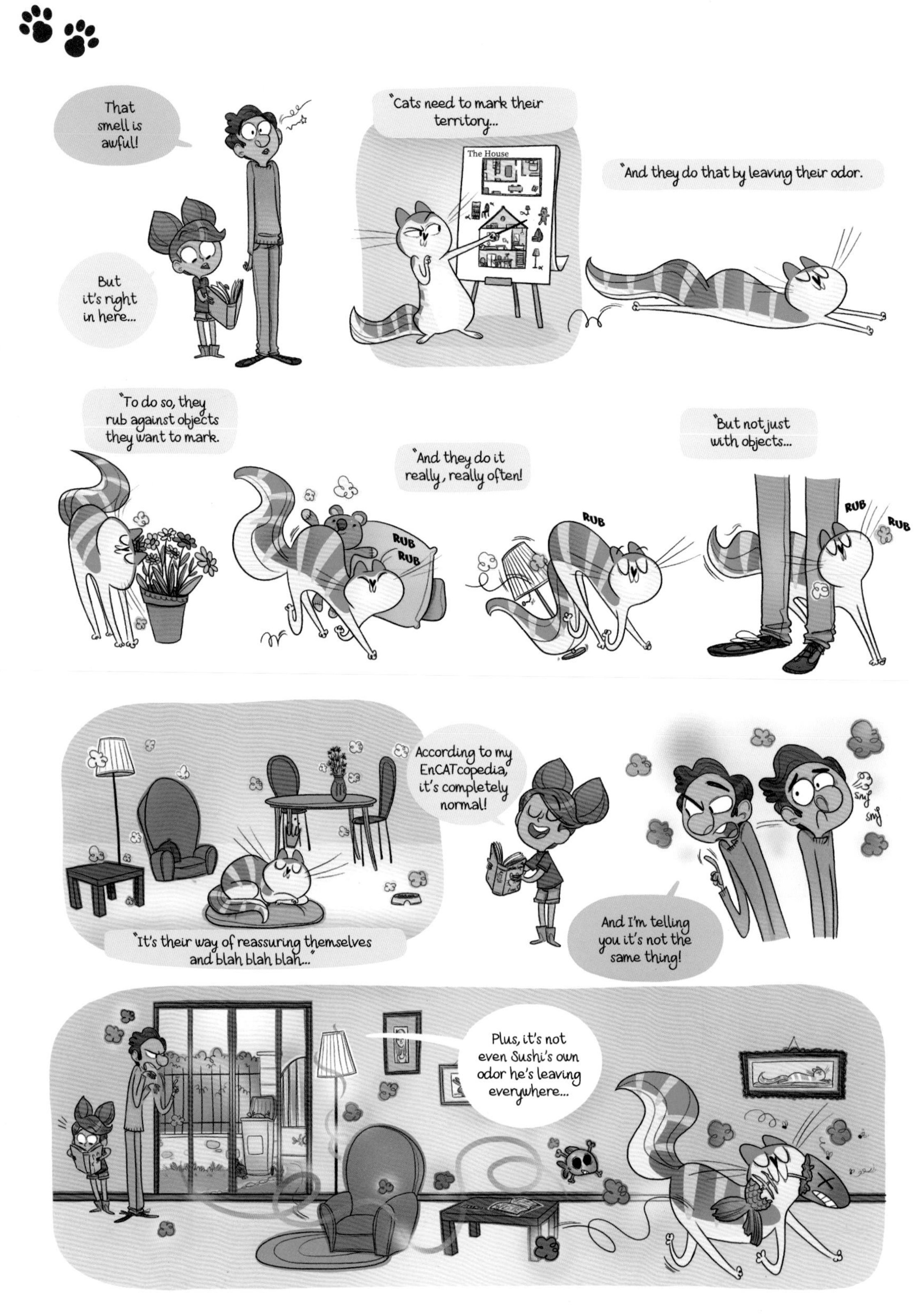
That smell is awful!
But it's right in here...
"Cats need to mark their territory...
The House
"And they do that by leaving their odor.
"To do so, they rub against objects they want to mark.
"And they do it really, really often!
RUB
RUB
RUB
"But not just with objects...
RUB
RUB
According to my EnCATcopedia, it's completely normal!
"It's their way of reassuring themselves and blah blah blah..."
And I'm telling you it's not the same thing!
Plus, it's not even Sushi's own odor he's leaving everywhere...

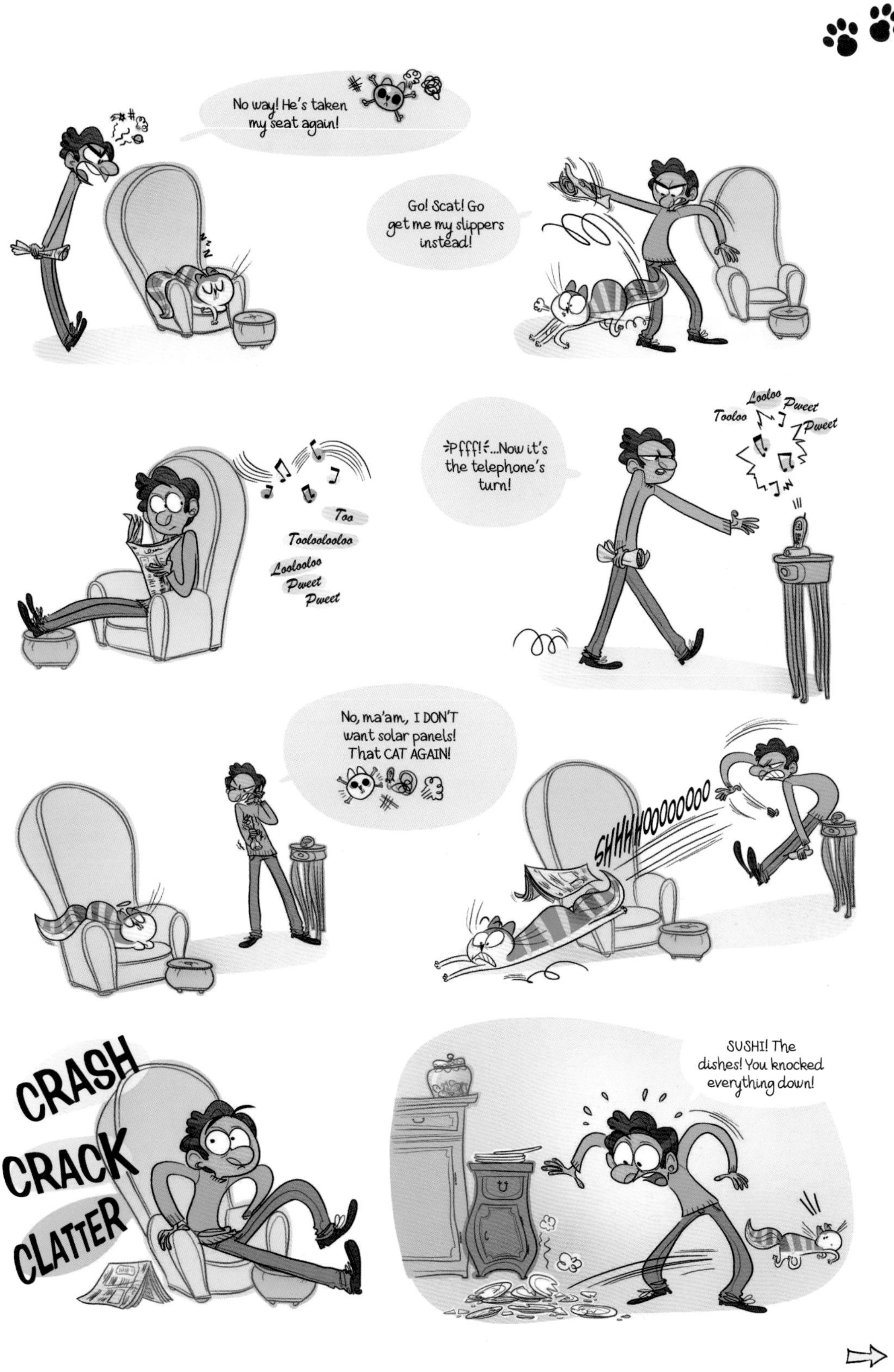

No way! He's taken my seat again!
Go! Scat! Go get me my slippers instead!
Too
Tooloolooloo
Loolooloo
Pweet
Pweet
Pfff! ...Now it's the telephone's turn!
Tooloo
Looloo
Pweet
Pweet
No, ma'am, I DON'T want solar panels! That CAT AGAIN!
SHHHHOOOOOOOOO
CRASH
CRACK
CLATTER
SUSHI! The dishes! You knocked everything down!

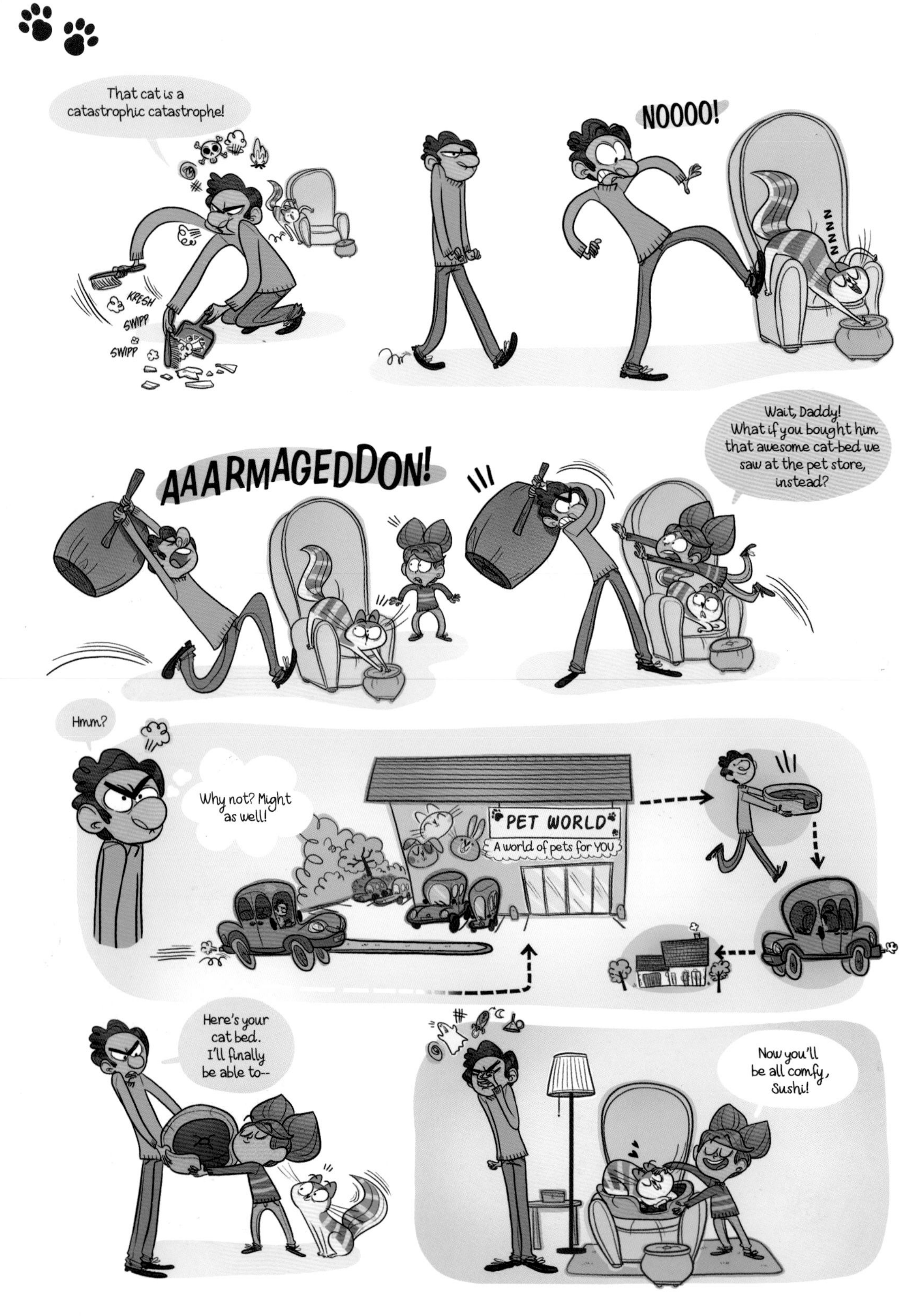
That cat is a catastrophic catastrophe!
KRESH
SWIPP
SWIPP
NOOOO!
AAARMAGEDDON!
Wait, Daddy! What if you bought him that awesome cat-bed we saw at the pet store, instead?
Hmm?
Why not? Might as well!
PET WORLD
A world of pets for YOU
Here's your cat bed. I'll finally be able to--
Now you'll be all comfy, Sushi!

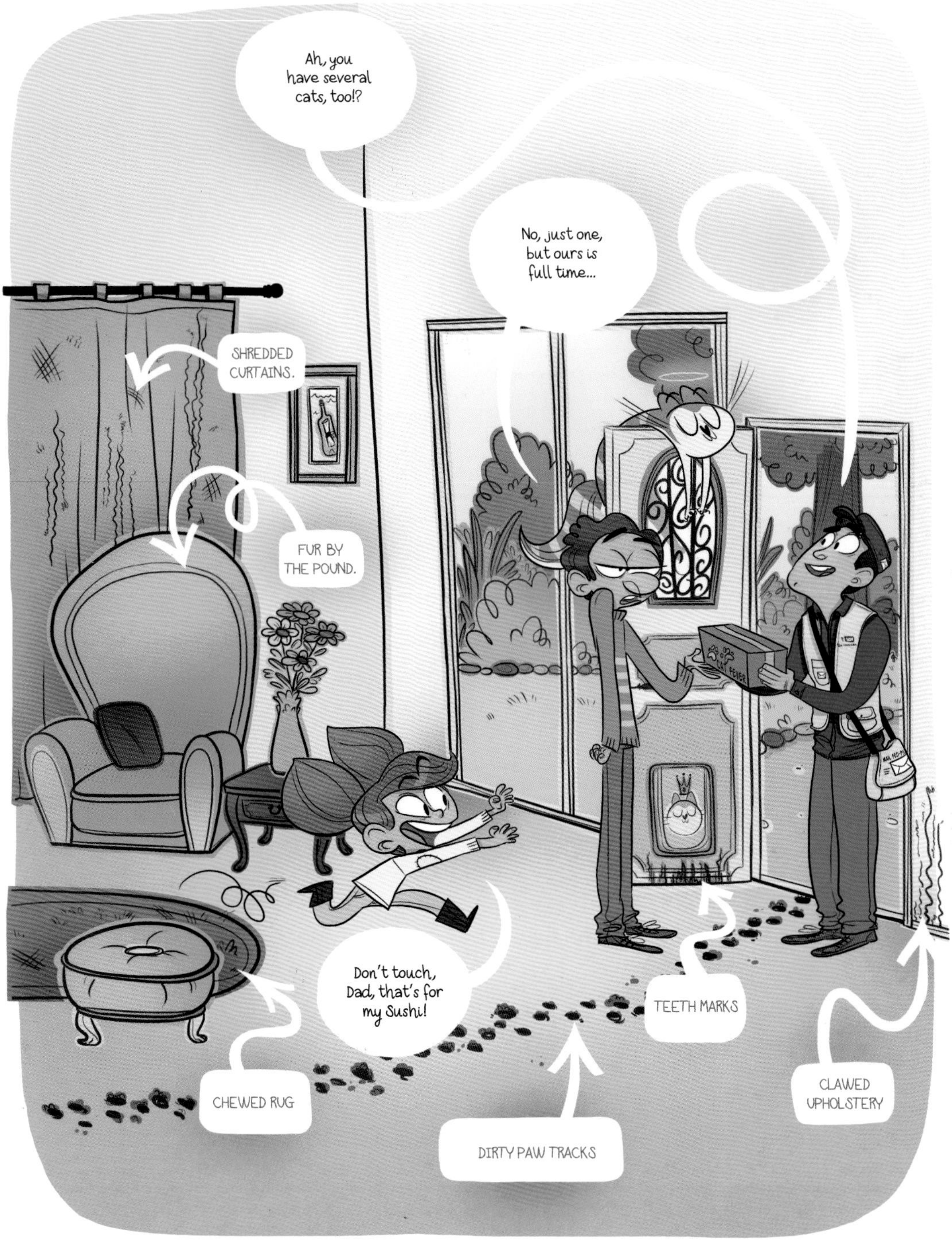
Ah, you have several cats, too!?
No, just one, but ours is full time...
SHREDDED CURTAINS.
FUR BY THE POUND.
Don't touch, Dad, that's for my Sushi!
TEETH MARKS
CHEWED RUG
DIRTY PAW TRACKS
CLAWED UPHOLSTERY

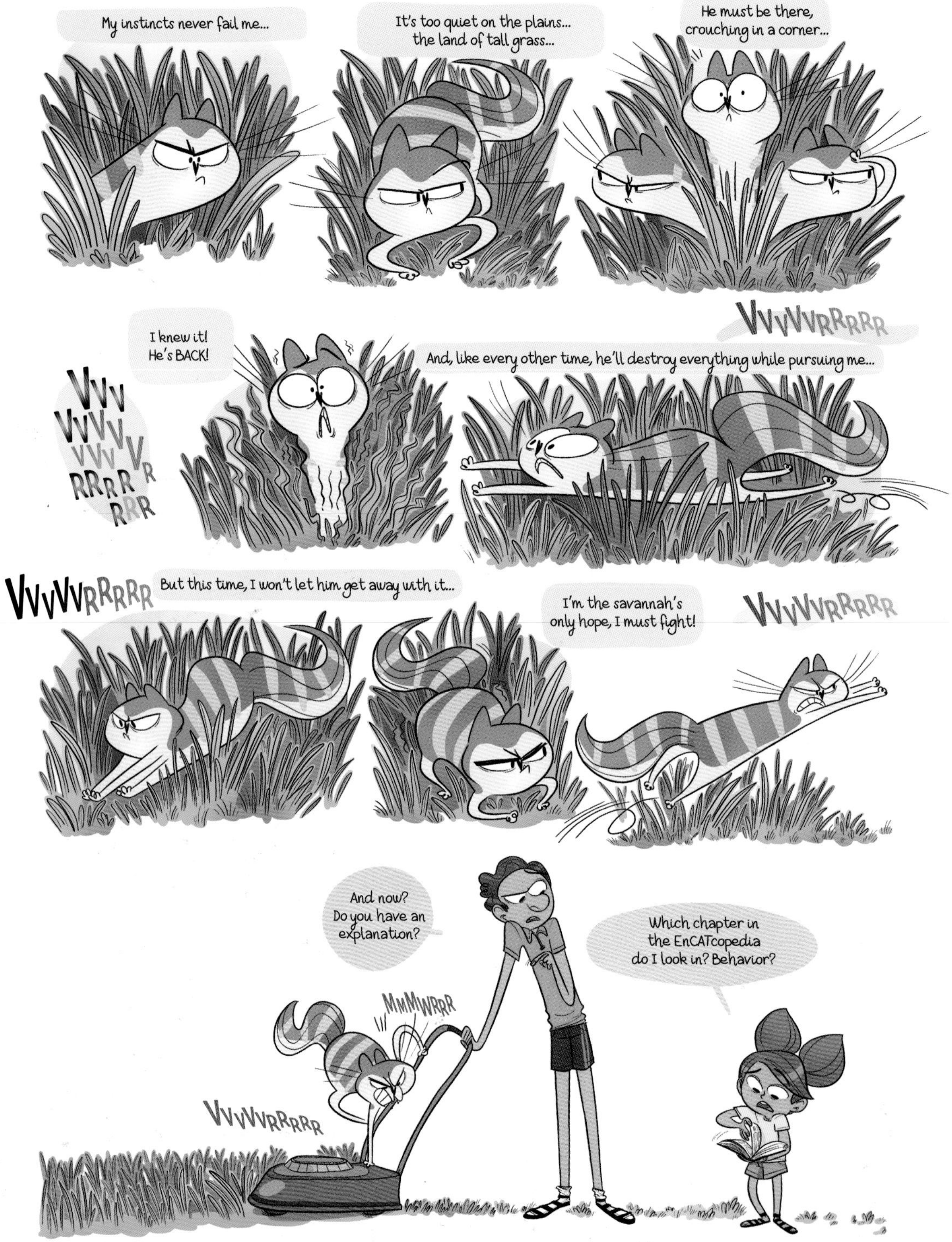
My instincts never fail me...
It's too quiet on the plains... the land of tall grass...
He must be there, crouching in a corner...
VvvVvRRRRR
I knew it! He's BACK!
VvvVVVVVvVRRRRRRRR
And, like every other time, he'll destroy everything while pursuing me...
VvvVvRRRRR
But this time, I won't let him get away with it...
I'm the savannah's only hope, I must fight!
VvvVvRRRRR
And now? Do you have an explanation?
Which chapter in the EnCATcopedia do I look in? Behavior?
MMMWRRR
VvvVvRRRRR

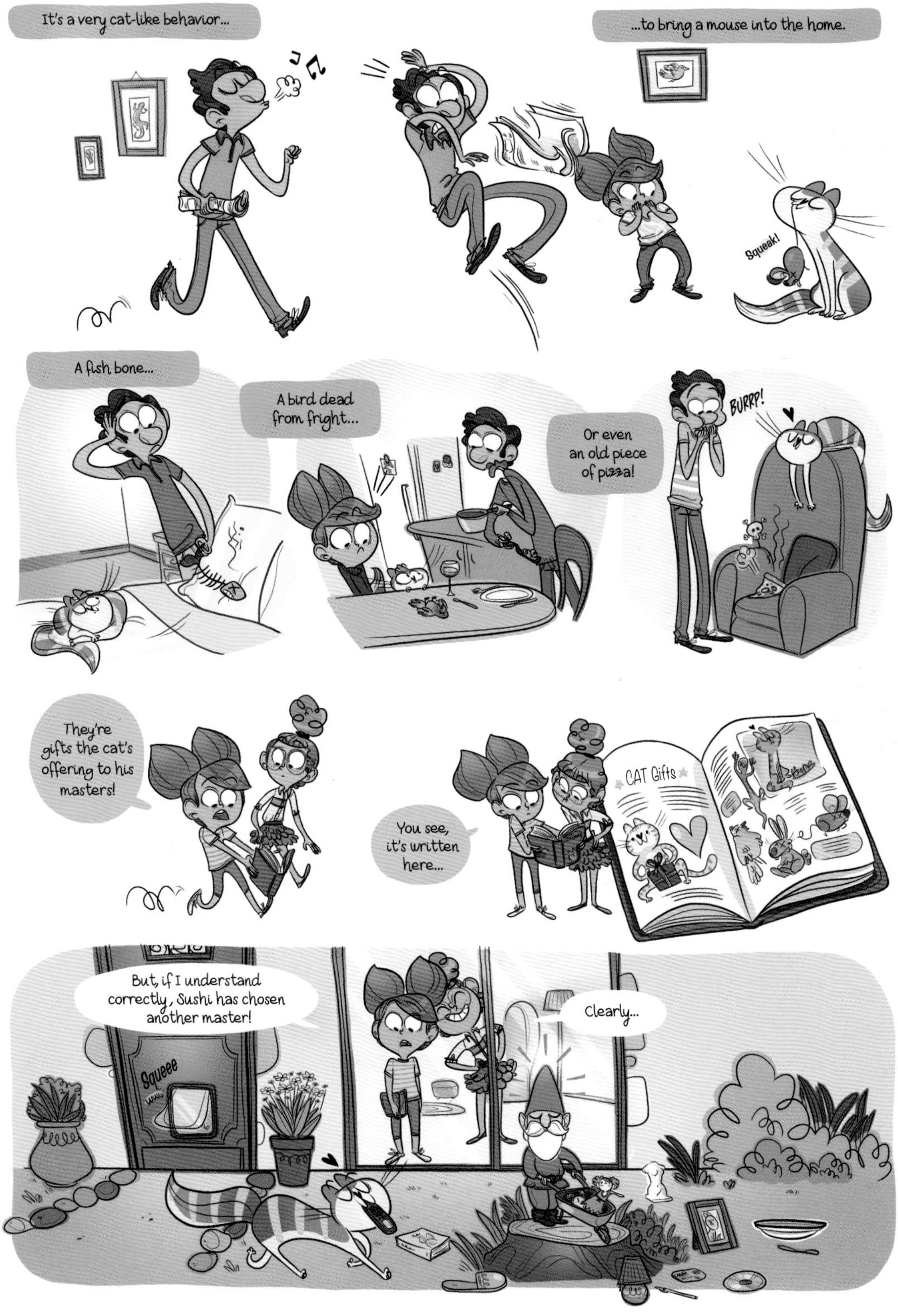
It's a very cat-like behavior...
...to bring a mouse into the home.
Squeak!
A fish bone...
A bird dead from fright...
Or even an old piece of pizza!
BURRP!
They're gifts the cat's offering to his masters!
You see, it's written here...
CAT Gifts
But, if I understand correctly, Sushi has chosen another master!
Clearly...
Squeee

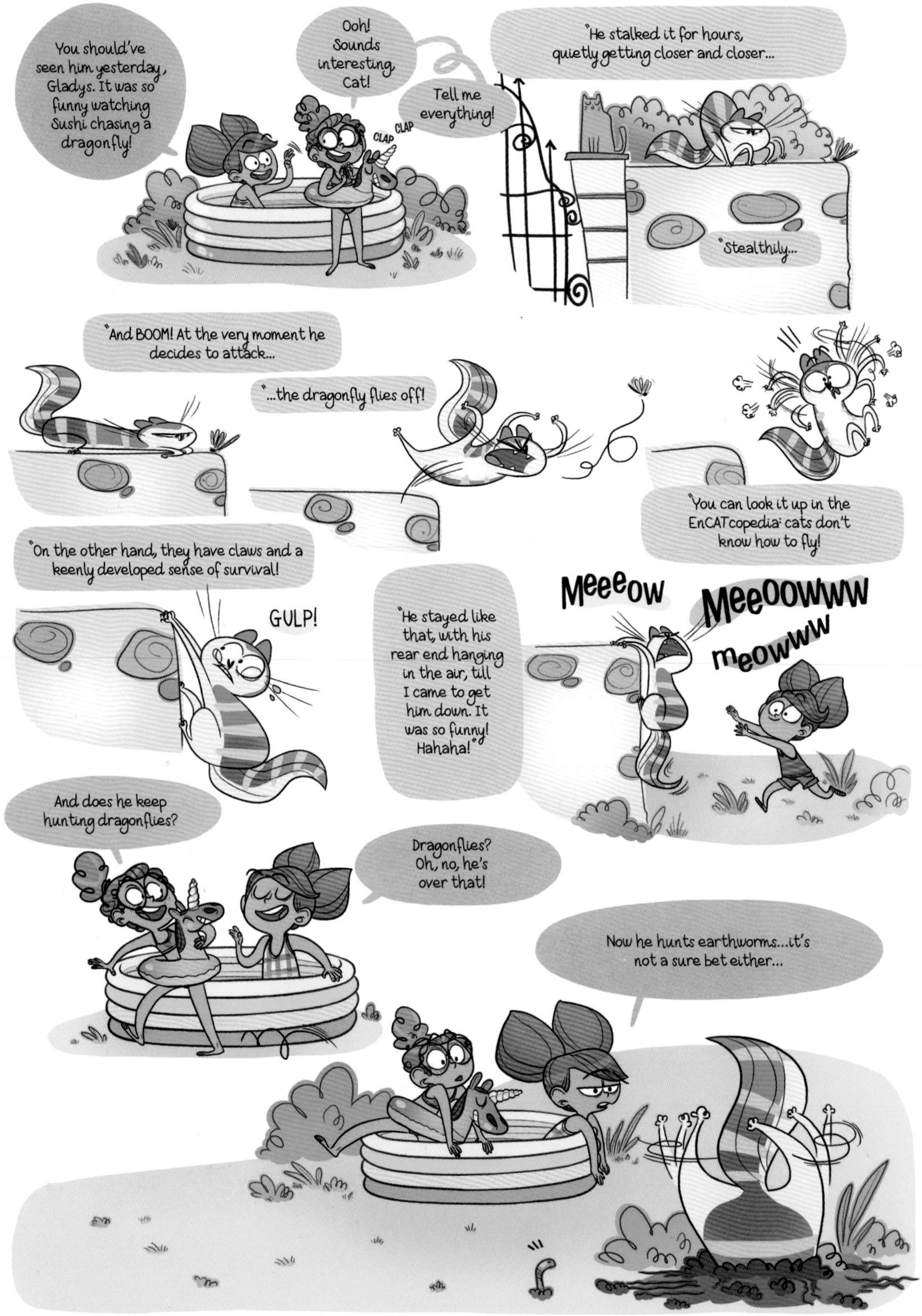
You should've seen him yesterday, Gladys. It was so funny watching Sushi chasing a dragonfly!
Ooh! Sounds interesting, Cat!
CLAP CLAP
Tell me everything!
"He stalked it for hours, quietly getting closer and closer...
"Stealthily...
"And BOOM! At the very moment he decides to attack...
"...the dragonfly flies off!
"You can look it up in the EnCATcopedia: cats don't know how to fly!
"On the other hand, they have claws and a keenly developed sense of survival!
GULP!
"He stayed like that, with his rear end hanging in the air, till I came to get him down. It was so funny! Hahaha!"
Meeeow
Meeoowww
meowww
And does he keep hunting dragonflies?
Dragonflies? Oh, no, he's over that!
Now he hunts earthworms...it's not a sure bet either...

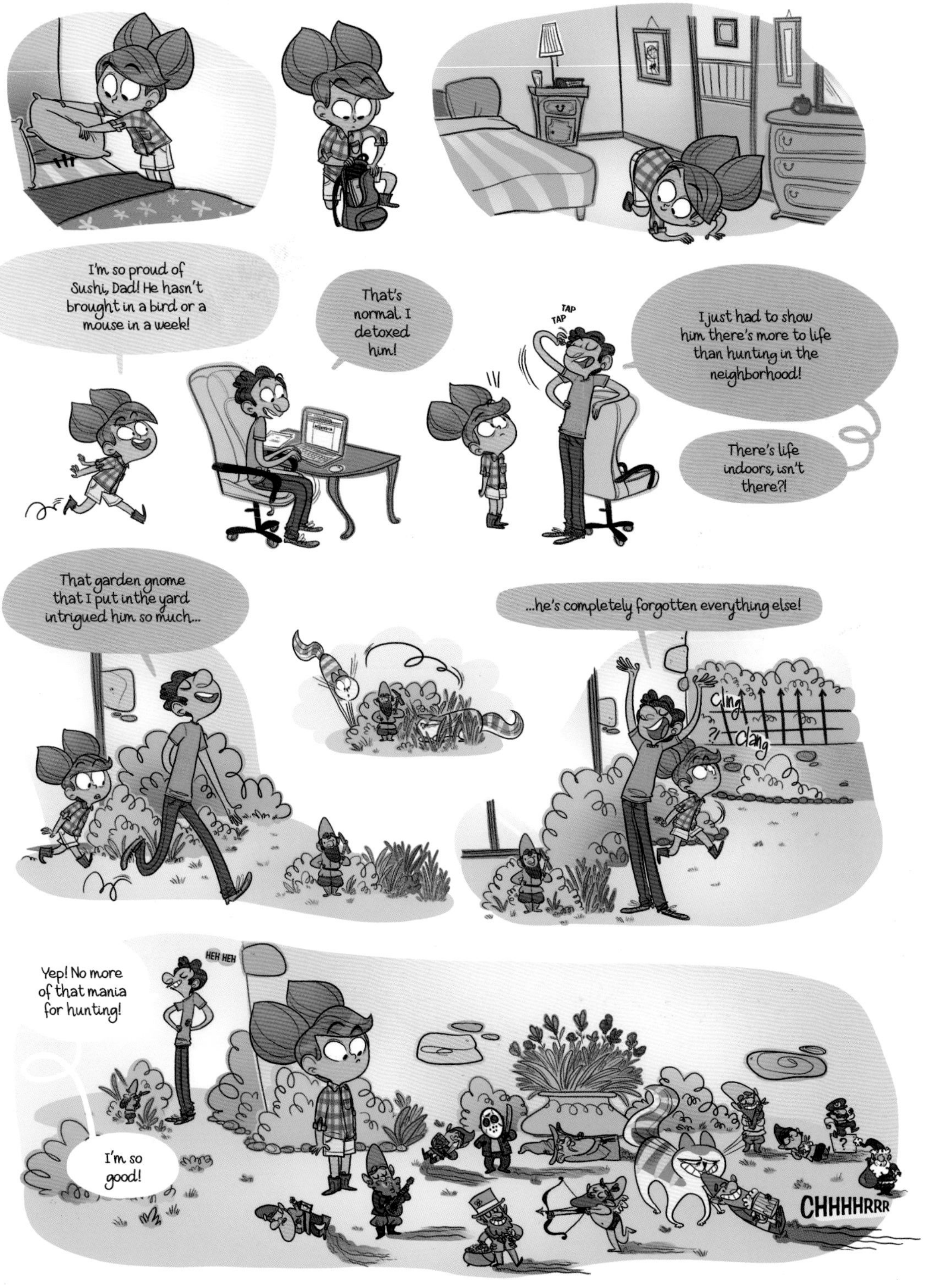

I'm so proud of Sushi, Dad! He hasn't brought in a bird or a mouse in a week!
That's normal. I detoxed him!
TAP TAP
I just had to show him there's more to life than hunting in the neighborhood!
There's life indoors, isn't there?!
That garden gnome that I put in the yard intrigued him so much...
...he's completely forgotten everything else!
Cling
?!
Clang
HEH HEH
Yep! No more of that mania for hunting!
I'm so good!
CHHHHRRR

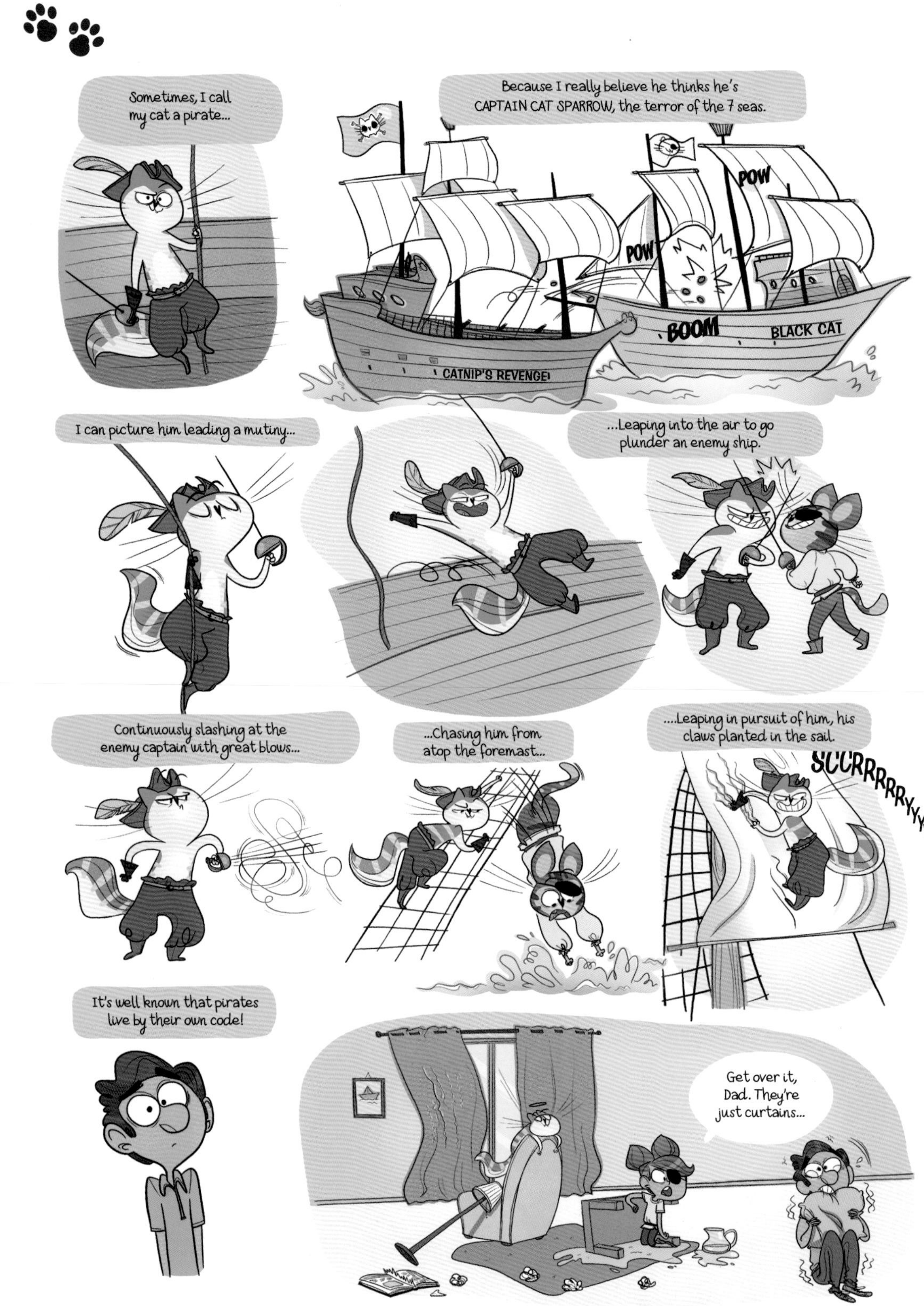

Sometimes, I call my cat a pirate...
Because I really believe he thinks he's CAPTAIN CAT SPARROW, the terror of the 7 seas.
POW
POW
BOOM
BLACK CAT
CATNIP'S REVENGE
I can picture him leading a mutiny...
...Leaping into the air to go plunder an enemy ship.
Continuously slashing at the enemy captain with great blows...
...Chasing him from atop the foremast...
....Leaping in pursuit of him, his claws planted in the sail.
SCCRRRRRRYYYYY
It's well known that pirates live by their own code!
Get over it, Dad. They're just curtains...

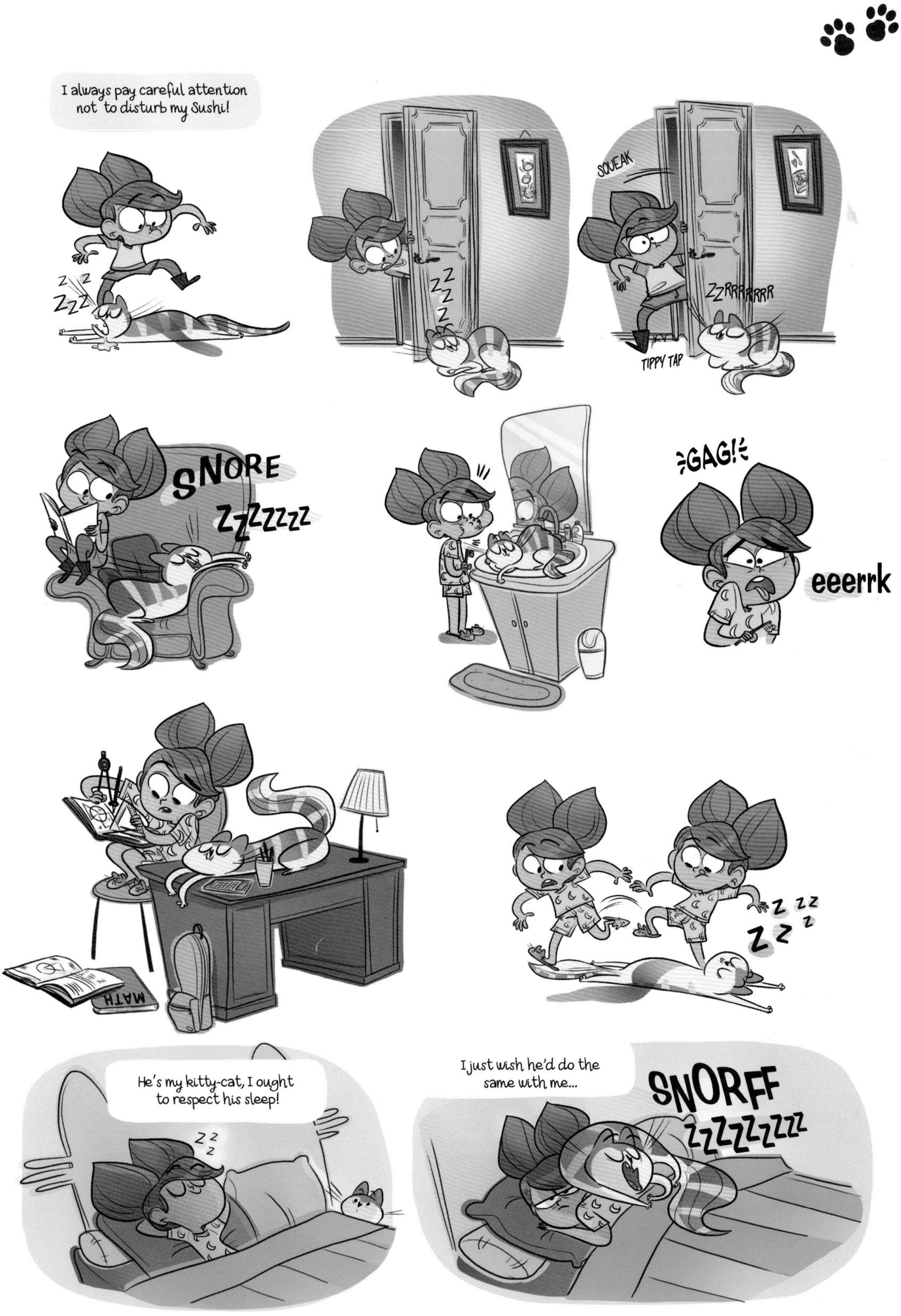
I always pay careful attention not to disturb my Sushi!
ZZZ
SQUEAK
ZZZZ
ZZRRRRRRR
TIPPY TAP
SNORE
ZZZZZZZ
GAG!
eeerrk
MATH
ZZZZZ
He's my kitty-cat, I ought to respect his sleep!
ZZZ
I just wish he'd do the same with me...
SNORFF
ZZZZZZZZZ

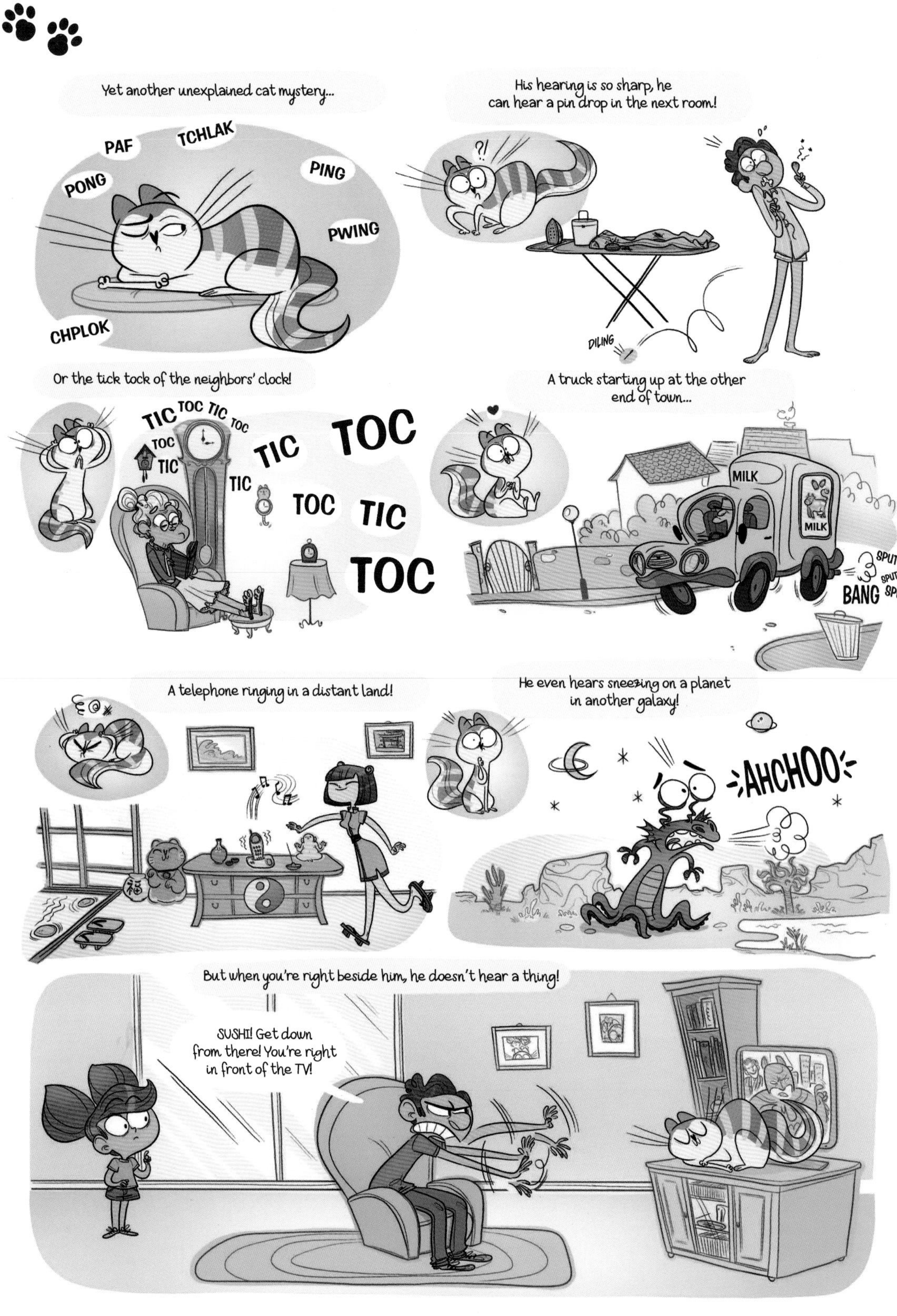
Yet another unexplained cat mystery...
PAF
TCHLAK
PONG
PING
PWING
CHPLOK
His hearing is so sharp, he can hear a pin drop in the next room!
?!
DILING
Or the tick tock of the neighbors' clock!
TIC TOC TIC TOC
TOC
TIC
TIC
TIC
TOC
TOC
TIC
TOC
A truck starting up at the other end of town...
MILK
MILK
SPUT
SPUTTER
BANG
SPUT
A telephone ringing in a distant land!
He even hears sneezing on a planet in another galaxy!
AHCHOO
But when you're right beside him, he doesn't hear a thing!
SUSHI! Get down from there! You're right in front of the TV!

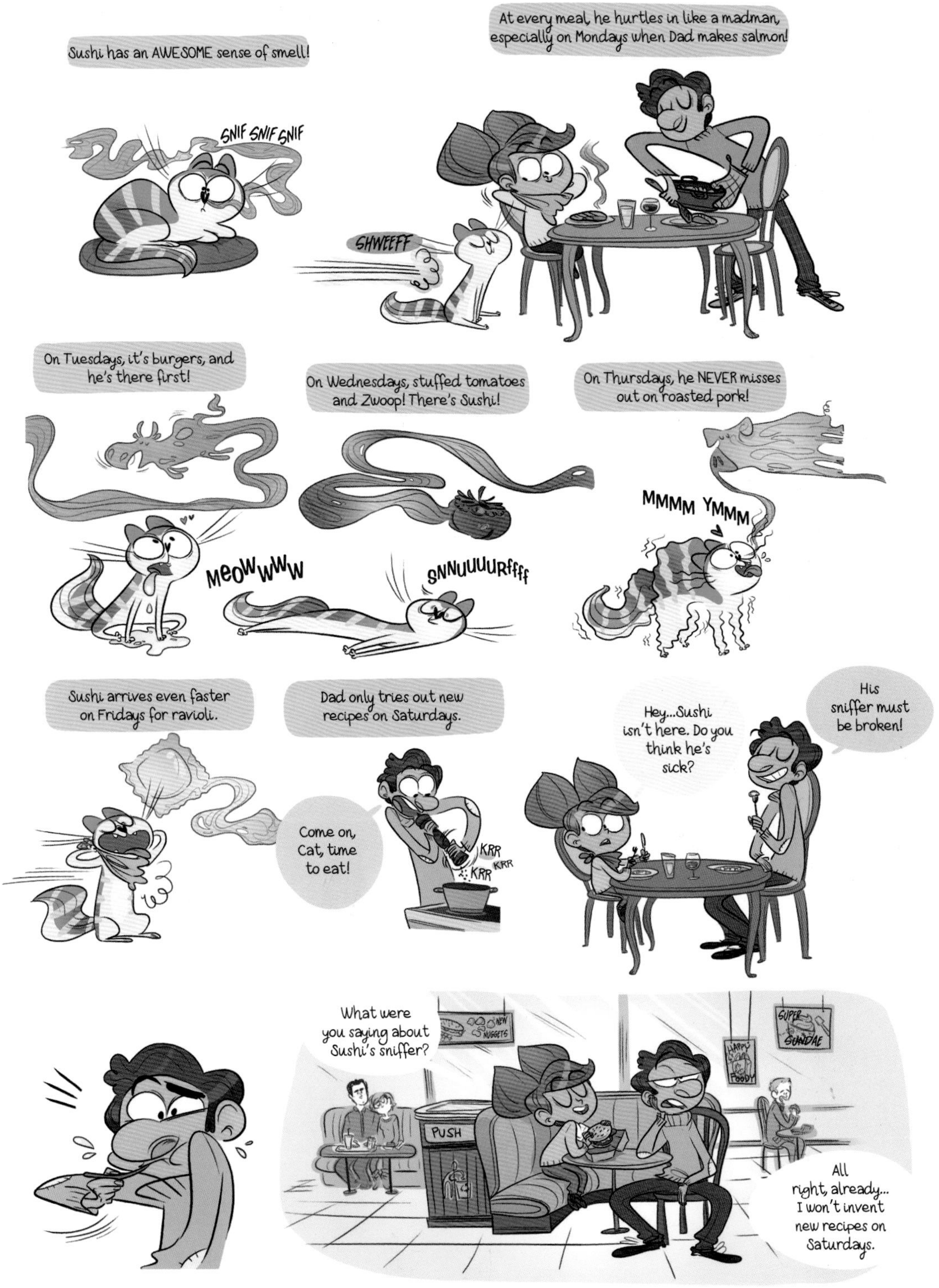

Sushi has an AWESOME sense of smell!
SNIF SNIF SNIF
At every meal, he hurtles in like a madman, especially on Mondays when Dad makes salmon!
SHWEEFF
On Tuesdays, it's burgers, and he's there first!
MEOWWWW
On Wednesdays, stuffed tomatoes and Zwoop! There's Sushi!
SNNUUUURffff
On Thursdays, he NEVER misses out on roasted pork!
MMMM YMMM
Sushi arrives even faster on Fridays for ravioli.
Dad only tries out new recipes on Saturdays.
Come on, Cat, time to eat!
KRR
KRR
KRR
Hey...Sushi isn't here. Do you think he's sick?
His sniffer must be broken!
What were you saying about Sushi's sniffer?
NEW NUGGETS
SUPER SUNDAE
PUSH
All right, already... I won't invent new recipes on Saturdays.

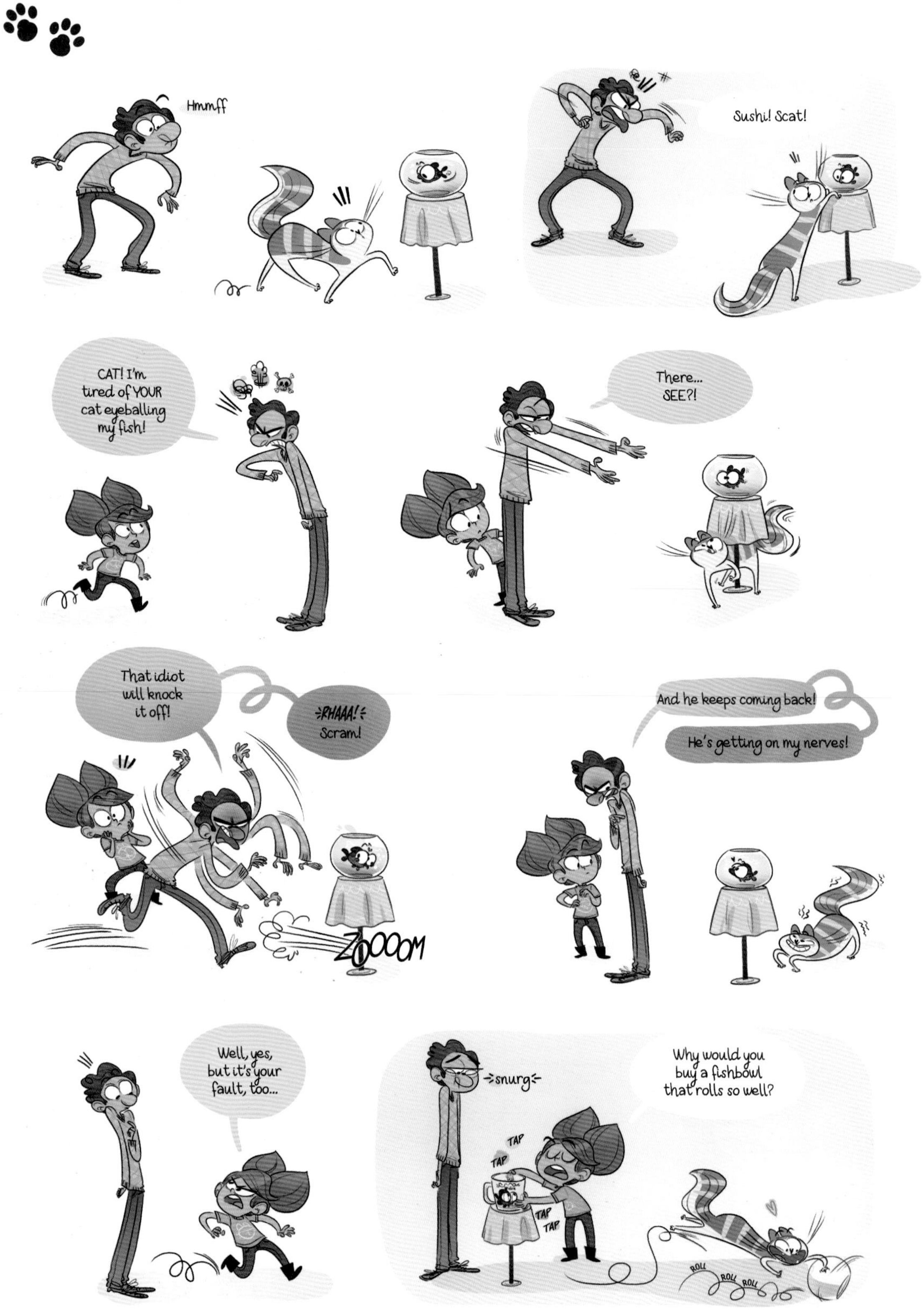
Hmmff
Sushi! Scat!
CAT! I'm tired of YOUR cat eyeballing my fish!
There... SEE?!
That idiot will knock it off!
RHAAA! Scram!
ZOOOOM
And he keeps coming back!
He's getting on my nerves!
Well, yes, but it's your fault, too...
snurg
Why would you buy a fishbowl that rolls so well?
TAP
TAP
TAP
TAP
ROLL
ROLL
ROLL

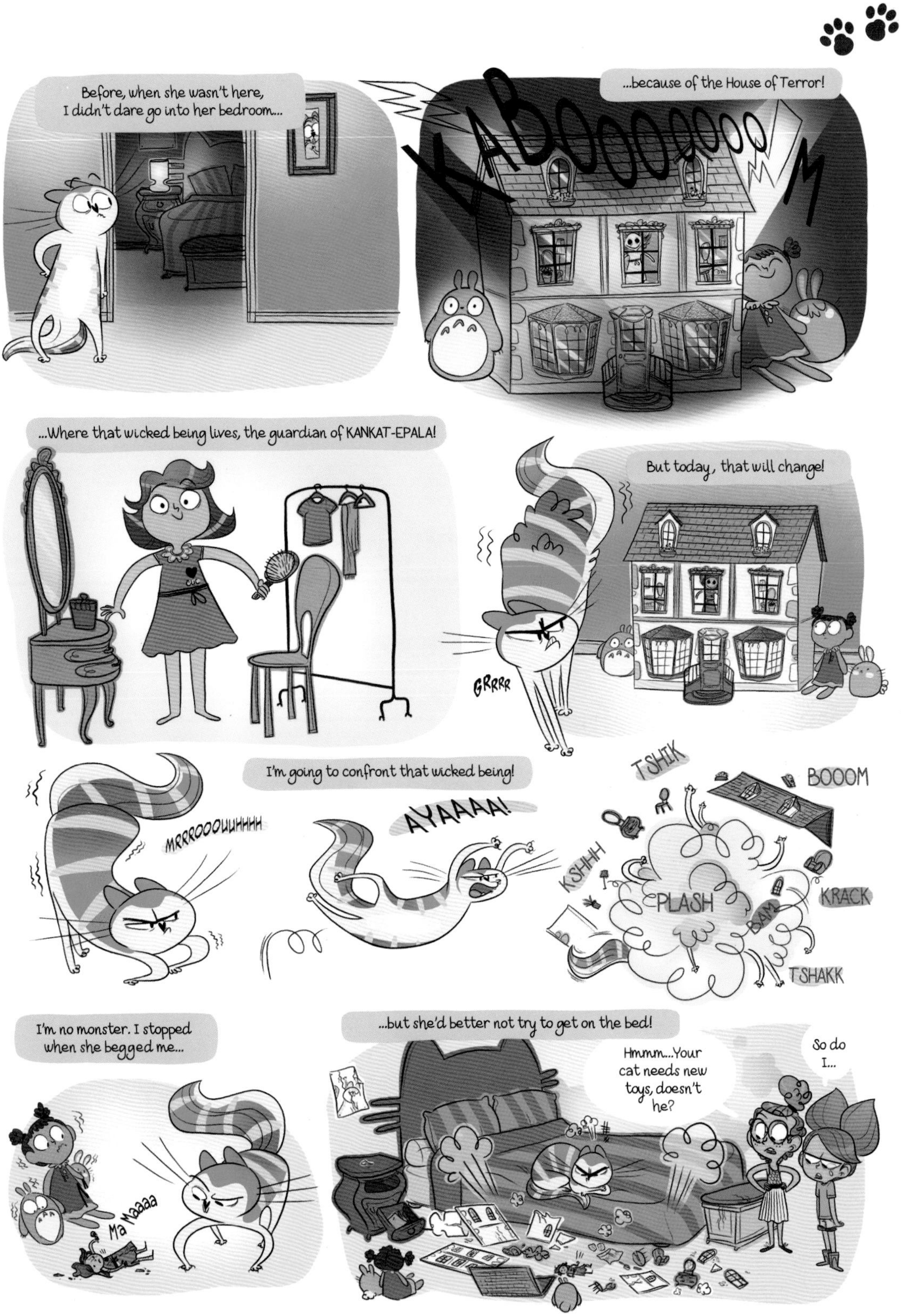

Before, when she wasn't here, I didn't dare go into her bedroom...
KABOOOOOOOM
...because of the House of Terror!
...Where that wicked being lives, the guardian of KANKAT-EPALA!
But today, that will change!
GRRRR
MRRROOOUUHHHH
I'm going to confront that wicked being!
AYAAAA!
TSHIK
BOOOM
KSHHH
PLASH
BAM
KRACK
TSHAKK
I'm no monster. I stopped when she begged me...
Ma Maaaa
...but she'd better not try to get on the bed!
Hmmm...Your cat needs new toys, doesn't he?
So do I...

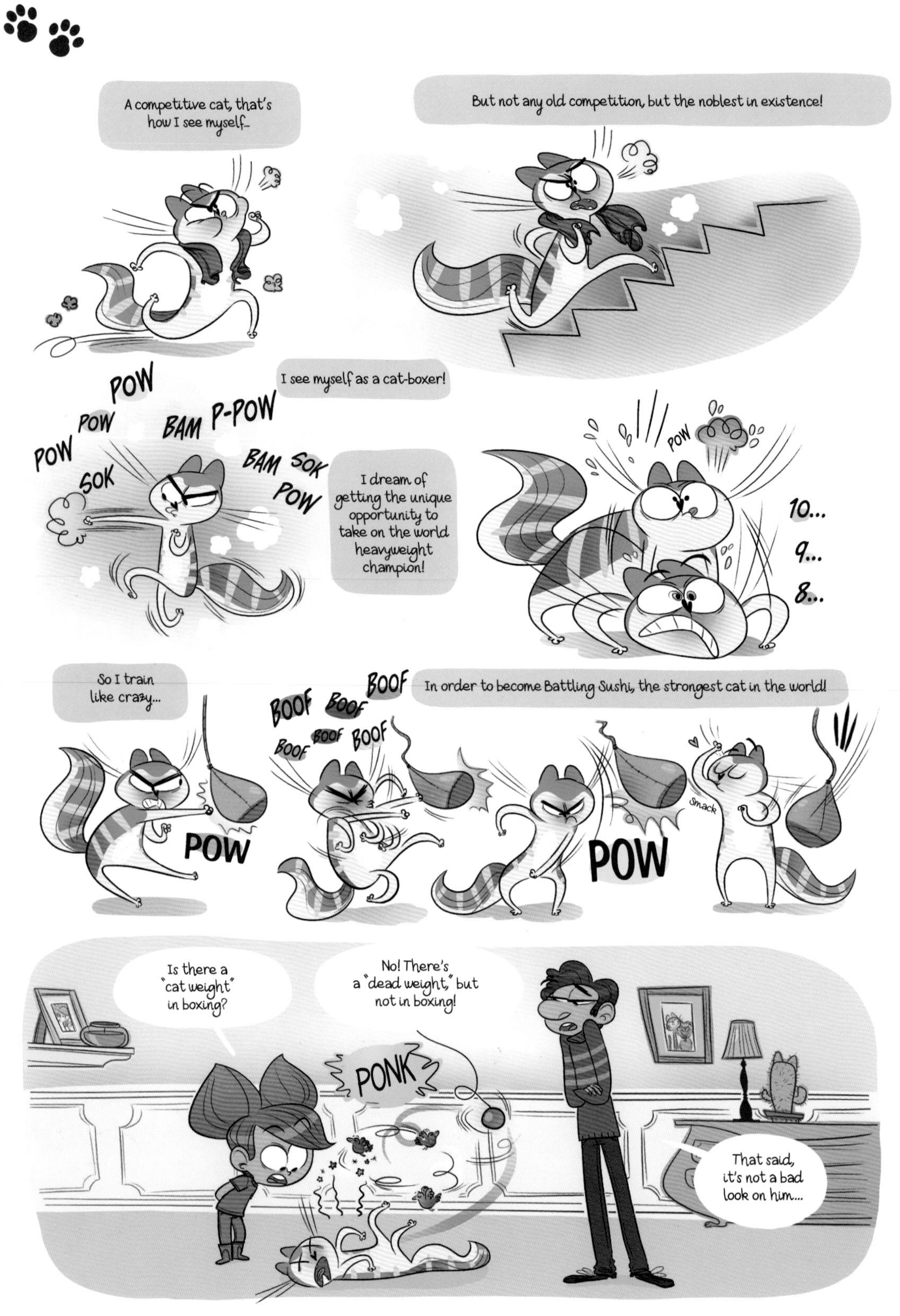

A competitive cat, that's how I see myself...
But not any old competition, but the noblest in existence!
I see myself as a cat-boxer!
POW
POW
POW
BAM
P-POW
SOK
BAM
SOK
POW
I dream of getting the unique opportunity to take on the world heavyweight champion!
POW
10...
9...
8...
So I train like crazy...
BOOF
BOOF
BOOF
BOOF
BOOF
BOOF
In order to become Battling Sushi, the strongest cat in the world!
POW
POW
Smack
Is there a "cat weight" in boxing?
No! There's a "dead weight," but not in boxing!
PONK
That said, it's not a bad look on him...

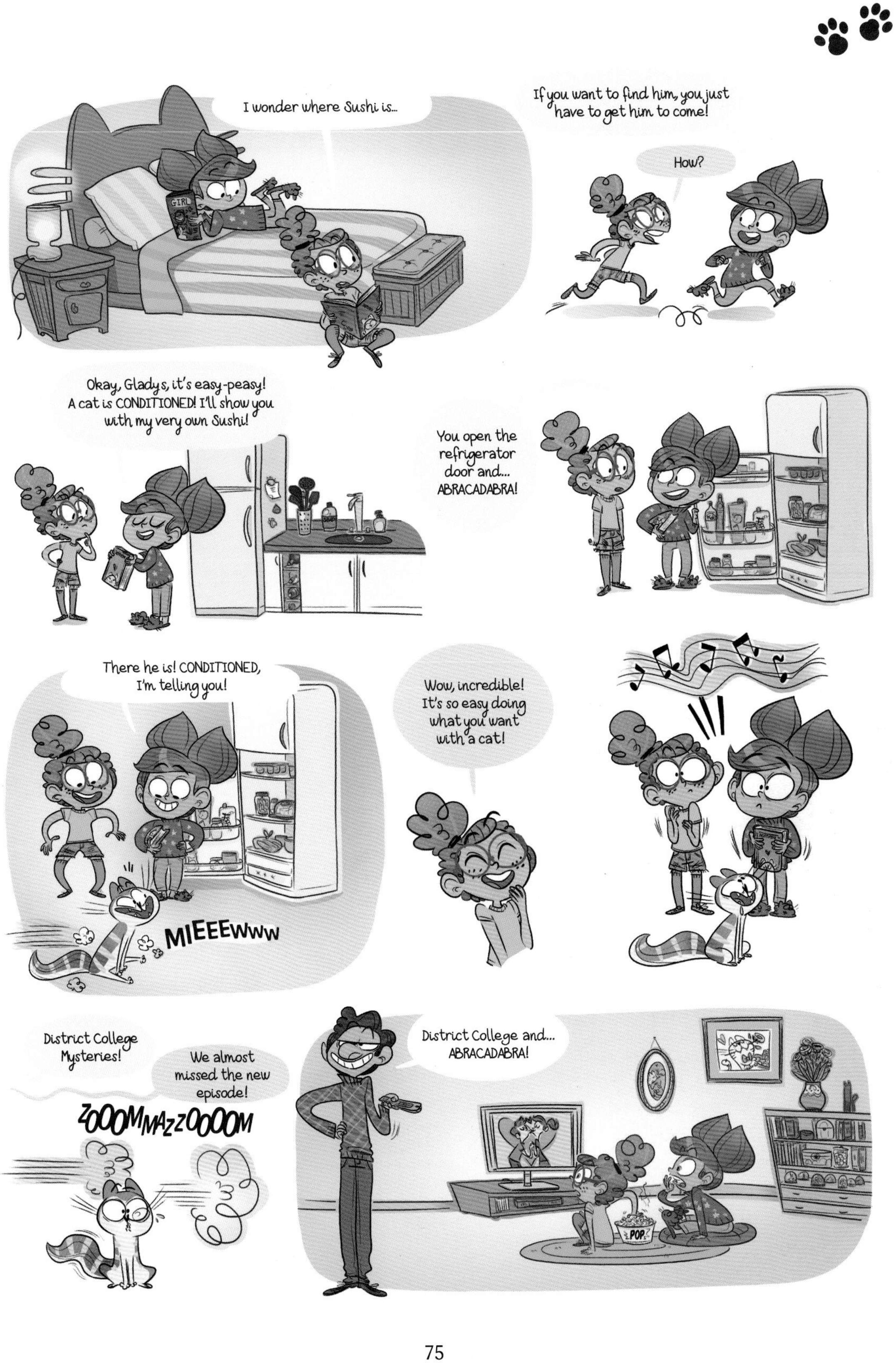
I wonder where Sushi is...
If you want to find him, you just have to get him to come!
How?
Okay, Gladys, it's easy-peasy! A cat is CONDITIONED! I'll show you with my very own Sushi!
You open the refrigerator door and... ABRACADABRA!
There he is! CONDITIONED, I'm telling you!
MIEEEWWW
Wow, incredible! It's so easy doing what you want with a cat!
District College Mysteries!
We almost missed the new episode!
ZOOOMMAZZOOOOM
District College and... ABRACADABRA!
POP

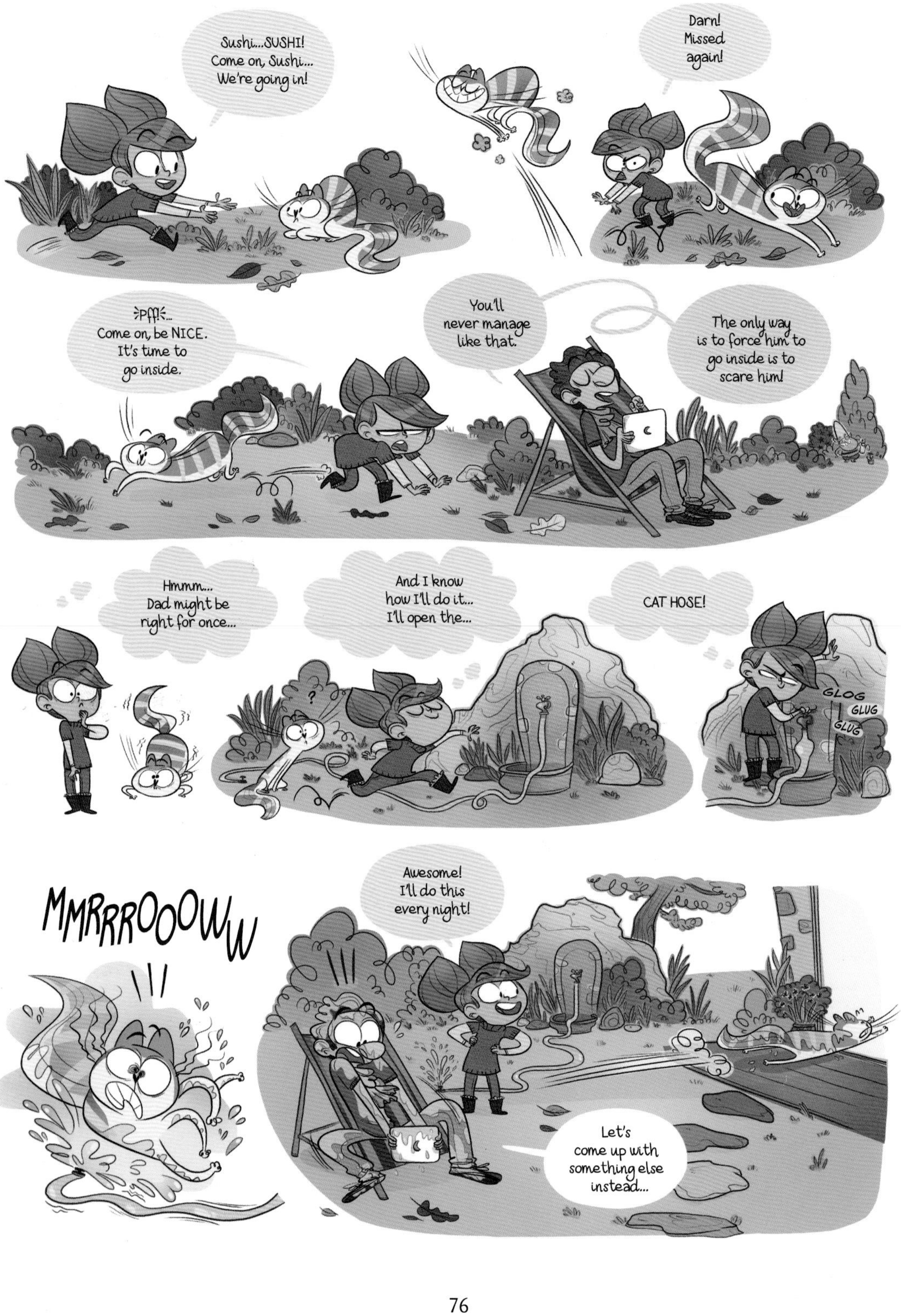
Sushi...SUSHI!
Come on, Sushi...
We're going in!
Darn!
Missed
again!
⋟Pff!⋞...
Come on, be NICE.
It's time to
go inside.
You'll
never manage
like that.
The only way
is to force him to
go inside is to
scare him!
Hmmm...
Dad might be
right for once...
And I know
how I'll do it...
I'll open the...
CAT HOSE!
GLOG
GLUG
GLUG
MMRRROOOWW
Awesome!
I'll do this
every night!
Let's
come up with
something else
instead...

?

COSTUME

What are you doing Cat?

I'm making a scary costume...

BOOOOOOO

COSTUME

That's fun... For Halloween?

COSTUME

No, to get Sushi to come inside! Hey, help me slip into my costume!

Dad told me not to try to catch him but to scare him instead...

Otherwise, it's impossible to get him to come in the house...

I understand!

Okay. Here goes!

COSTUME

CATMAGGEDON!

But, Dad...Why are you keeping Sushi from coming in?!

HEEHEEHEE

Plop

CLAK CLAK CLAK CLAK CLAK CLAK CLAK CLAK CLAK CLAK CLAK

MEEEEQOW

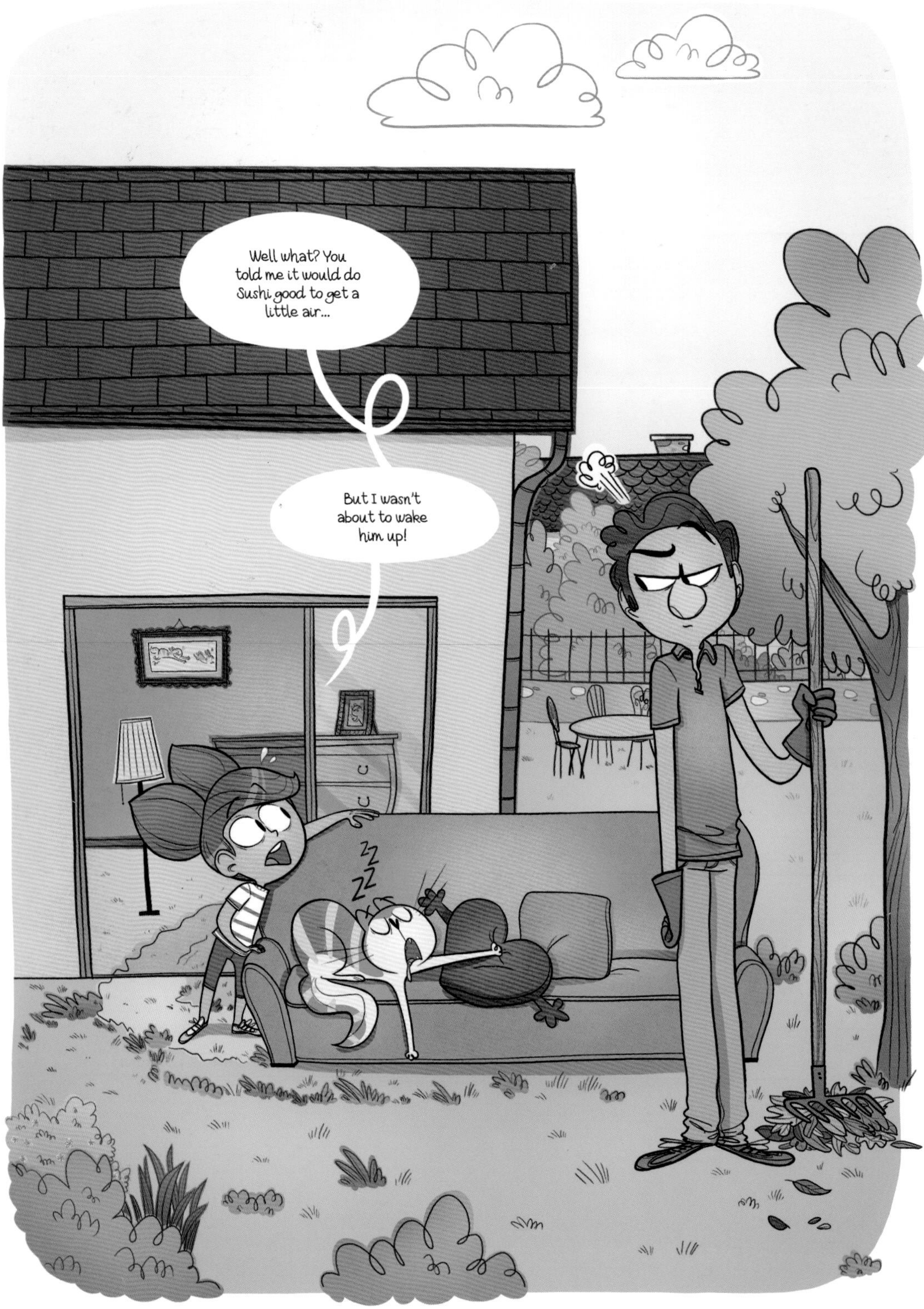
Well what? You told me it would do Sushi good to get a little air...
But I wasn't about to wake him up!
ZZZ

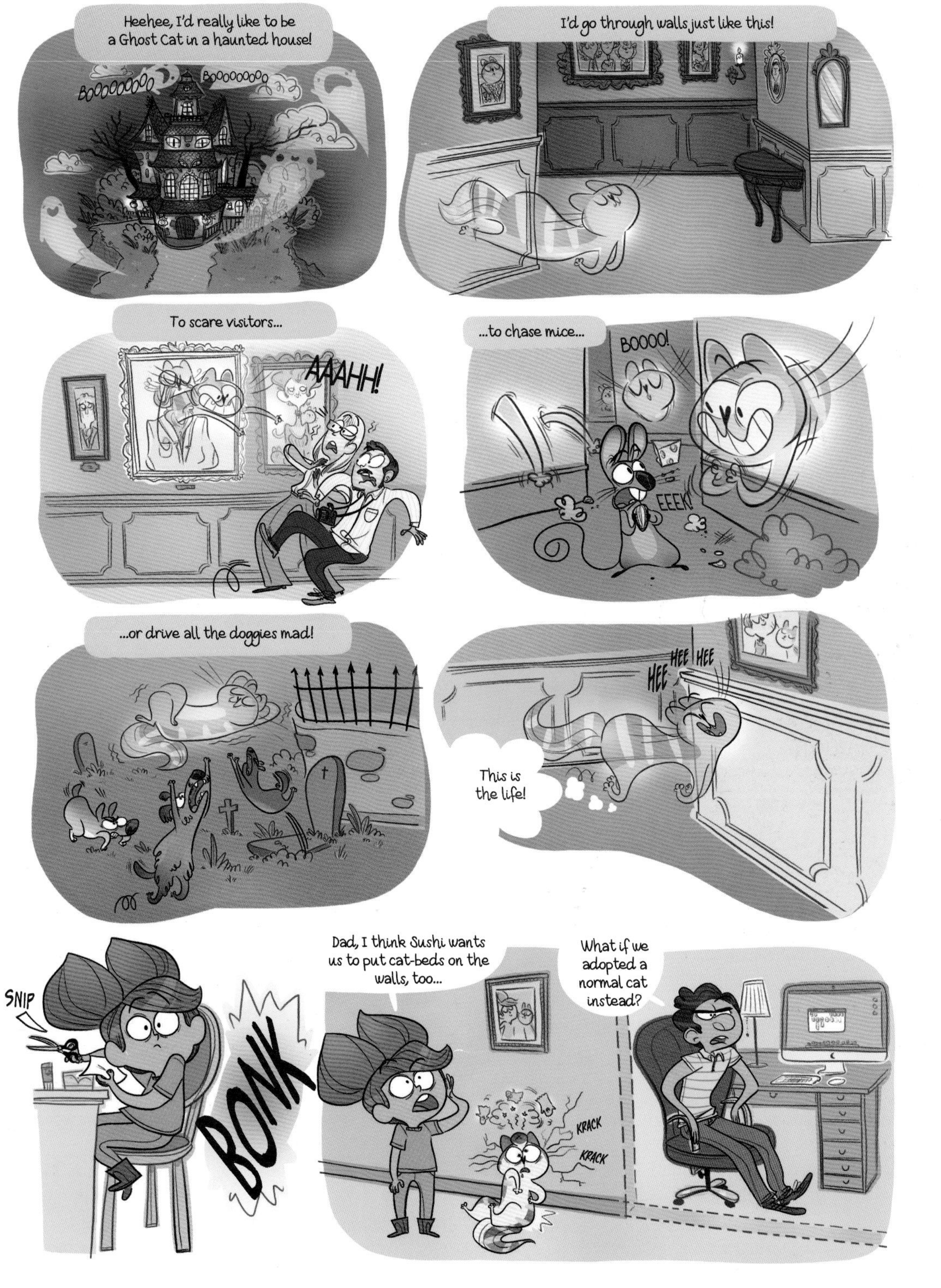
Heehee, I'd really like to be a Ghost Cat in a haunted house!
BOOOOOOOOO
BOOOOOOOOO
I'd go through walls just like this!
To scare visitors...
AAAHH!
...to chase mice...
BOOOO!
EEEK!
...or drive all the doggies mad!
HEE HEE HEE
This is the life!
SNIP
BONK
Dad, I think Sushi wants us to put cat-beds on the walls, too...
KRACK
KRACK
What if we adopted a normal cat instead?

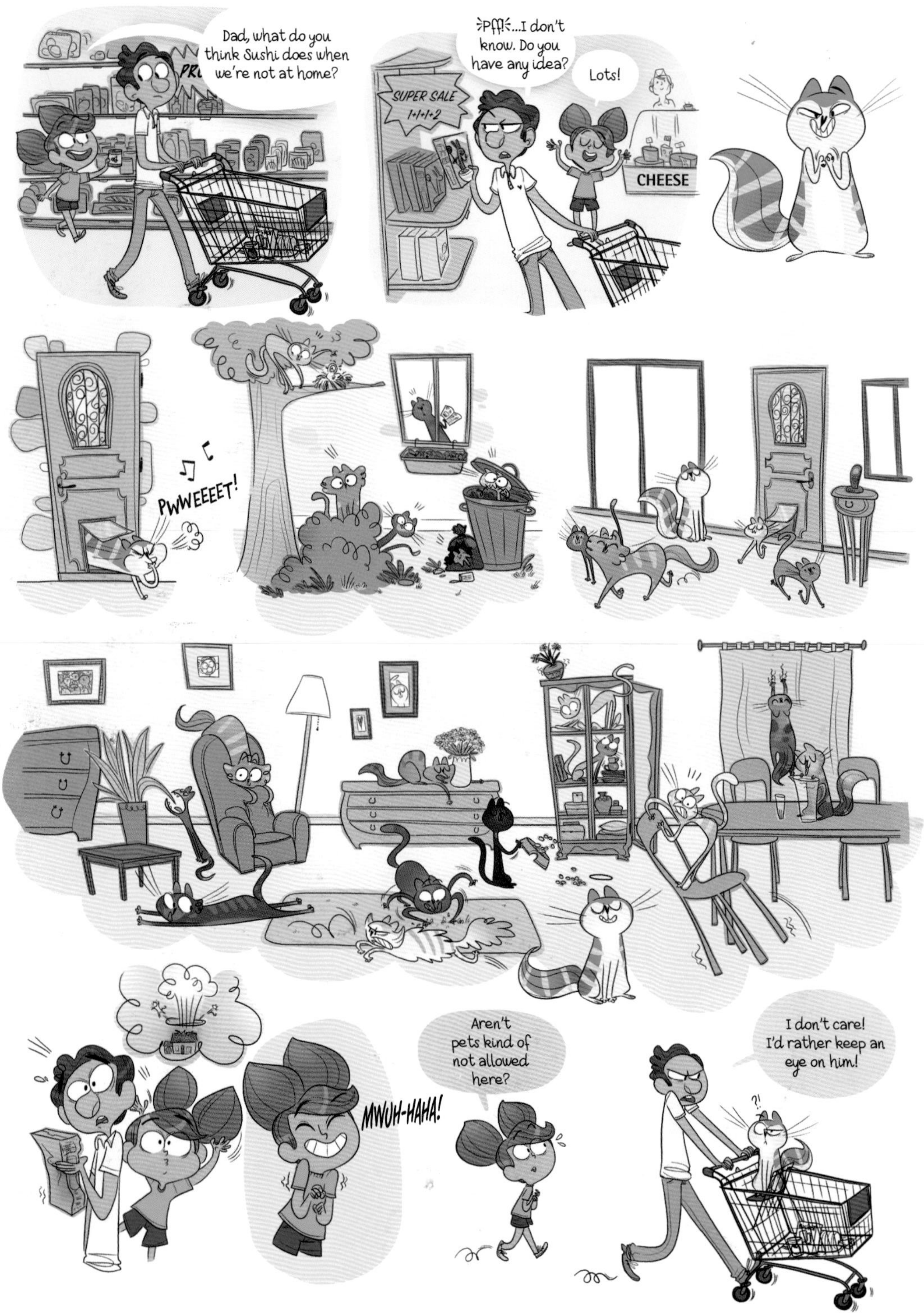
Dad, what do you think Sushi does when we're not at home?
SUPER SALE
1+1+1+2
Pff!...I don't know. Do you have any idea?
Lots!
CHEESE
PWWEEEET!
MWUH-HAHA!
Aren't pets kind of not allowed here?
I don't care! I'd rather keep an eye on him!
?!

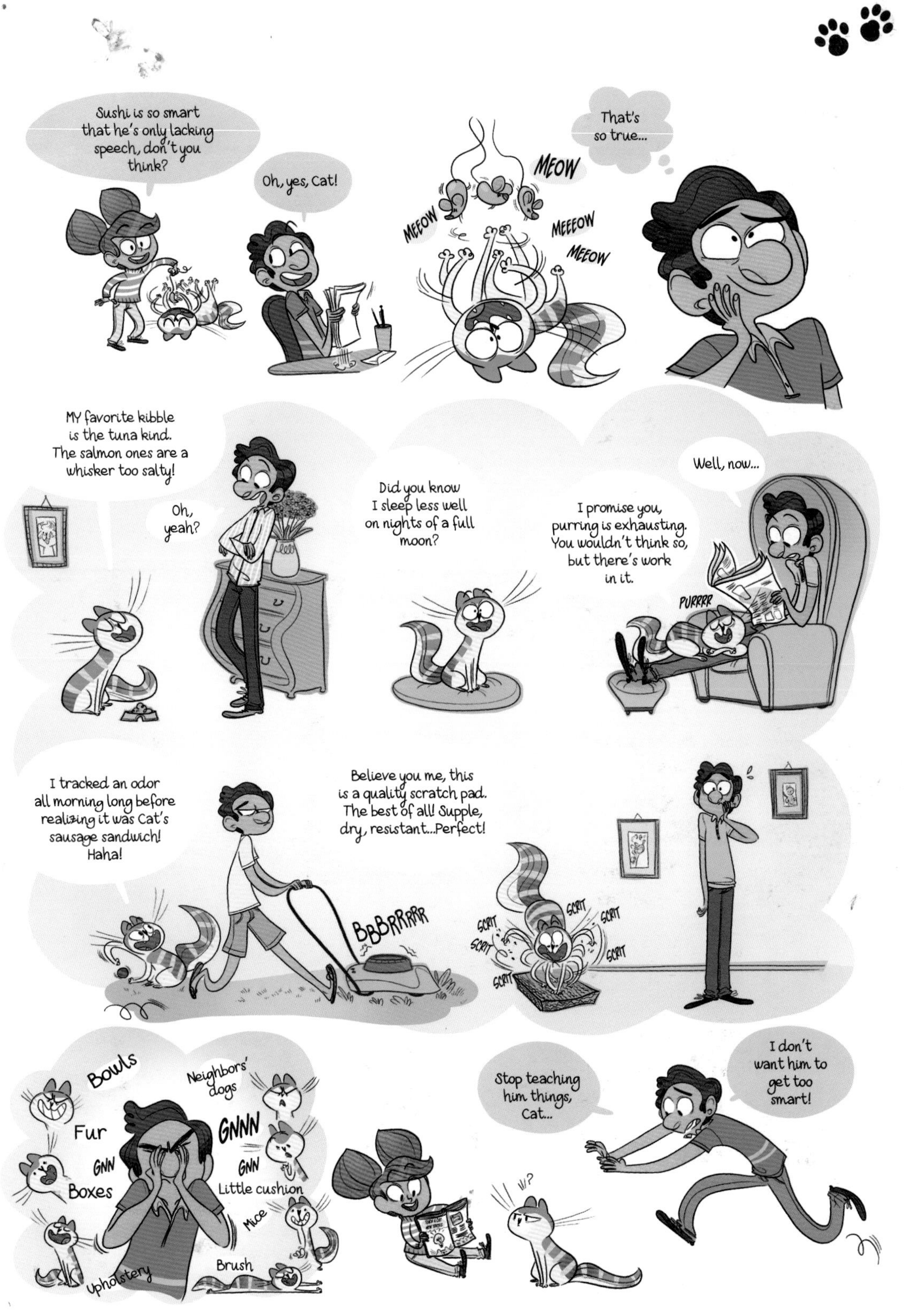

Sushi is so smart that he's only lacking speech, don't you think?
Oh, yes, Cat!
MEOW
MEEOW
MEEEOW
MEEOW
That's so true...
MY favorite kibble is the tuna kind. The salmon ones are a whisker too salty!
Oh, yeah?
Did you know I sleep less well on nights of a full moon?
I promise you, purring is exhausting. You wouldn't think so, but there's work in it.
PURRRR
Well, now...
I tracked an odor all morning long before realizing it was Cat's sausage sandwich! Haha!
BBBRRRRR
Believe you me, this is a quality scratch pad. The best of all! Supple, dry, resistant...Perfect!
SCRIT
SCRIT
SCRIT
SCRIT
SCRIT
SCRIT
Bowls
Neighbors' dogs
Fur
GNNN
GNN
GNN
Boxes
Little cushion
Mice
Upholstery
Brush
?
Stop teaching him things, Cat...
I don't want him to get too smart!

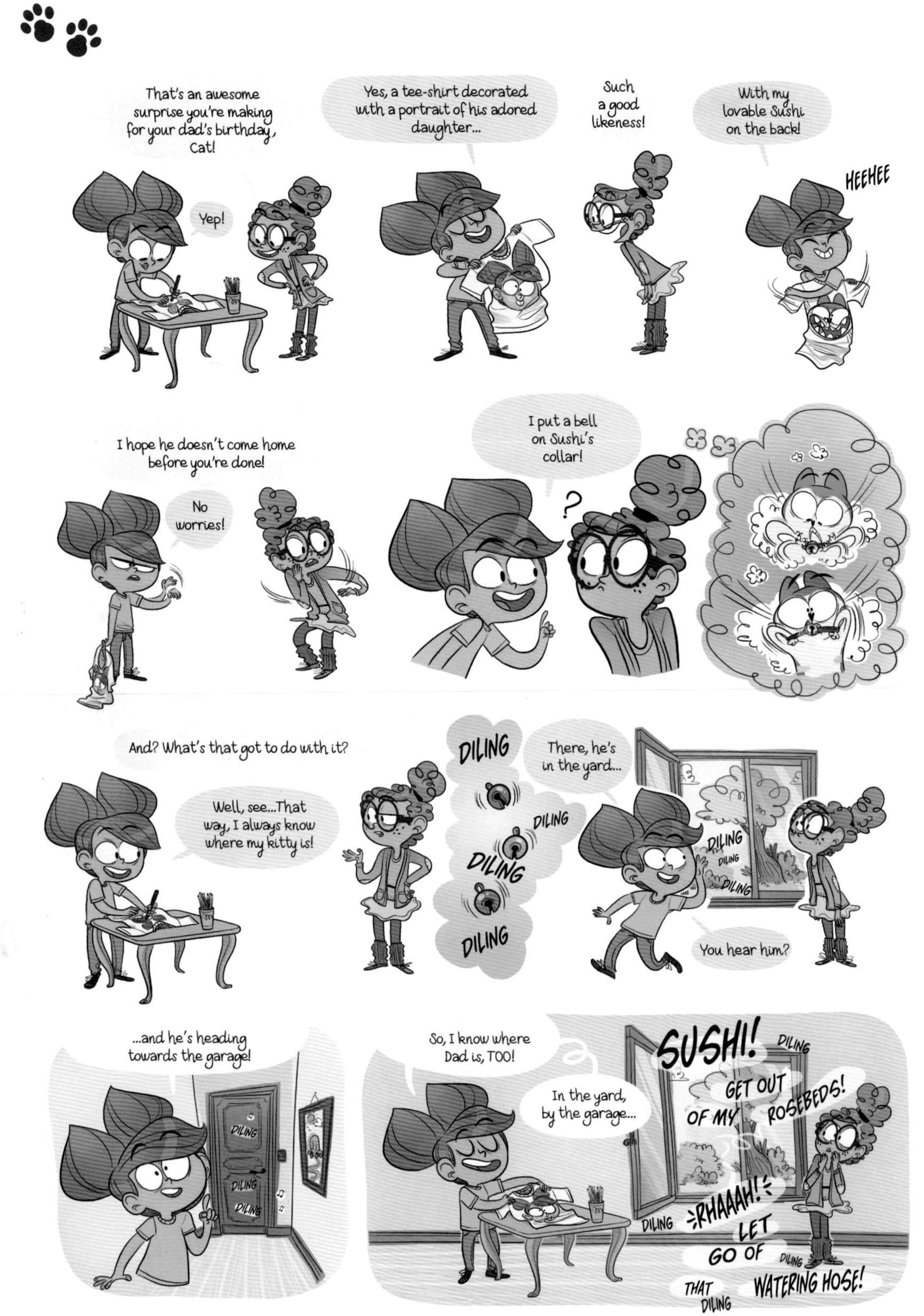
That's an awesome surprise you're making for your dad's birthday, Cat!
Yep!
Yes, a tee-shirt decorated with a portrait of his adored daughter...
Such a good likeness!
With my lovable Sushi on the back!
HEEHEE
I hope he doesn't come home before you're done!
No worries!
I put a bell on Sushi's collar!
?
And? What's that got to do with it?
Well, see...That way, I always know where my kitty is!
DILING
DILING
DILING
DILING
There, he's in the yard...
DILING
DILING
DILING
You hear him?
...and he's heading towards the garage!
DILING
DILING
DILING
So, I know where Dad is, TOO!
In the yard, by the garage...
SUSHI!
DILING
GET OUT OF MY ROSEBEDS!
DILING
RHAAAH!
LET GO OF THAT WATERING HOSE!
DILING
DILING

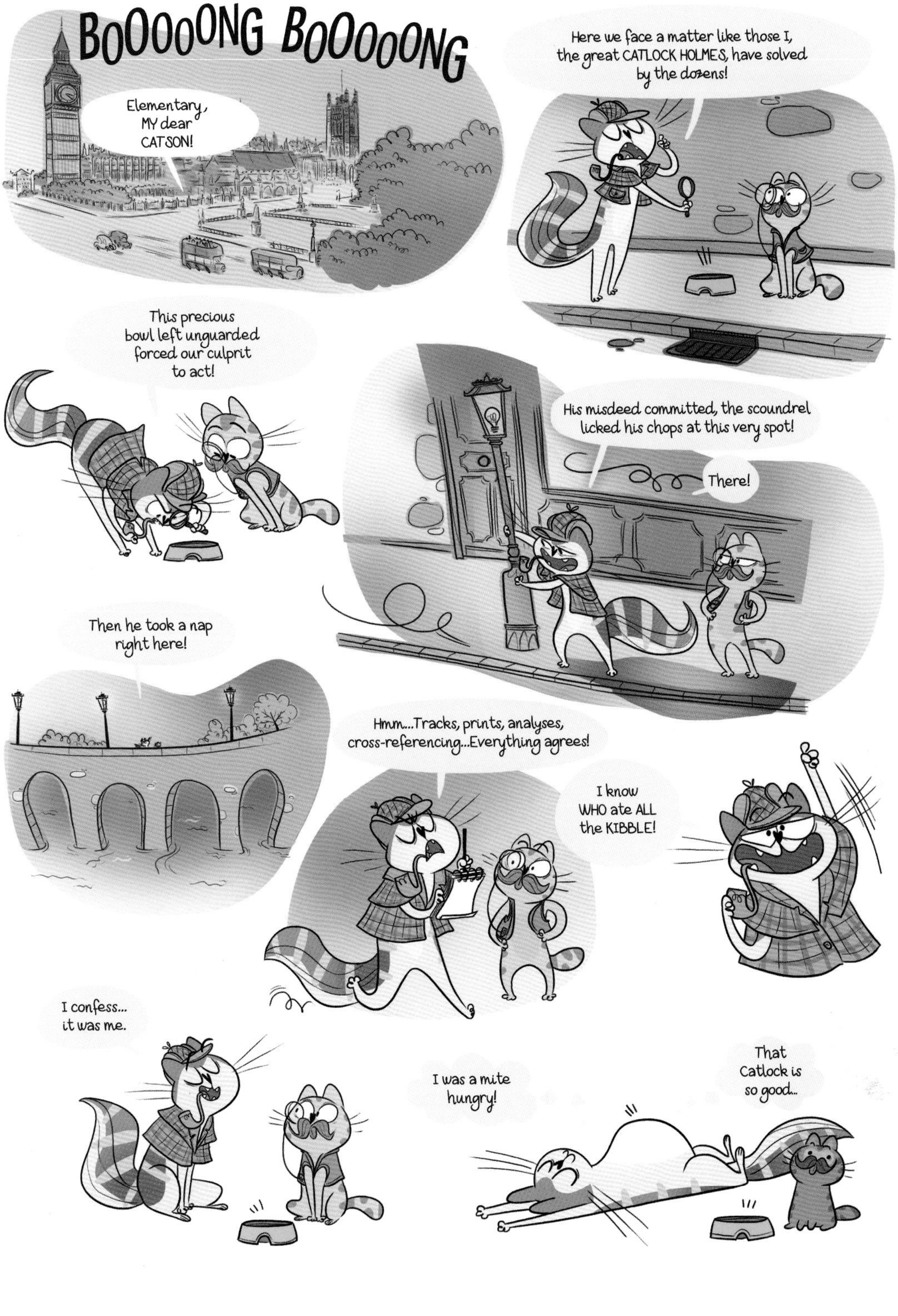
BOOOOONG BOOOOONG
Elementary, MY dear CATSON!
Here we face a matter like those I, the great CATLOCK HOLMES, have solved by the dozens!
This precious bowl left unguarded forced our culprit to act!
His misdeed committed, the scoundrel licked his chops at this very spot!
There!
Then he took a nap right here!
Hmm...Tracks, prints, analyses, cross-referencing...Everything agrees!
I know WHO ate ALL the KIBBLE!
I confess... it was me.
I was a mite hungry!
That Catlock is so good...

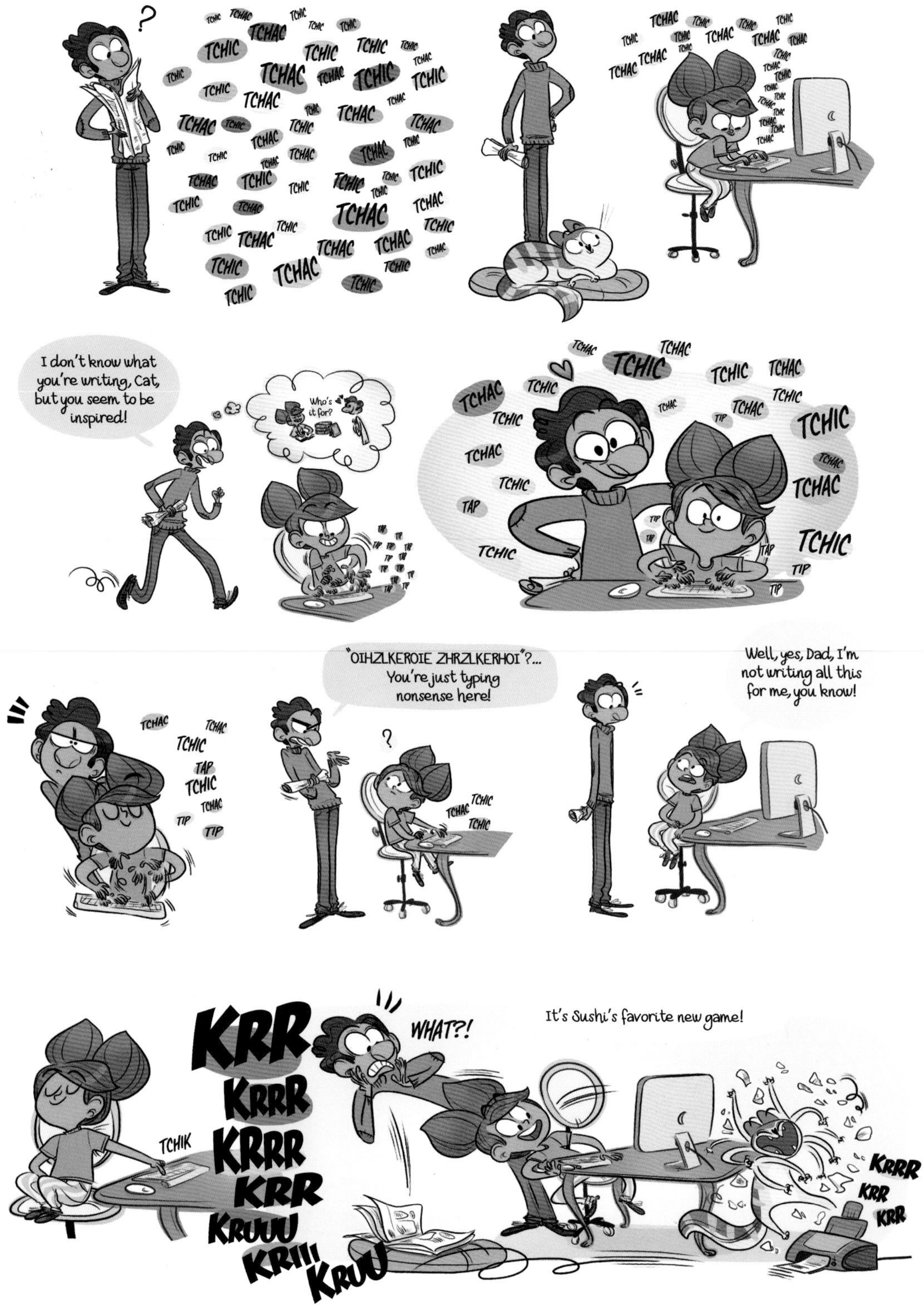
?
TCHIC TCHAC TCHIC TCHAC TCHIC TCHAC
TCHAC TCHIC TCHAC TCHIC TCHAC
I don't know what you're writing, Cat, but you seem to be inspired!
Who's it for?
TAP TIP
TCHAC TCHIC TCHAC TCHIC TCHAC TCHIC TCHAC TIP TAP TCHIC
TCHAC TCHAC TCHIC TAP TCHIC TCHAC TIP TIP
"OIHZLKEROIE ZHRZLKERHOI"?... You're just typing nonsense here!
?
TCHAC TCHIC TCHIC
Well, yes, Dad, I'm not writing all this for me, you know!
TCHIK
KRR KRRR KRRR KRR KRUUU KRIII KRUU
WHAT?!
It's Sushi's favorite new game!
KRRR KRR KRR

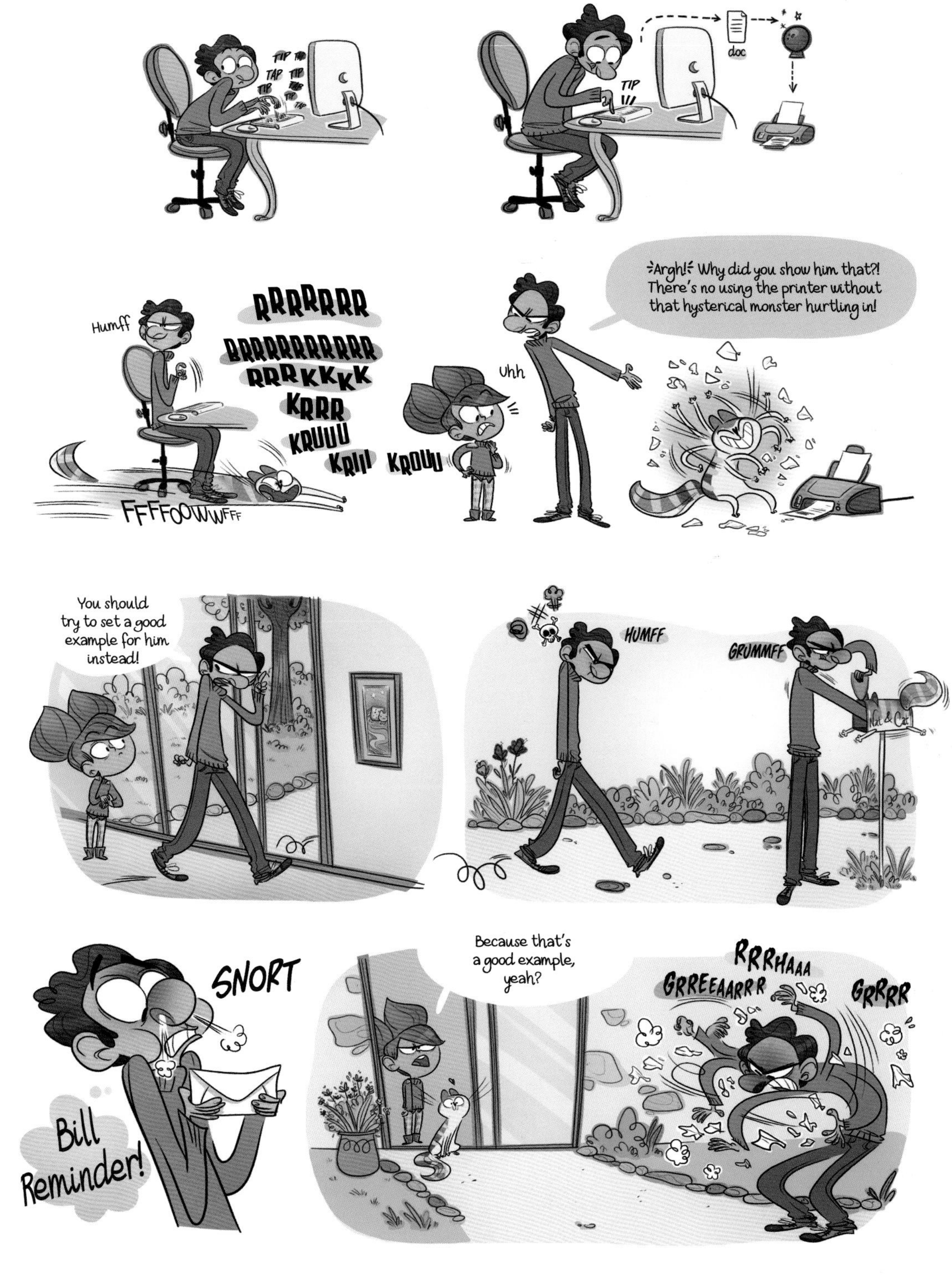

TIP TAP TIP
doc
TIP
Humff
RRRRRRR
BRRRRRRRRRR
RRRKKKK
KRRR
KRUUU
KRIII
KROUU
FFFFOOWWFFF
Uhh
Argh! Why did you show him that?! There's no using the printer without that hysterical monster hurtling in!
You should try to set a good example for him instead!
HUMFF
GRUMMFF
Nat & Cat
SNORT
Bill Reminder!
Because that's a good example, yeah?
RRRHAAA
GRREEAARRR
GRRRR

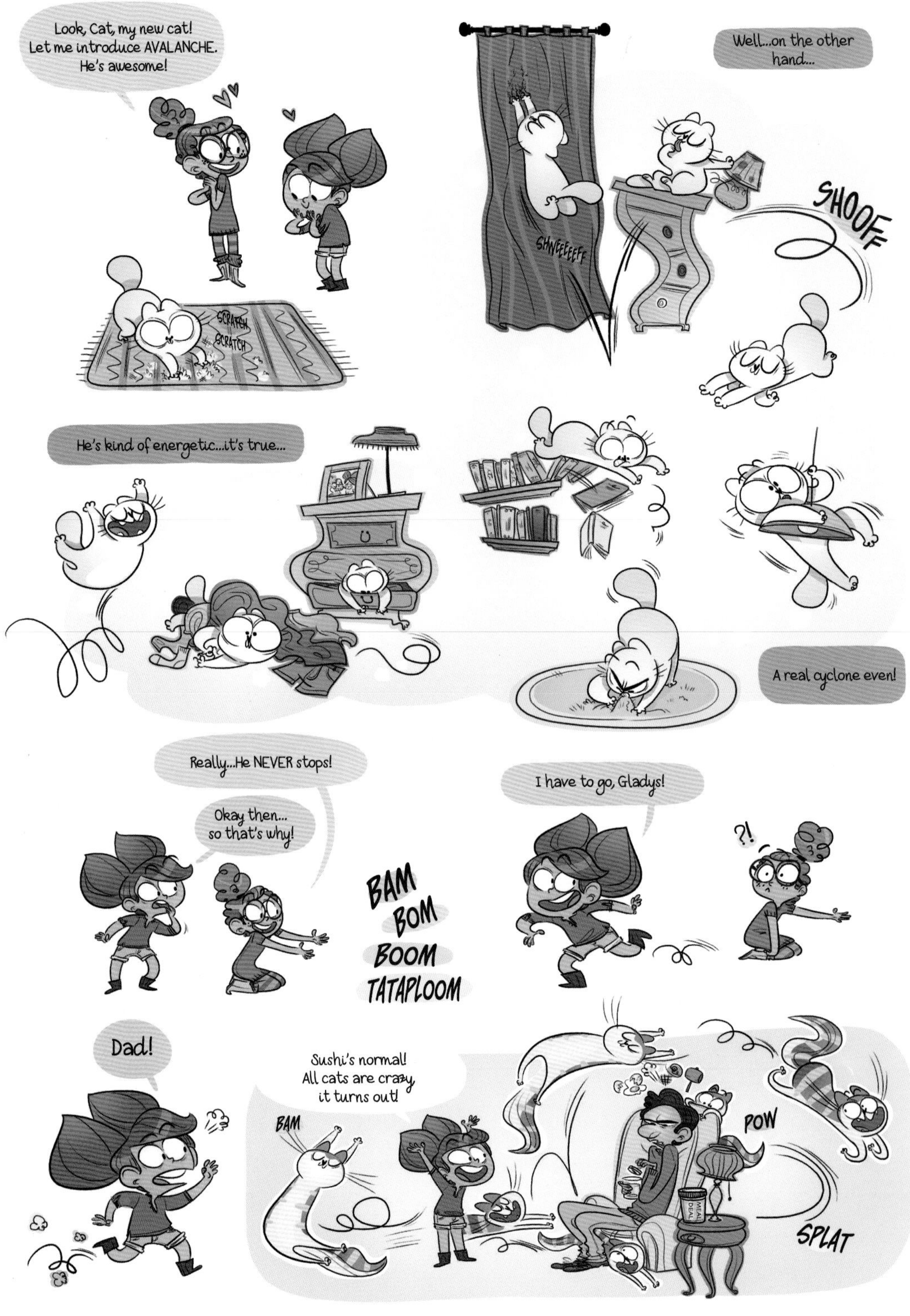
Look, Cat, my new cat!
Let me introduce AVALANCHE.
He's awesome!
SCRATCH
SCRATCH
Well...on the other hand...
SHOOFF
He's kind of energetic...it's true...
A real cyclone even!
Really...He NEVER stops!
Okay then...
so that's why!
BAM
BOM
BOOM
TATAPLOOM
I have to go, Gladys!
?!
Dad!
Sushi's normal!
All cats are crazy,
it turns out!
BAM
POW
SPLAT

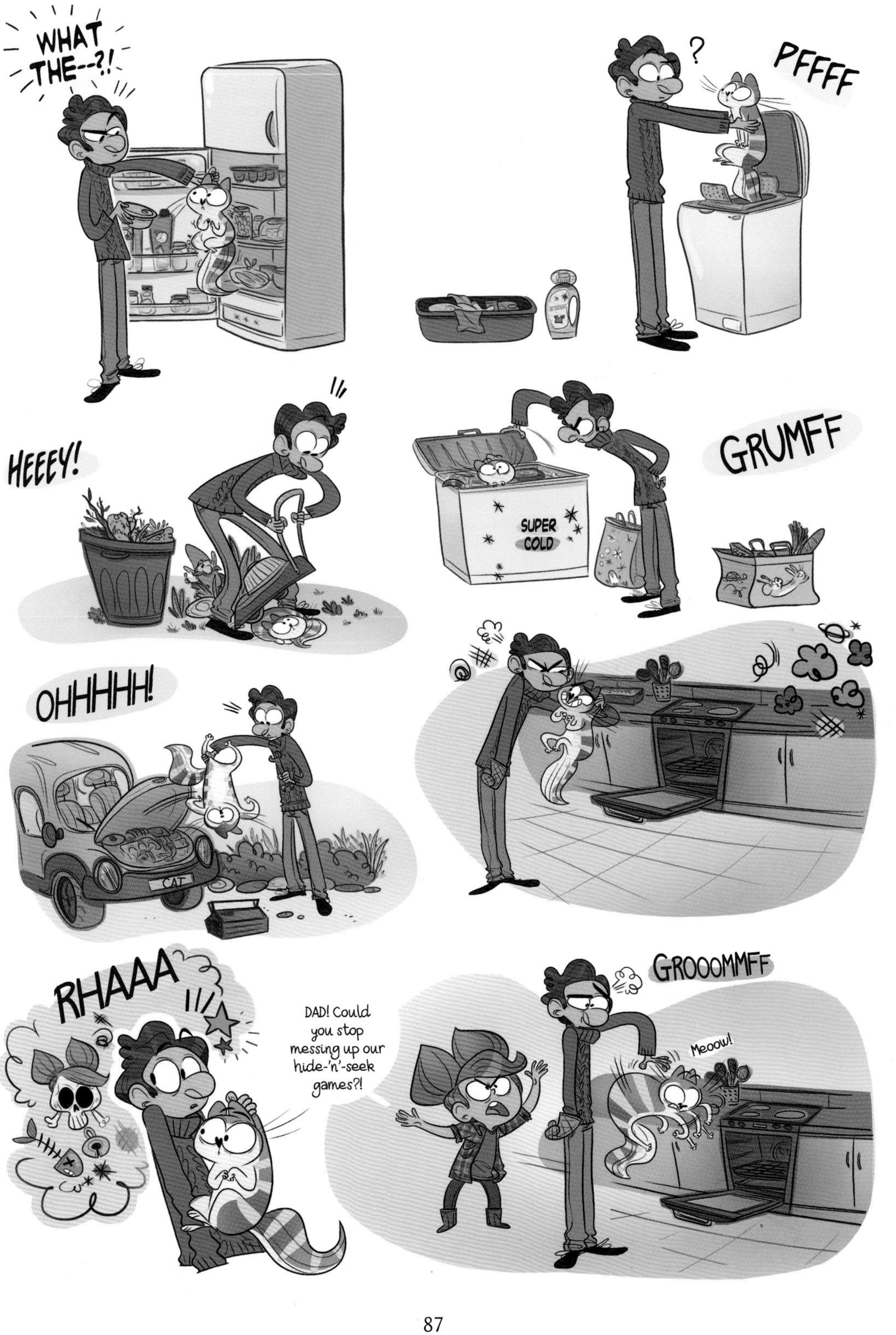
WHAT THE--?!
?
PFFFF
HEEEY!
SUPER COLD
GRUMFF
OHHHHH!
CAT
RHAAA
DAD! Could you stop messing up our hide-'n'-seek games?!
GROOOMMFF
Meoow!

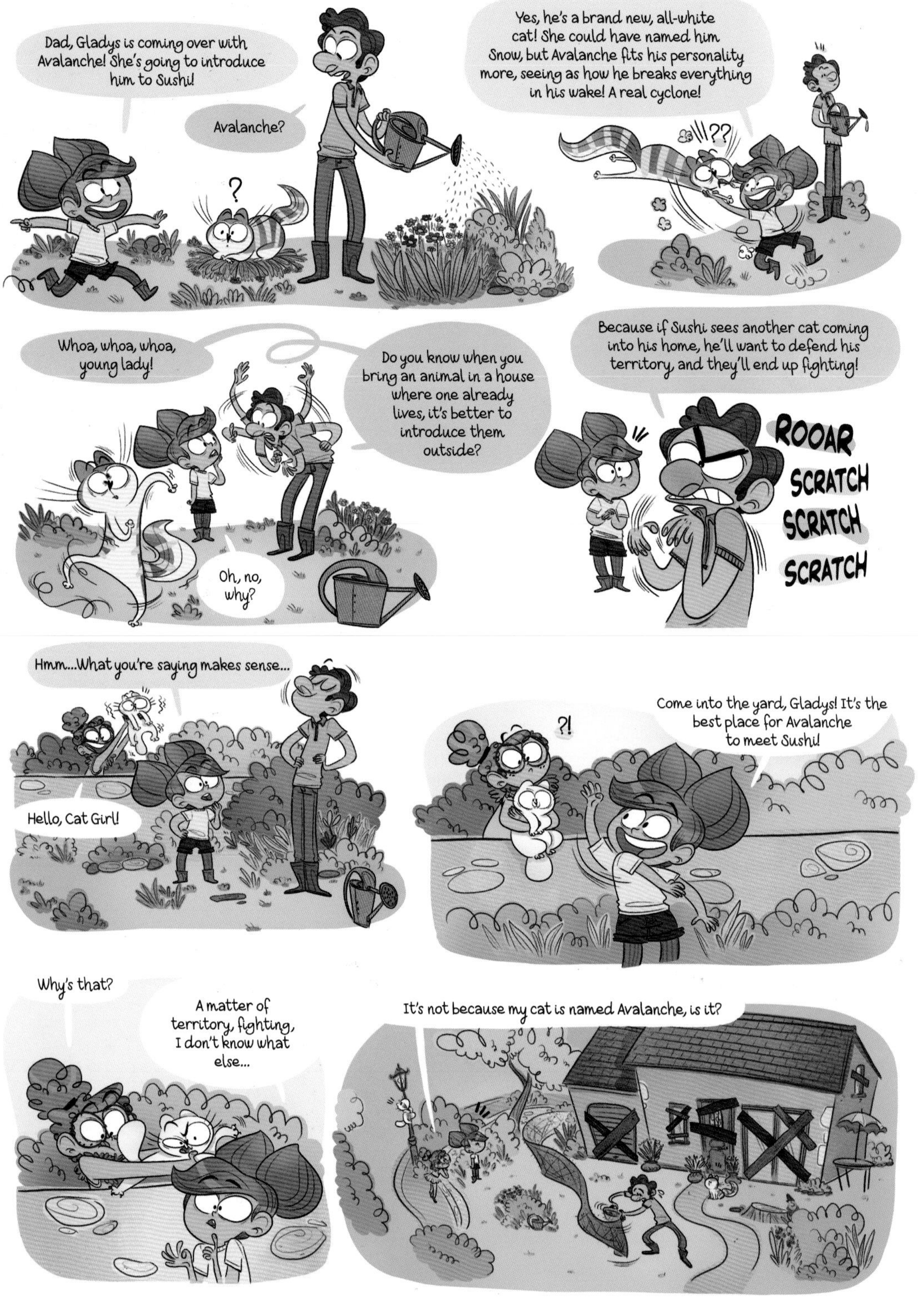
Dad, Gladys is coming over with Avalanche! She's going to introduce him to Sushi!
Avalanche?
?
Yes, he's a brand new, all-white cat! She could have named him Snow, but Avalanche fits his personality more, seeing as how he breaks everything in his wake! A real cyclone!
??
Whoa, whoa, whoa, young lady!
Do you know when you bring an animal in a house where one already lives, it's better to introduce them outside?
Oh, no, why?
Because if Sushi sees another cat coming into his home, he'll want to defend his territory, and they'll end up fighting!
ROOAR
SCRATCH
SCRATCH
SCRATCH
Hmm...What you're saying makes sense...
Hello, Cat Girl!
?!
Come into the yard, Gladys! It's the best place for Avalanche to meet Sushi!
Why's that?
A matter of territory, fighting, I don't know what else...
It's not because my cat is named Avalanche, is it?

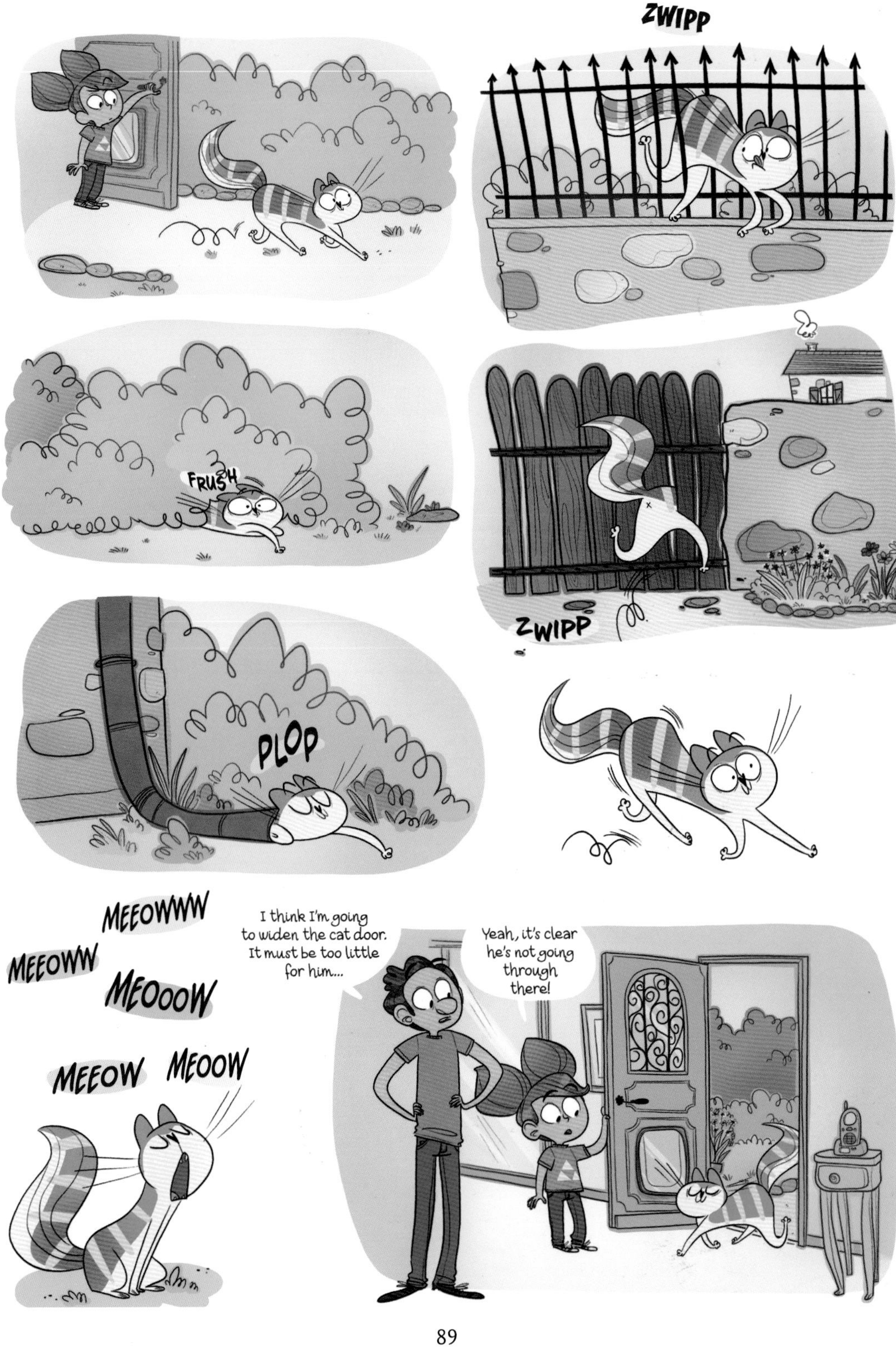
ZWIPP
FRUSH
ZWIPP
PLOP
MEEOWWW
MEEOWW
MEOOOW
MEEOW
MEOOW
I think I'm going to widen the cat door. It must be too little for him...
Yeah, it's clear he's not going through there!

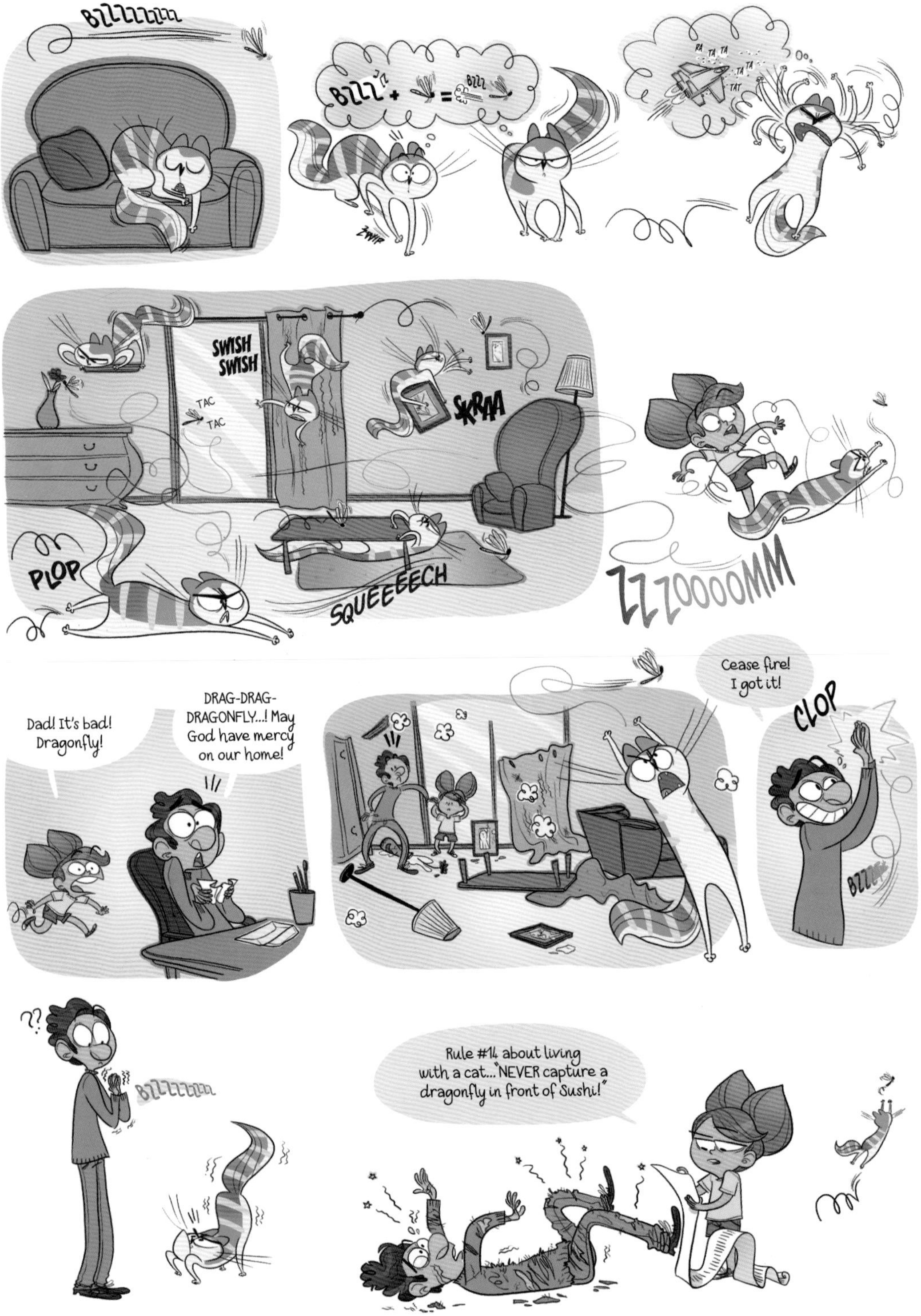
BZZZZZZZZ
BZZZ + = BZZZ
ZWIP
RA TA TA TA TA TAT
SWISH SWISH
TAC TAC
SKRAA
PLOP
SQUEEEECH
ZZZOOOOMM
Dad! It's bad! Dragonfly!
DRAG-DRAG-DRAGONFLY...! May God have mercy on our home!
Cease fire! I got it!
CLOP
BZZZ
??
BZZZZZZZZ
Rule #14 about living with a cat... "NEVER capture a dragonfly in front of Sushi!"

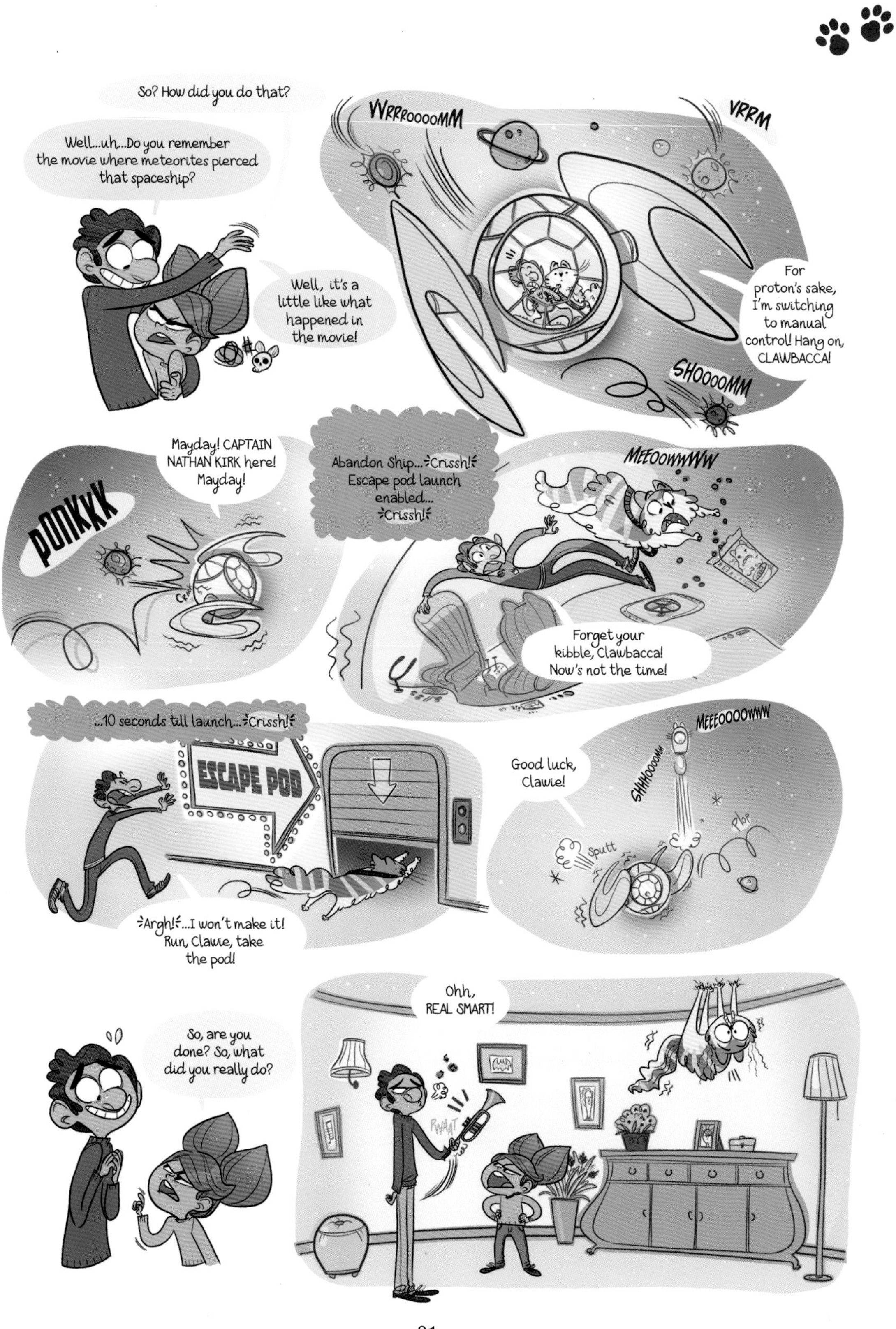
So? How did you do that?
Well...uh...Do you remember the movie where meteorites pierced that spaceship?
Well, it's a little like what happened in the movie!
VVRRROOOOMM
VRRM
For proton's sake, I'm switching to manual control! Hang on, CLAWBACCA!
SHOOOOMM
PONKKK
Mayday! CAPTAIN NATHAN KIRK here! Mayday!
Abandon Ship...Crissh! Escape pod launch enabled... Crissh!
MEEOOWWWW
Forget your kibble, Clawbacca! Now's not the time!
...10 seconds till launch...Crissh!
ESCAPE POD
Argh!...I won't make it! Run, Clawie, take the pod!
Good luck, Clawie!
MEEEOOOOWWW
SHHHOOOOMM
Sputt
Plop
So, are you done? So, what did you really do?
Ohh, REAL SMART!
PWAAT

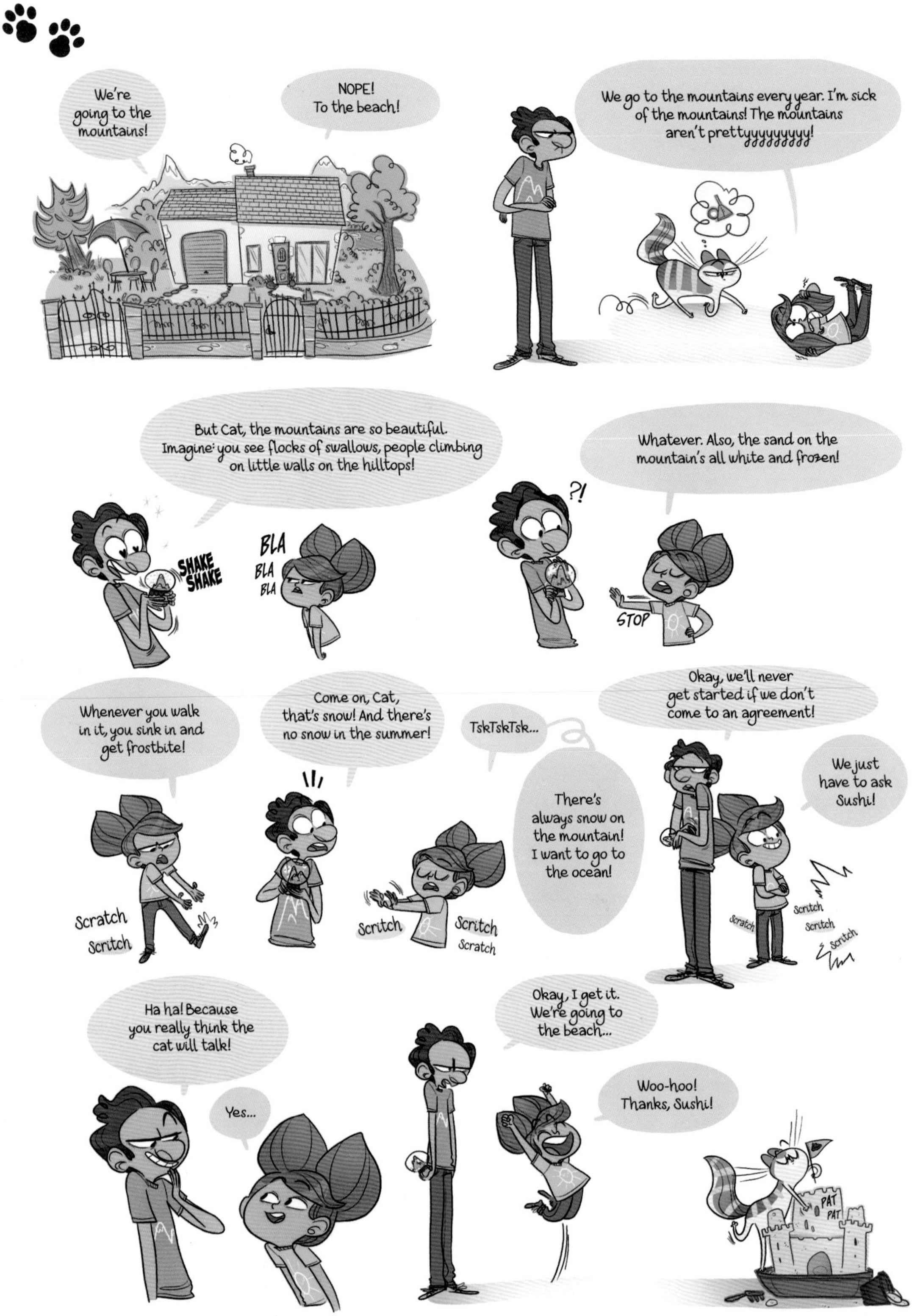
We're going to the mountains!
NOPE! To the beach!
We go to the mountains every year. I'm sick of the mountains! The mountains aren't prettyyyyyyyyy!
But Cat, the mountains are so beautiful. Imagine: you see flocks of swallows, people climbing on little walls on the hilltops!
SHAKE SHAKE
BLA BLA BLA
?!
Whatever. Also, the sand on the mountain's all white and frozen!
STOP
Whenever you walk in it, you sink in and get frostbite!
Scratch Scritch
Come on, Cat, that's snow! And there's no snow in the summer!
TskTskTsk...
There's always snow on the mountain! I want to go to the ocean!
Scritch Scritch Scratch
Okay, we'll never get started if we don't come to an agreement!
We just have to ask Sushi!
Scratch Scritch Scritch Scritch
Ha ha! Because you really think the cat will talk!
Yes...
Okay, I get it. We're going to the beach...
Woo-hoo! Thanks, Sushi!
PAT PAT

WATCH OUT FOR PAPERCUTZ™

Welcome to the first feline & family-friendly CAT & CAT graphic novel, by Christophe Cazenove & Hervé Richez, writers, and Yrgane Ramon, artist, from Papercutz, those animal-lovers dedicated to publishing great graphic novels for all ages. I'm Jim Salicrup, the Editor-in-Chief and litter-box-cleaner, here to talk about cats. Seems that there are so many cats featured in our graphic novels, that it's often suggested that we change our name to *Papercatz*. Obviously, we must love cats, with CAT & CAT simply being the latest addition to our feline line-up. Here's a list of some of the other cats you'll find at Papercutz...

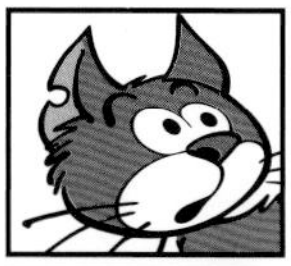

Azrael – This naughty kitty belongs to the Smurfs's archfoe, Gargamel. Azrael would love nothing better than to eat a Smurf! You can find Azrael in THE SMURFS graphic novels by Peyo (writer/artist).

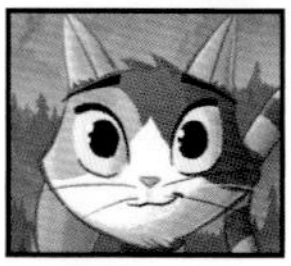

Brina – A two-year-old city cat, named Brina, takes a summer vacation in the country with her owners. Here she meets a group of stray cats who call themselves "The Gang of the Feline Sun," who convince her to runaway with them and live life as a free cat. While Brina enjoys her newfound freedom, her young owners are distraught over losing her, someone they consider a member of their family. Brina is terribly conflicted and must choose to return to her owners or to continue to live free in the wild. Find out more in the preview, by Georgio Salati, writer and Christian Cornia, artist, on the next page.

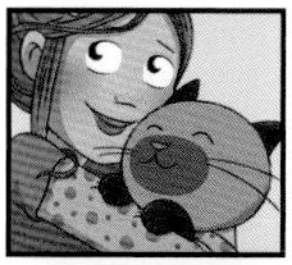

Cartoon – Is a pretty happy cat, and he lives with Chloe and her family. CHLOE, by Greg Tessier (writer) and Amandine (artist) is published by Charmz, a Papercutz imprint focused on young love. Even though Cartoon is a minor character in CHLOE, he's proven so popular that he'll soon have a graphic novel of his very own: CHLOE & CARTOON!

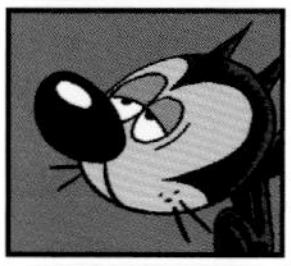

Cliff – Is the pet cat of the Loud family and is just one of the many occupants of THE LOUD HOUSE. There's Lincoln Loud, his ten sisters (Lori, Leni, Luna, Luan, Lynn, Lucy, Lisa, Lola, Lana, and Lily), his parents (Rita and Lynn Sr.), and the other pets, Charles (a dog), El Diablo (a snake), Hops (a frog), Walt (a bird), and Geo (a hamster). Cliff may not be the star of THE LOUD HOUSE, but the fact is that the Nickelodeon animated series is a big hit, as are the Papercutz graphic novels, so who's to say he's not a part of what's making THE LOUD HOUSE so successful?

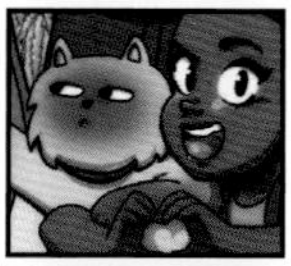

Hubble – Is the snarky pet cat of the Monroe family, and the unofficial mascot of the GEEKY F@B 5. Hubble has watched sisters Lucy and Marina Monroe, start up the Geeky F@b 5 with their friends, Zara, A.J., and Sofia, and tackle all sorts of problems, including finding homes for pets when the local animal shelter suffers major damage from a tornado. Even Hubble must admit that when girls stick together, anything is possible! Written by mother/daughter writing team, Liz & Lucy Lareau, and drawn by artist Ryan Jampole.

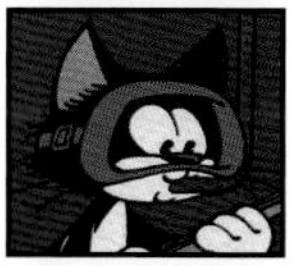

Pussycat -- Before Peyo created THE SMURFS he wrote and drew the adventures of PUSSYCAT. Pussycat is a lovable, mischievous tuxedo cat who spends his time chasing after milk and snacks and framing other members of his family for his shenanigans Warning: our hero Pussycat is a real cat. He does not speak (he just meows) and his main passions in life are eating, hunting mice, avoiding dogs, and meowing at night. All of Pussycat's adventures were collected in one deluxe volume entitled, PUSSYCAT.

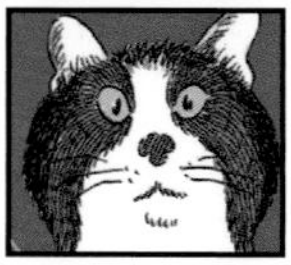

Scarlett – Scarlett, as revealed in SCARLETT "Star on the Run" by Jon Buller (author/artist) and Susan Schade (author/artist), is a small, harlequin-colored cat and a huge movie star. And what's more — she talks! Unfortunately she's also abused by her producer, so she dreams of only one thing: escaping! When the occasion presents itself, she runs for her life.

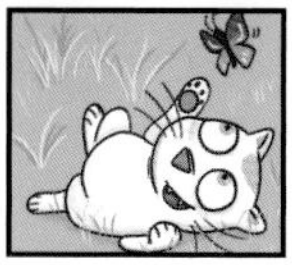

Sybil – Is the cute cat owned by fourteen-year-old (soon to be fifteen) Amy Von Brandt. Amy's life is never dull, and you can find out all about her and Sybil in AMY'S DIARY by Véronique Grisseaux (writer) and Laëtitia Ayné(artist), based on the novels by India Desjardins, and published by Charmz.

We could go on and on, but we think you get the point! (We didn't even mention Geronimo Stilton's purr-sistant foes, the Pirate Cats, who in the GERONIMO STILTON graphic novels, are always trying to rewrite history to their advantage!) Instead, we'll just ask you to keep an eye out for the next CAT & CAT graphic novel, and to watch out for Papercutz!

Thanks,
Jim

STAY IN TOUCH!

EMAIL:	salicrup@papercutz.com
WEB:	www.papercutz.com
TWITTER:	@papercutzgn
INSTAGRAM:	@papercutzgn
FACEBOOK:	PAPERCUTZGRAPHICNOVELS
FANMAIL:	Papercutz, 160 Broadway, Suite 700, East Wing, New York, NY 10038

Here's a special preview BRINA the CAT The Gang of the Feline Sun #1

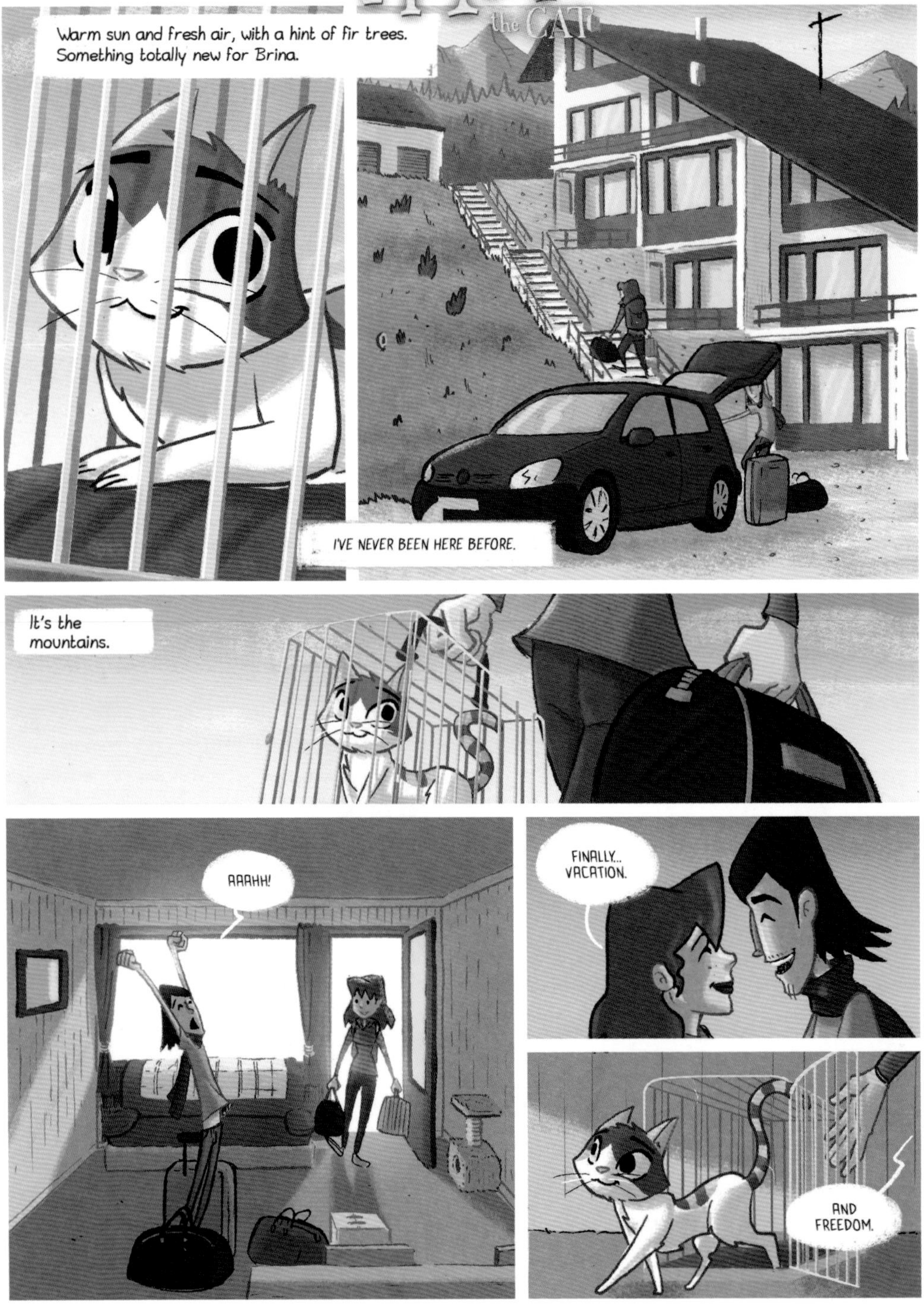
Warm sun and fresh air, with a hint of fir trees. Something totally new for Brina.
I'VE NEVER BEEN HERE BEFORE.
It's the mountains.
AAAHH!
FINALLY... VACATION.
AND FREEDOM.

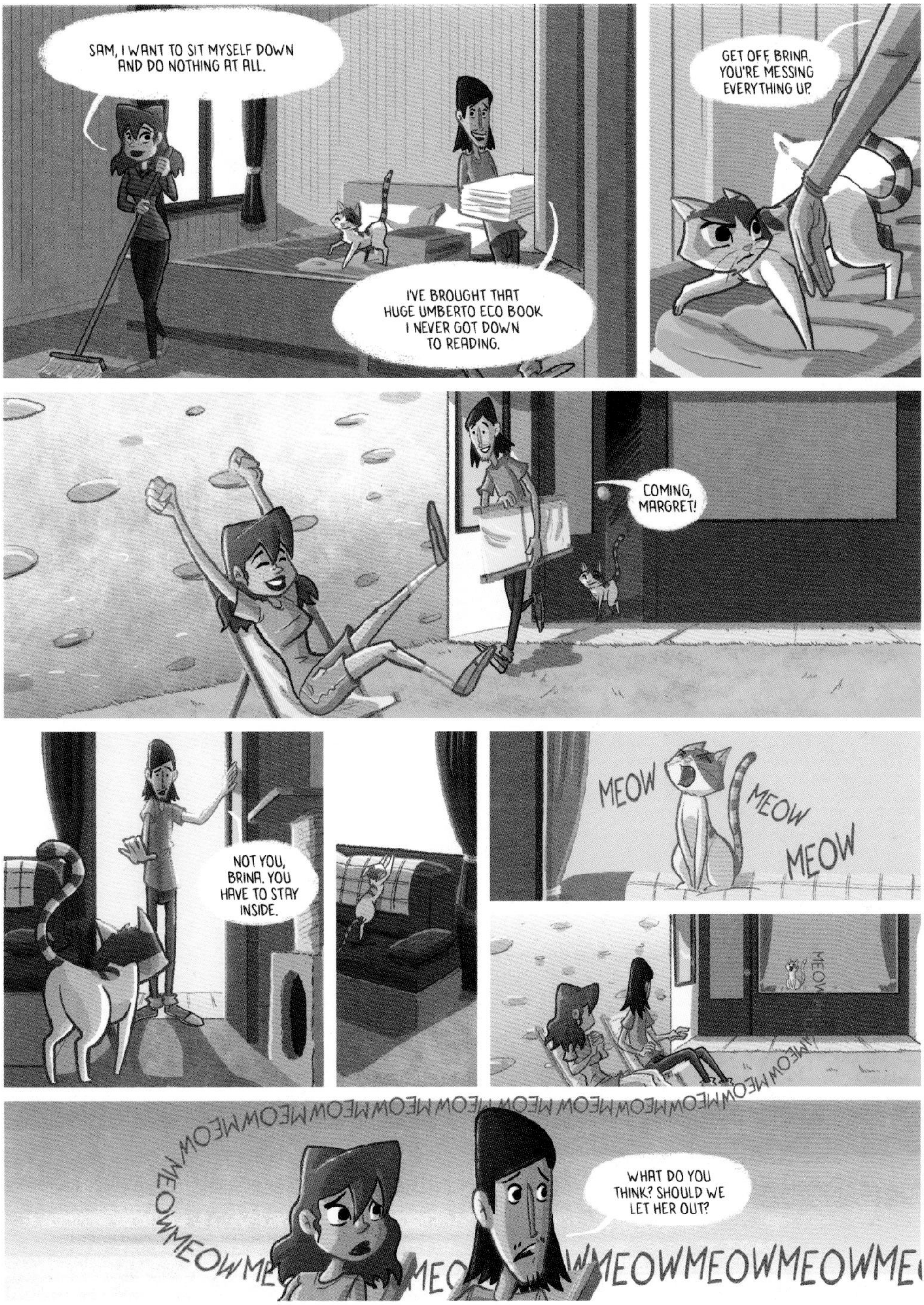
SAM, I WANT TO SIT MYSELF DOWN AND DO NOTHING AT ALL.
I'VE BROUGHT THAT HUGE UMBERTO ECO BOOK I NEVER GOT DOWN TO READING.
GET OFF, BRINA. YOU'RE MESSING EVERYTHING UP.
COMING, MARGRET!
NOT YOU, BRINA. YOU HAVE TO STAY INSIDE.
MEOW
MEOW
MEOW
MEOW
MEOWMEOWMEOWMEOWMEOWMEOWMEOWMEOWMEOW
WHAT DO YOU THINK? SHOULD WE LET HER OUT?
MEOWMEOWMEOWMEOWMEOW

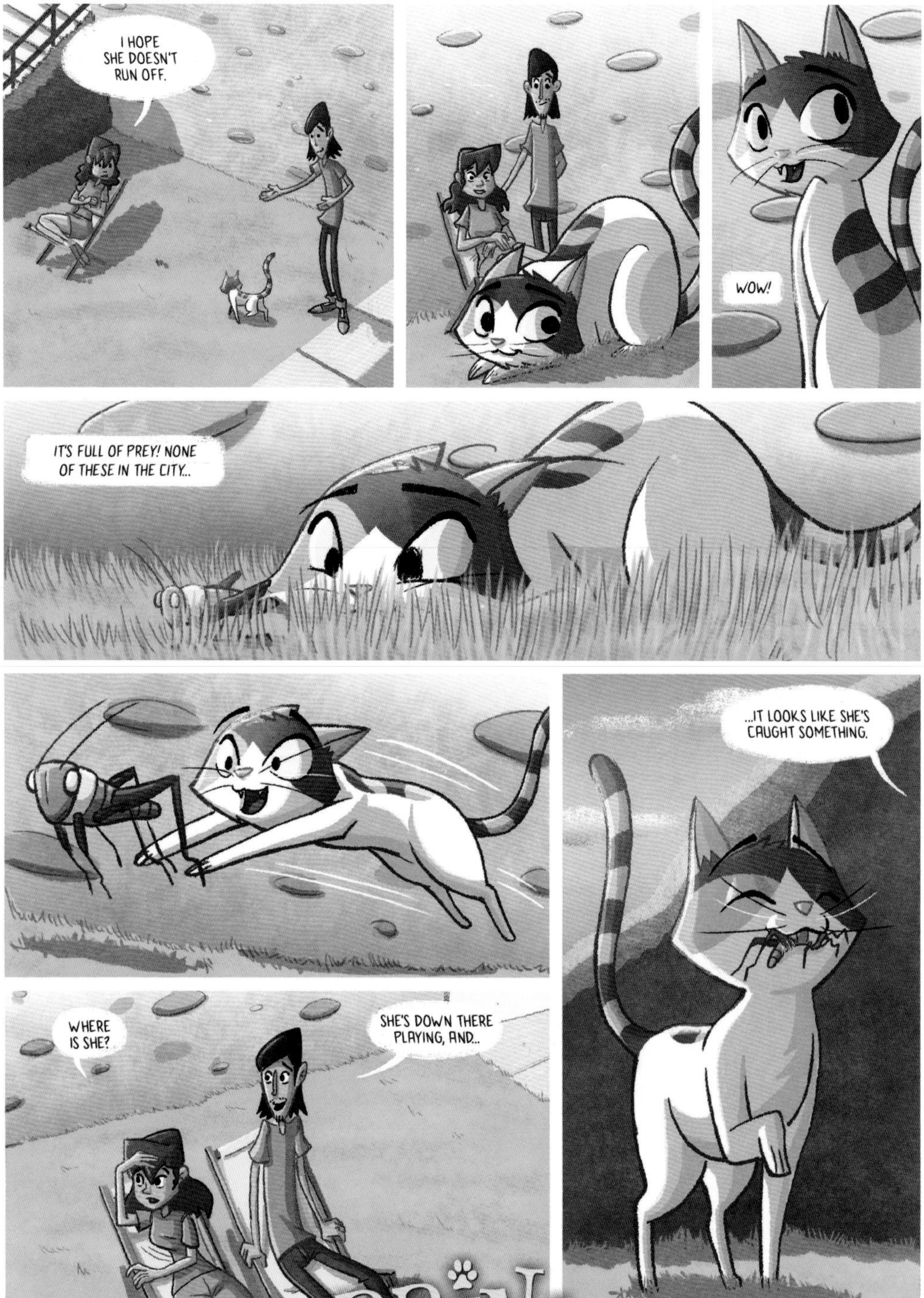
I HOPE SHE DOESN'T RUN OFF.
WOW!
IT'S FULL OF PREY! NONE OF THESE IN THE CITY...
...IT LOOKS LIKE SHE'S CAUGHT SOMETHING.
WHERE IS SHE?
SHE'S DOWN THERE PLAYING, AND...